Suede to Rest

"Toile, taffeta, and trouble! There's a new material girl in town! Poly may have an eye for fashion but she's also a resourceful and gutsy sleuth. Diane Vallere skillfully blends two mysteries in this smart and engaging tale that will keep you guessing to the very end."

— Krista Davis, *New York Times* bestselling author
of the Domestic Diva Mysteries

"In *Suede to Rest*, Diane Vallere has fashioned a terrific mystery, rich with detail and texture. Polyester Monroe is a sassy protagonist who will win your hearts with her seamless style and breezy wit. The first in the series promises readers hours of deftly-woven whodunit enjoyment."

— Daryl Wood Gerber, Agatha Award–winning author
of the nationally bestselling Cookbook Nook Mysteries

"Diane Vallere has stitched up an engaging new series with an intelligent, resourceful heroine in Polyester Monroe, plus a great supporting cast and a clever plot. Vallere's knowledge of the fashion business adds an extra layer of authenticity. *Suede to Rest* is a strong addition to the cozy mystery genre."

— Sofie Kelly, *New York Times* bestselling author
of the Magical Cats Mysteries

"In the Material Witness Mystery Series, Diane Vallere weaves a tapestry of finely knit characters, luxurious fabrics, and . . . murder."

— Janet Bolin, national bestselling author
of the Threadville Mysteries

continued . . .

Suede
to Rest

DIANE VALLERE

BERKLEY PRIME CRIME, NEW YORK

THE BERKLEY PUBLISHING GROUP
Published by the Penguin Group
Penguin Group (USA) LLC
375 Hudson Street, New York, New York 10014

USA • Canada • UK • Ireland • Australia • New Zealand • India • South Africa • China

penguin.com

A Penguin Random House Company

SUEDE TO REST

A Berkley Prime Crime Book / published by arrangement with the author

Berkley Prime Crime Books are published by The Berkley Publishing Group.
BERKLEY® PRIME CRIME and the PRIME CRIME logo are trademarks of
Penguin Group (USA) LLC.

For information, address: The Berkley Publishing Group,
a division of Penguin Group (USA) LLC,
375 Hudson Street, New York, New York 10014.

ISBN: 978-0-425-27057-8

PUBLISHING HISTORY
Berkley Prime Crime mass-market edition / November 2014

PRINTED IN THE UNITED STATES OF AMERICA

10 9 8 7 6 5 4 3 2 1

Cover illustration by Matthieu Forichon.
Cover design by Sarah Oberrender.
Interior text design by Tiffany Estreicher.

To my family

ACKNOWLEDGMENTS

Thank you to: my parents for loaning out family names for characters and for not telling me I need a "real job." Extra thanks to my mom, Mary Vallere, the true fabric expert in the family, for being my consultant.

Krista Davis and Daryl Wood Gerber, who helped set the whole thing in motion; Peg Cochran, Janet Bolin, Sophie Kelly, Leslie Budewitz, and Gigi Pandian, for your cheering along the way. Jessica Faust, for support, guidance, and suggestions to make the proposal even better; Katherine Pelz, for seeing the series potential; and Janet Robbins, for knowing what to do with sticky things like hyphens and commas.

Brittany Pollard, for sharing experiences from your own life and inspiring Poly's backstory; The Sew and Sew in Glendora, California, for answering my questions about the running of a fabric store; Randy and Ben at Mood Fabrics, Los Angeles; and Grace Topping, Richard Goodman, and

Dru Ann Love for your highly valued and appreciated input and feedback.

And lastly, my inner circle: Kendel Flaum, for being a friend like no other; and Josh Hickman, without whom life would be one big graymare.

One

A breeze rippled through the trees to the left and the right of the storefront. I stood across the street, taking in the blacked-out windows and the once-magnificent sign now covered in bird poop, decades of grime, and spray-painted curse words. *Land of a Thousand Fabrics*, it said. I wondered briefly if that had ever been true, if my great-aunt, Millie, and great-uncle, Marius, had ever actually counted the bolts of fabric in their inventory or amassed that number in order to avoid false advertising. And now that it had been left to me, I wondered if that would become my concern.

"Do you want to go inside or are you going to stand here all day?" asked Ken Watts. He looked very official in his navy-blue double-breasted blazer with *Watts Realtor Agency* embroidered over the left breast pocket in gold threads. More official than I remembered him looking the last time I saw him: at our high school graduation ten years ago, when he wore his football uniform under his cap and gown.

"Nobody's been in there for years, right?"

Ken flipped through the pages on his brown clipboard. "Right. Since Mildred Monroe was murd—" He stopped talking midsentence. "I'm sorry. I shouldn't have brought that up."

"Don't be sorry. Nobody in my family ever wants to talk about Aunt Millie, but I don't mind." I took a deep breath and lowered my head, preparing myself to march across the street, into the store. Times like these I wished I had a cascade of hair to hide my face, but my short reddish-brown hair, so overdue for a maintenance cut that it was starting to look like a shag, did little more than tickle my forehead when the wind blew.

"Poly, you don't have to do this if you don't want to. I can arrange for you to sell the store without ever having to go inside." He stared at me. "You probably didn't even have to make the trip. I could have faxed the paperwork to your office in Los Angeles. You could have signed it, faxed it back, and it would all be over and done with."

"I wanted to come back. I would have come back ten years ago for Aunt Millie's funeral or memorial service, only there wasn't one. And now that Uncle Marius is gone, the store is the only thing left of them."

"A lot of people were mad at your uncle because he didn't have a service for her."

"My parents said he couldn't admit she was gone. That's why he never sold the store."

"He wasted a lot of money paying down the mortgage on this place when there was no income. Turned down a lot of solid offers on it, too."

"If it protects your memories and keeps your heart from breaking, can it really be considered a waste of money?" I asked, looking again at the once-glamorous sign.

"That's one way of looking at it."

"He's my great-uncle, and that's *my* way of looking at it."

"Suit yourself."

A truck loaded down with ladders, orange cones, and men in yellow construction hats drove past us, obstructing my view of the storefront. A thin old man with a cane approached from the left. He stopped in front of the store, studied me for a few seconds, then nodded at Ken and continued past us.

"Who was that?"

"Mr. Pickers. He's head of the Senior Patrol. They're a group of retirees who keep an eye on things around San Ladrón."

I watched the man continue down the street. It was just after four, between the lunch and the dinner crowds I expected would fill up the restaurants on the street, and, now that the head of the Senior Patrol had moved on to other pressing matters, it was just Ken and me.

"Can I have the keys?"

"You know she was murdered in the store, and you still want to go in? I have the paperwork right here. You don't have to see a thing if you don't want to."

"Isn't that my name on the will?"

He looked down at his clipboard again and tapped the form. " 'New owner: Polyester Monroe.' Your uncle Marius either really loved you or really hated you." He looked back at the dingy gray storefront. "Right now I can't tell which." Ken juggled his clipboard and pen with a set of keys until he found the one he wanted. "I wouldn't expect much," he added.

We crossed the road in the middle, blatantly jaywalking. I might have walked to the light and waited for the signal to change if I were alone, but figured there was safety in numbers if any traffic cops decided to make an example out of us. Ken fed the key into the gate, a collapsible metal fence that had been pulled shut over the front door of the store and left locked. The key turned but the gate refused to open.

Rust at the intersecting joints left it as stiff as the tin woodsman and here we were, armed with keys, legal papers, and a flashlight, but no oilcan.

"Is there a back door?"

"Let's see."

As we hiked down the block then around to the back, I noticed a shiny black Mercedes sedan with dark-tinted windows sitting alone in a parking lot at the corner. The sounds of talk radio blurred as we passed the car, the only indication that someone was inside the vehicle. The front license plate read *MCM*. Distracted from the path, I tripped over an uneven seam in the sidewalk and landed facedown in the gravel.

I pushed myself back up and slapped the dirt from my black turtleneck and black velvet jeans. I wore black a lot these days. It hid most of the grime I picked up from sketching, repairing sewing machines, and using a glue gun, but it wasn't so good for hiding evidence of my klutziness.

Ken didn't notice I was missing from his side until he reached the back door and turned around to look at me.

"I'm okay," I said, then jogged a few steps to catch up with him.

"Still as uncoordinated as you were in high school. Remember how you tripped over the hem of your prom dress during the 'Electric Slide'?" He laughed.

"Just unlock the door, please."

Ken and I had attended the same high school in the neighboring town of Glendora. Upon graduation, he had moved to San Ladrón and gone to work in his father's real estate agency, while I moved to Los Angeles and attended FIDM. I started working at To The Nines when I graduated and hadn't been back since.

He turned the key and pushed the door inside. A stench of stale air, mildew, and something I immediately associated with wet metal hit me. Ken, who had been in front of me, stepped back and let me pass through. "I'll wait here," he said, waving his hand in front of his face.

"Fine." I pulled the collar of my turtleneck over my nose and mouth to filter out some of the smell, clicked on the flashlight, and entered.

Tiny dust particles floated through the beam of the flashlight. As I moved farther inside, my eyes adjusted enough to make out large square tables piled high with bolts of fabric. The walls were fitted with shelves about four and a half feet deep, housing stacks upon stacks of round rolls of fabric, too. I only knew the depth of the shelf because I knew a bolt of fabric was generally forty-eight to fifty-six inches long. At least, the fabrics I bought for To The Nines, the downtown Los Angeles dress company where I worked, were that length. The job wasn't what I dreamed of when I graduated from the Fashion Institute, but it was solid work in the garment district, and as my boyfriend, Carson, liked to tell me, a steady paycheck is worth more than a treasure chest of dreams.

As a little girl, I used to play in the store, and "playing" included climbing the fixtures and hiding between the bolts of fabric. And before I outgrew the fun of playing hide-and-seek in the store, I outgrew the fixtures. By sixth grade I was five feet tall; by graduation I was only a few inches shy of six.

The interior of the store appeared smaller than I remembered, and not just because my memories were from childhood. I noticed a dividing wall that hadn't been there on my last visit over ten years ago. An unpainted wooden door was in the middle of the makeshift partition. I crossed the room and tried the doorknob. It was locked. I looked behind me for Ken with his janitor-like key ring, but he was still MIA.

"Ken? Can you come here with your keys?" I called out the back door. "I want to see what's behind this door." There was no answer.

Above the door was a small square window. I pulled a three-rung folding metal ladder under it, climbed up, and tried to look through, but the glass was too filthy. "You break it, you bought it," I said under my breath. "Good thing I'm the owner." I swung the flashlight against the glass. It shattered on impact and fell to the floor on the other side of the wall, creating tinkling harmonies in the process. I looked through the hole but made out nothing of interest, nothing that would have been the reason for closing off a third of the store. There must be something back there, I reasoned. Before I decided whether or not I was keeping the store, I wanted to know what it was.

I jumped down and found a pair of scissors under the dust-coated register. After cutting a long strip of faux zebra fur and throwing it over my shoulder, I sliced off two more strips and wrapped them around each fist. I climbed back on the footstool, punched the bigger pieces of remaining glass to the floor, and threw the larger piece of fur over the bottom of the sill. I fed my head, arms, and shoulders through the opening and fumbled with the flashlight with my fur-wrapped hands. It dropped to the floor and landed on the pile of glass. The light flickered a few times, and then went out.

I leveraged myself against the opposite side of the window with my zebra paws, but the opening of the window was doing direct battle with the size of my hips. My feet lost touch with the footstool as I wriggled, trying to fit through.

"Just what the heck do you think you're doing up there?" said a muffled voice behind me.

There was little I could do in my Pooh Bear–like pose, other than kick my legs in an effort to reconnect with the footstool.

"Ken? Is that you? Can you help me?" I called. "I'm stuck."

"Hold on."

Positioned as I was, halfway through a broken window four feet above the ground, I didn't really see that I had much choice and considered saying as much, but I bit my tongue. I only hoped Ken was a quick thinker, because the pressure of the windowsill against my midsection was creating an impending need for a bathroom.

The locked door swung open. I heard a click of a switch, and seconds later the secret room was flooded with light. I shut my eyes immediately, too late. I was temporarily blinded and still stuck in the window. Things were not improving.

As my vision cleared I realized the man who stepped into the room in front of me was a stranger. His light brown hair was cut short and parted on the side. He wore a white turtleneck and a navy-blue cotton peacoat over khaki trousers and white sneakers, and looked as if he'd just returned from an afternoon on his yacht. It was bad enough to be caught dangling through a window, even if it was *my* window, but worse because it seemed I was on the verge of making a very bad first impression.

"Do you think you can fit through the window if I pull you?"

"I don't—maybe."

" 'Maybe' might not be good enough. You could get stuck more than you already are."

"I can push her from behind," said Ken's muffled voice from, well, behind.

"Nobody's pushing anything!" I said. "You, pull. I'm almost through."

The stranger stepped in front of me and paused for a second before grabbing my zebra-wrapped hands. My center of gravity had shifted, more of me through the window than not, and I knew there was no going back. As the stranger pulled, my hips popped through the opening and I fell on top of him, knocking him to the floor next to the chalk outline of a body.

Suddenly, I knew why Uncle Marius had divided off this portion of the store.

I didn't know if *Thank you* or *I'm sorry* was the more appropriate response to knocking someone into the scene of a ten-year-old homicide, so I said nothing. For the second time that day I stood up and dusted myself off, then unwrapped the fur from my right hand and offered it to the stranger to help him stand. He ignored the offer and stood up on his own.

"You're on private property," he said.

"Actually, *you're* on private property, if we're going to get into specifics, but considering you just rescued me from a tight spot I'm willing to look the other way," I said. I didn't know if he'd seen the outline of the body or not, but at the moment I wanted out of that room.

He took a step closer and looked down at me. I wasn't used to men looking down at me, since I was five foot nine, but he did. "Do you want to tell me what you're doing on my father's property?"

I stepped backward. "Who's your father?" I asked.

"Vic McMichael."

"Who?"

At that moment Ken burst through the door. His blazer flapped open, the crest on his breast pocket partially hidden under the lapel. "You should have called to tell me you were coming here," he said to the stranger.

"Which one of you is going to tell me what is going on?" I demanded.

The stranger looked between Ken and me. "Who are you again?" he asked.

"Poly Monroe," I answered and held out my hand for the second time. This time he shook it.

"Vaughn McMichael." The intensity that I'd seen in his features moments ago melted into an expression that was just shy of a smile. His eyes, a mixture of green flecked with gold, held my own for a second longer than felt comfortable, but I fought the urge to look away. His handshake was firm enough to mean business, but the softness of his hand cocooned my own. I returned the pressure of the handshake equally. I didn't know why, but I sensed that Vaughn McMichael wasn't sure what to make of my presence. As we shook hands, a roll of pink-and-white gingham fell from the table behind him and landed on the floor. It rolled halfway across the room and came to a stop by Ken's foot.

Vaughn dropped my hand and looked at Ken. "Sorry if I jumped the gun. Take your time. I'll be in touch." He turned around and left through the wooden door that had kept us from being inside the hidden room.

I followed him out of the store, keeping a few steps behind and watching to see where he headed. He approached the black sedan that had been idling in the adjacent parking lot, tapped twice on the back window, and the door opened up. Before he got inside he turned around and looked directly at me. I went back into the store as the car pulled away.

"What was that all about?" I asked Ken.

"That, my friend, was the son of the man who owns half of San Ladrón."

"How did he get in? And why was he here? And why did he say that I was on private property, and that his father owned the store?"

Ken ignored my questions. "Come with me." We walked to the front of the store and Ken unlocked the door from the inside. Again the metal fence kept us prisoners inside the store. In the distance, I heard the rapid-fire rhythm of a jackhammer against asphalt.

Ken cursed. He led me out the back door, around the block, and back in front of Land of a Thousand Fabrics. "See that?" he pointed to the vacant building on the left of the store. "Mr. McMichael owns that."

"So?"

"See that?" He pointed to the building on the right of the store. "Mr. McMichael owns that, too."

"Okay, I get it."

"See that?" Ken continued, ignoring me. "And that? And that?" he said, pointing to various buildings around the fabric store. "He owns them all. In fact, there's only one building on this street he doesn't own. Care to guess which one?"

"Okay, so he's interested in buying the fabric store. Why did his son act like he already owns it?"

Ken pulled a folder out from the bottom of the clipboard and balanced it on the back of a metro bench next to us. He flipped through a few sheets of paper until he reached a piece of thick stationery with a monogram on the top. *MCM*, it said, just like the license plate.

"When Mr. McMichael heard you'd inherited the store, he made an offer. A generous offer. I know you're only here through the weekend, so I took the liberty of drawing up the paperwork."

Ken was either the most efficient real estate agent I'd ever met, or I was being rushed into making a decision. Not one to be bullied, I crossed my arms and dug in for answers.

"What does Mr. McMichael plan to do with the store? Is he connected to the fashion industry? Does he even like fabric? Can he tell the difference between wool challis and gabardine? Did he know Uncle Marius and Aunt Millie? Or my parents? Does he know my parents? Has he talked to them about this?"

Ken signed. "Are you going to stop for a breath? Poly, this is business. He's not asking for your hand in marriage. Mr. McMichael is a developer, and this property is worth a lot to him. He can't do anything with the rest of the block unless he has this one location."

"How does he know I own it?"

"It's public knowledge. Besides, this isn't the first offer Mr. McMichael has made on the property."

"So Uncle Marius wouldn't sell to him?"

"Apparently not."

I looked across the street at the bird-poop-stained façade. "Then maybe I shouldn't sell, either."

"Don't be stupid. What are you going to do—give up your job in Los Angeles and move to San Ladrón?" He stepped back and scanned my outfit, from boots to turtleneck. "No offense, but you don't seem like the small-town type."

"I probably don't seem like the type to make a rash decision, either. Give me the night to think it over."

Ken folded the letter into thirds along already-established creases and handed it to me. "Mr. McMichael has brought a lot of jobs to the city by the properties he's developed. This would be no different. Consider that along with his offer. It's not all about you, but it's partially about you. That money might give you a chance to quit producing pageant dresses and do something real with your life."

I had a choice. Defend my crappy job with the steady paycheck or admit that I wanted to do something more with my life. I did neither. Instead, I folded the paper in half again, and tucked it into the back pocket of my dusty jeans.

"The keys?" I asked.

Ken removed three keys from his full key ring and dropped them into my open palm. "I'll call you tomorrow. Noon?"

"Sure," I answered.

"Poly, just because your uncle got caught up in what the store meant to him doesn't mean you have to get caught up in it, too. Do the sensible thing." Ken turned away and unlocked his shiny black Lexus by remote. He drove away seconds after getting into it and left me standing on the sidewalk, staring after him.

I watched him drive away. Maybe Ken was right. Maybe the sensible thing was to sign away the store and go home. It had been ten years since I'd last been in San Ladrón, and it had changed a lot in that time. I looked up at the façade of Land of a Thousand Fabrics. To the right of it was an antiques store that specialized in Polynesian collectibles. To the left was another antiques store divided into cubicles of stuff left over from a hundred different garage sales. I didn't remember either of those stores being there the last time I was here. I looked up and down the street, at a hardware store, a salon, and a gas station. The only thing I remembered from this vantage point was the traffic light at the intersection of San Ladrón and Bonita Avenue.

I walked down the block to the meter where I'd parked my own car, a semiautomatic yellow VW Bug from the early eighties. I'd bought it with the first thousand dollars I'd made at To The Nines. Even though Los Angeles was filled with people driving perfectly maintained luxury cars, I liked everything about the one I owned: the ecru leather interior, the chrome handles, the small round gearshift.

But at the moment, there was something new about my car, something I definitely didn't like. The cluster of colored wires dangling from the steering column.

Two

I stuck the key into the ignition and turned it, even though I had a pretty good idea what would happen. A whole lot of nothing. And a whole lot of nothing was exactly what I got. I pulled my AAA card from my wallet and called the number. As I waited for the phone to connect, I noticed a faded sign farther down the street, *Charlie's Automotive*.

I disconnected and hopped from the car, pulling a man's black oversized suit jacket from the backseat and shrugging into it before slamming the door shut. The door required slamming. After a minor encounter with a particularly narrow parking space, I'd dented it by the hinges and never bothered having it fixed. And now the dent in the door was certainly not my priority.

I looked up and down the street for signs of vandals. Should I call the cops to report the crime? That's what Carson had done when his car had been vandalized last year, but it hadn't done any good. Vandalized cars fell pretty low on the scale of crime, and as far as I could tell, nothing was missing. I looked back at the automotive shop. Getting the car fixed seemed to be the higher priority.

The afternoon sun was behind the auto shop, casting the building in a shadow. I hurried to the lot in front but saw no cars. If it weren't for the pair of legs sticking out from under a car in the garage and the Van Halen blaring from the small CD player, I would have considered it closed and walked away.

"Excuse me," I said. "My car's about half a block up the street and it looks like somebody got creative with my wiring."

The round toes of the heavy black work boots moved slightly, as did the blue pant legs above them. I leaned down, closer to the bumper. "Hello? Can you hear me?"

I would have walked away if it weren't something of an emergency. Instead, I crossed the concrete floor and unplugged the CD player. When I turned around, the person under the car was halfway out. Seconds later I was staring down at a woman in a dirty blue zip-front jumpsuit.

"Oil changes for twenty-five dollars. Barely pays the rent on this place." She wiped the back of her arm across her forehead and left a grease stain on her pale skin. "You got a problem with your car or are you looking for directions?"

"My car. It's parked across the street. Looks like someone tampered with the electrical while I was otherwise engaged."

"Where were you?"

"In the fabric store."

She made no secret of the once-over she gave me, looking at my riding boots, my dirty velvet jeans, my turtleneck, and my oversized man's blazer. I ran my fingers through my auburn hair, tucking a few tendrils behind my ears while she stared at me. I'd long since chewed off my trademark cranberry lipstick, but at least I knew my eyeliner and mascara had been applied as generously as hers.

"How'd you get into the fabric store?"

"The back door."

"I mean, how'd you get permission? I don't think anybody's been in there for ages."

"I inherited it."

"Who are you again?" she asked. She sat upright.

"Poly Monroe."

"As in Pollyanna?" she asked.

"As in Polyester."

"I'm Charlie." She held out a hand and I pulled her up. Her thick, wild black hair was held in a messy ponytail on the top of her head. Her features were angular but sexy, full red lips and dark eyes. Her eyeliner was heavy on the upper lids, drawn into a point at the edge of each eye, Cleopatra-like. She wiped her hands on an already filthy rag and extended her hand a second time, which I shook.

"Polyester Monroe." She tipped her head slightly as she considered this. "Related to Marius and Millie Monroe?" she asked.

I nodded.

"You say your car was vandalized?"

"Looks that way."

She craned her neck and looked outside. "Yellow VW Bug?"

"That's the one."

She slammed the hood on the car she was working on, unzipped her jumpsuit, and stepped out of it. She wore a faded chambray shirt and jeans underneath. She hung the jumpsuit on a hook by a calendar of half-naked firemen. "It's time for me to close up. Watch the joint while I take a powder?"

"What about my car?"

"I'll fix it in the morning." She pulled down the hinged metal doors in the front of her shop and threw the locking mechanism. Before I could answer, she disappeared behind a small door on the back corner of the garage. I stood in the front, not sure exactly what it was I was supposed to be doing. I heard a knock on the front door and turned around to find two men in the doorway. The one in front wore a dirty white T-shirt and faded jeans and steel-toed boots. The second one was dressed the same except his T-shirt was black. They both held yellow hard hats.

"Can I help you?" I asked.

"I don't know. Where's Charlie?"

"She's closing up. If you want to talk to her about a job, come back in the morning."

"Sure, yeah, that's why we're here. About a job." They laughed.

The air felt crisp with tension. The two men stayed at the door, but I sensed if I weren't there they would have come inside. I crossed the shiny garage floor and stepped directly in a trail of oil that led to the drain. The guy in the white T-shirt stood in the doorway.

"Like I said, she's closed for business." I put one hand on the door and the other on the frame. I was the same height as the guy in front of me and I looked him straight in the eyes. I kept my voice steady. I pointed over his shoulder to a gas station where a black-and-white police cruiser was parked. "Looks like there's an on-call mechanic across the street. If it's an emergency, they can probably accommodate you."

White T-shirt stepped back. He looked at his friend. "It can wait."

We stood face-to-face. The guy in the front stepped backward and the two of them started down the street. I waited out the better part of a minute before I stepped back and locked the door. It was then that I realized how hard my heart was pounding in my chest.

"I asked you to watch the place, not lock the doors," Charlie said behind me. She unlocked the door and poked her head out. I suspected the two guys were within her sight, but didn't know for sure. She stood upright, then shut and relocked the door.

"They came here?"

"They said they had a job. I said you were closed and recommended the mechanic across the street."

She looked out the front door at the police cruiser parked in the gas station lot. "You told them to go there? That's rich."

"Why? Who were they?"

"Our very own local bad boys, or at least that's what they'd like you to think. They tend to fly under the radar with small stuff that nobody reports."

"Like tearing the wires out of my car?"

"Could be. That's their idea of fun."

"What did they want from you?"

"I've got flies buzzing around me all the time. The more you swat 'em away, the more they keep coming back. Comes with the territory," she said, tipping her head toward the interior of the auto shop.

"If your flyswatter doesn't work, you can always get one of those electric bug zappers. Might leave more of an impression."

She studied me. "Polyester Monroe, you just got a whole lot more interesting. Follow me. Happy hour's on. You have someplace to be? Need the number for a rental car company?"

I looked across the street at Land of a Thousand Fabrics. When I left Los Angeles, I'd led my boyfriend Carson to believe I was coming to San Ladrón to sign paperwork to inherit the store, and then sign paperwork to give Ken power of attorney to sell it. But I hadn't counted on how it felt to be inside the store after all these years. It might be nice to stick around, spend the night in the apartment over the store, and pretend my great-aunt and uncle were still alive.

"You said you can fix it tomorrow?"

"I won't know for sure until I look at it, but nothing's going to happen tonight."

"That's fine. I think I'm going to spend the night in San Ladrón."

"Great. Since you're not going anywhere, you want to join me for a drink?"

What the heck, I thought. It wasn't like I had any other plans, And if a couple of local bad boys wanted to scare me into leaving, they were pretty dumb to tamper with my car.

Charlie led the way past Antonio's Ristorante, past two hair salons named after someone named Angie and someone named Susie, a dentist's office, and a hardware store. The fabric store was across the street and I slowed my pace and stared at the front of it. It was flanked by antiques stores, both of which sported bright white trim and welcoming exteriors. Land of a Thousand Fabrics looked like the equivalent of the creepy house of the neighborhood that spawns stories to be told around a campfire.

Charlie noticed that I wasn't keeping pace. She retraced her steps until she was next to me and followed my stare. "I bet the inside is something else," she said.

"It is."

"C'mon, you can tell me all about it." She nudged me forward with her elbow and I dropped back in step.

We crossed a side street and entered an unmarked building through a back door. The interior was dimly lit. Two men shot darts next to a vacant pool table. A mirror behind the bar was painted with the words *The Broadside Tavern* in gold paint. Charlie took a seat at the bar and gestured for me to sit next to her. When the bartender appeared, she ordered.

"Irish Car Bomb. You want one, too?" she asked me.

I wasn't sure exactly what it was, so I shook my head. "I'll have a beer," I said, even though I'd never developed a taste for it.

The drinks arrived. A shot glass and a tall mug of dark

brown beer for her, and a pale ale for me. Charlie dropped her shot glass into her beer and drank half of the resulting mixture.

"So, what was it like?" she asked.

"What was what like?"

"The store. You said you were inside. I've always wondered about that place."

"Why?"

"I've been staring at the gate since I opened my auto shop."

Staring at a closed gate was a pretty lackluster excuse for what seemed to be more than passing interest in the store, but if I weren't sitting in the bar talking to Charlie, I wasn't sure where I'd be. The possibility existed that I'd be sitting in the bar by myself, and that wasn't something I was used to doing.

"It's still filled with fabric, though there's a good chance most of it's damaged. I'll have to go through the inventory pretty carefully to see if any of it can be salvaged, but that's a big job."

"You actually care about the fabric?" she asked, taking another pull of her drink. Her eyes flickered to my barely touched beer and I gulped as much as I could, satisfying my thirst before the bitter taste kicked in.

"I work for a dress company in Los Angeles. There's a big market for stuff like that, even if it's damaged. Depends on how bad it is. The inventory has been in there for a while, so I don't really know what I'm going to find when I start digging through it."

"So you plan to stick around long enough to dig through the inventory?"

"As opposed to what?"

"Selling and going back home."

It was like she and Ken had compared notes and agreed to push the same buttons. "That store has been in my family for a long time. I'm not selling until I know what I'm selling."

"Interesting."

I bristled. "I don't think it's all that interesting. I think most people would do what I'm doing."

"That's where you're wrong, Polyester. Most people would take the money and run." She took another drink. "It's an old store that's been closed for a decade. Hard to believe there's something in there that might be of value."

"Even harder to believe at one time the metal gate actually opened."

"Rust?"

I nodded.

"Nothing a little motor oil and determination can't fix. I bet you have bigger problems than the gate."

"Like what?"

"You'll find out soon enough if you stick around. And if you don't want to stick around, I'm sure you can find a buyer."

"I've already had an offer," I said, my lips loosened by the beer. "But I don't want to make a rash decision. I feel like it's my heritage, my family. My great-uncle left it to me, and I don't want to rush into any kind of deal that takes it away from me."

"That's smart. You should take your time, do your thing. Check out the inventory and decide what *you* want to do with it. Maybe you should keep it and move here. This town needs another Monroe. With your uncle Marius gone, it's up to you."

"You knew my uncle?"

"I knew *of* your uncle. Smart man." She finished off her dark brown drink and motioned to the bartender for two more before I had finished half of my first.

"What do you mean by that?"

"He was willing to take on old man McMichael. It's a

tough job but somebody's got to do it. A word of warning, though. Be careful."

"Of what?"

"Of things that go bump in the night," she said mysteriously.

I knew she wanted me to ask what she meant, but I wasn't going to take the bait. Inheriting the store felt personal to me, and talking about it like this, over beer and Irish Car Bombs, devalued the importance of it.

To make a good showing with my new tough friend, I drank more of my beer. I wasn't accustomed to drinking quickly and I already felt it in my system, the alcohol making my arms sluggish and my head woozy. I hadn't eaten much since arriving in San Ladrón. Drinking my dinner didn't seem like a very good idea.

The bartender carried two red plastic baskets past us, each filled with a burger and fries. He set them down by the men playing darts. The greasy scent called out to me like a bouquet of roses. I took another sip before realizing I'd already decided not to do so.

"Look, I can already tell you're a lightweight and I know you're not driving back to Los Angeles tonight considering your car's out of commission. You got a place to stay?"

I hadn't really thought of that. When I drove up from Los Angeles, I figured it would take a couple of hours tops to check out the store and sign Ken's paperwork. I'd brought my messenger bag, filled with my wallet, dark red lipstick, emergency sewing kit, notebook, and pen. There might have been a couple of stale ginger candies in the bottom. Not exactly enough for a spontaneous getaway. I pushed my hands into the pockets of my black blazer and my fingers closed around the keys Ken handed off earlier. "I think I have a place."

Charlie pulled a business card out of the breast pocket of her chambray shirt. "Got a pen?"

I handed her the rhinestone-encrusted pen I carried around with me, hand-bejeweled one day at To The Nines when I was testing a cheap batch of glue my boss told us to use on the dresses we produced. She stared at it a few seconds before taking it and rolling it between her palms. Three rhinestones fell off. She brushed them from her lap onto the floor, then scribbled something on the back of the card.

"Call me if you can't work it out on your own. I have a sofa you can crash on."

I took the card and thanked her but already knew I wouldn't take her up on the offer. I wanted to be alone to process everything.

She tossed a ten-dollar bill on the counter and left. I ordered a burger and fries to go and paid the balance of our tab. The sun had dropped by the time I walked out of the small bar. The historic downtown area, mostly antiques stores, hair salons, and the occasional office space, was eerily lit by streetlamps that cast a faint orange glow over the fake western storefronts. I approached my car and checked to be sure the doors were locked and then looked across the street. The metal gate to Land of a Thousand Fabrics was dark and foreboding in the evening light.

I walked to the crosswalk, to the end of the block, into the alley, and to the back door. The second of the three keys on my key ring unlocked the lock. I carried my burger and fries to the small metal control panel mounted by the back door and flipped a bunch of switches until the interior was bright with artificial light. Odd, I thought, that the electric worked. I knew Uncle Marius had kept up the mortgage and tax payments but couldn't imagine why he'd paid the electric bill all these years, too.

Now I could see the store, really see it, and focus on what I had inherited. I felt a connection to the bins of fabric, to the walls lined with rolls of brightly colored taffetas and silks, the tables loaded down with rolls of synthetic fur, suede, leather, and damask.

It wasn't what I'd learned at the Fabric Institute that had landed me the job at To The Nines, it was what I'd learned while growing up surrounded by material. During my interview with Giovanni, I mentioned that I'd learned to identify fabric from the feel of it when I was ten years old. He gave me an impromptu test, handing me a dozen swatches from a stack behind his desk, and I proved my knowledge. It wasn't until after I started working for him that I learned the swatches of fine fabrics by his desk were for appearance's sake, and that most of our inventory was as polyester as my name.

I crossed the concrete floor to the white laminate cutting station, and placed the keys in the drawer below the dusty cash register. A small teal notebook sat in the drawer, the word *Resources* written across the fabric cover in red marker. I hoisted myself up on the flat surface right by where a metal yardstick had been mounted for measuring cuttings of fabric, unwrapped my burger, and paged through the notebook. Someone, probably my great-aunt, Millie, had logged details of various bolts of fabric in the inventory. *Red velvet, Spain, 12 yards. Burgundy georgette, Lyon, 50 yards (slight imperfection at selvage). Assortment of toile, Paris. Bolt of blue silk taffeta, 17 yards, India.*

Additional pages were filled with similar entries. I imagined my relatives visiting exotic countries, purchasing fabrics to sell in the store. What it must have been like for them to run this place together in the late forties, when Christian Dior had shown his New Look to Parisian high society, when ready-to-wear started replacing true couture, when the idea of homemade glamour appealed to women everywhere. My great-aunt and great-uncle had made that dream a reality for women by stocking something better than the kind of cheap poly-satin blends we used to make dresses at To The Nines.

If I had access to fabrics like these when developing a concept for Giovanni, it would have been a whole different job. Sure, I established the direction our design team would go each season and outsourced the materials to make it happen, but with inexpensive, flammable cuts of fabric that would show wear after one use. I could look at a roll of poly-satin and know exactly what kind of dress it should become. But these fabrics were different. Being in the same room with them, even in what I could only imagine to be damaged condition, was like being on a magic carpet that would take me to another time, another place, another reality.

I cut a couple of yards from a bolt of royal-blue suede and draped it over the wrap stand like a tablecloth. I leaned over the fabric and ate my burger and most of the fries, then balled up the wax paper, the brown carry-out bag, and tied the blue suede around it like a hobo sack. Fabrics were known to absorb whatever nearby scent lingered in the air, and I didn't want the place smelling like a fast-food joint. A small plastic bin was nestled under the register, overflowing with fabric scraps and faded pieces of paper. I hopped down from the cutting table, rested the blue bundle on top of the bin, and carried it out back. Outside, it had grown dark. Weird shadows took on distorted forms. I scampered to the Dumpster, lifted the lid, and turned the trash can upside down, shaking out the contents. When I pulled it out and lowered the lid, I saw a strange man watching me from end of the alley.

Three

He started toward me. I turned around and ran to the back door, tripping over my own feet in the process. I face-planted on the gravel like I had earlier. I scrambled for footing, coughed a few times, and grabbed the doorknob. I glanced behind me to see if the man had gotten closer. He hadn't. He stood at the end of the alley, silhouetted by headlights from a car idling in the lot behind him. I shut and locked the door behind me, flipped the switches on the control panel to off, and backed away slowly, continuing to stare at the doorknob. Something sounded against the door, like nails on a chalkboard. I grabbed the keys from the drawer under the register and ran to the corner of the store, to a circular staircase that led to the apartment above the store. I fumbled with the keys, almost dropping them twice. When I found one that fit, I unlocked the door and locked it behind me. I sank to the floor at the end of the rose-pink floral carpet runner that led down the hall and hugged my knees, scared to be alone.

As I sat with my back against the door, I listened for sounds—any sounds that indicated that I hadn't imagined that someone was outside, waiting to break in. I heard nothing but silence.

This was silly. Just because my car had been vandalized and a person was standing at the end of the alley behind the store didn't mean I had anything to worry about. I was safe in the apartment.

I waited a few minutes, and then crept back downstairs. My cell phone sat on the corner of the wrap stand. I picked it up and carried it to the staircase, sitting on the third rung from the bottom. I pulled up my favorites menu and called Carson in Los Angeles. Though it now seemed like I was safe inside the store, I wanted to talk to someone who could comfort me, who would tell me everything would be okay.

"Poly? Hold on, this is a bad connection. Let me get to the kitchen."

Carson, I figured correctly, was at our apartment. The cell phone reception was variable at best, and we'd learned which rooms better served our conversations. "Can you hear me now?"

"Yes. Listen, my battery's low and I don't have my charger," I said in a hushed voice.

"Why are you whispering?"

"I'm trapped inside the fabric store and I think there might be somebody outside trying to get me."

"What do you mean, you're trapped in the store?"

I thought about Charlie's warning. "I went outside to throw out the trash and saw a man in the alley watching me. And after I locked the door I thought I heard something at the door."

"Calm down. You always had an active imagination. Did you call the cops?"

"No, I called you."

"There's not a lot I can do from Los Angeles."

"I don't want you to *do* anything, I just wanted to hear your voice. Maybe I did imagine the whole thing. Can't we just talk for a couple of minutes?"

"We could have talked over dinner if you'd come home like I expected you to. It's Friday. I got frittatas."

"I'll eat them when I get back," I said absentmindedly, listening from the stairs for sounds of forced entry in progress.

"Frittatas don't keep. Are you even listening to me?"

"What?"

"Don't try to be cute."

I had a very strong urge to say I wasn't trying, but it seemed Carson wasn't in a playful mood. Carson was rarely in a playful mood, at least not lately. But turn him loose at happy hour with the rest of his banker friends and he was the life of the party. He used to be that way with me, and I figured we'd get back there someday when I got serious about the "marriage and our future" discussion.

"What time do you expect to be back tomorrow?" he asked.

"I don't know if I'll be back tomorrow."

"I thought this was a cut-and-dried case of inheritance and resell?"

"It's a little more complicated than that," I said. "My car was vandalized. Before you say anything, I took it to a mechanic. It'll be ready in the morning."

"Did you call the police?"

"It's no big thing, Carson. Some locals decided to play a joke on me. So I get it fixed and I leave in the morning. This just gives me time to check out the store and decide what I want to do."

"You should sign a couple of papers to take ownership then sign a couple of papers to give the agent your permission to resell it. Although I can't imagine who would want to buy a warehouse filled with rotting fabrics."

"It's my store now and maybe I want to keep it," I said, surprising myself.

"Poly, don't be a fool. Somebody would probably pay a pretty price to get that location."

I don't know what stopped me from telling him that I already had an offer, but I kept the info to myself. I knew Mr. McMichael was demonstrating solid business sense in his offer and I was demonstrating an irrational connection to the past by not accepting it, but I wasn't ready to walk away from what Uncle Marius had protected all these years. Maybe he and Aunt Millie were together again in that great fabric store in the sky, but just in case they needed a little time to find each other, I didn't want to be the one to trash the thing that kept them connected.

"Carson, did you move to a different room?"

"No. Why?" he asked through a crystal clear connection.

"You're breaking up. I better go. I'll call you tomorrow." I ended the call and turned my phone off to conserve what was left of the battery.

I climbed the stairs and entered the apartment a second time. Large white sheets were draped over the furniture. I remembered staying here, in the spare bedroom across the hall from Uncle Marius and Aunt Millie's room. I walked down the hall to the bathroom and turned the faucets. Pipes below the sink made a clunking sound followed by a sputter. No water came from the spigot. I glanced at the mirror and wiped my palm across the dusty reflective surface. My hair was mussed up, but that was the beauty of keeping it short. I could go an extra day without a shower. Not having a toilet was a different problem.

I turned off the light. Aunt Millie had kept a basket in the closet filled with blankets and stuffed animals made from scraps of fabric from the store. In the dark, I found the closet and pulled out a furry tiger-striped pillow and a zebra-fur quilt. I felt like an intruder into someone else's life, but I was tired: from the beer, from defending my interest in the store, from running away from a strange man in an alley who I may or may not have imagined. I pulled the sheet off the sofa and created a makeshift bed, then promptly fell asleep.

I awoke to the sound of sirens.

It was a couple of seconds before I remembered where I was. A thin border of bright sunlight framed the heavy curtains that covered the front windows of the apartment, winning the battle of daylight versus darkness when I pulled the cord that opened them. A sheriff's car was angled in front of the store. A portly man in a dark uniform stood next to the car. He held a white megaphone in his right hand. Ken's Lexus pulled up behind the cop car and Ken got out.

I wrapped myself in the zebra-fur blanket and left the apartment, scampering down the cold metal stairs in my bare feet. I opened the front door and bright sunlight blinded me, along with pulsating blue and red lights circulating at even intervals.

"Come out of there with your hands up!" called the uniformed man through the megaphone. "Hands up. Step away from the door."

I looked to my left and my right to see who he was talking to, but saw no one. "You—in the zebra fur. Yes, I'm talking to you."

Me?

"I can't come out; the gate is rusted shut." I continued shivering even though I still had the zebra-fur blanket draped over my shoulders. I opened my arms up with fists on the corners of the blanket, feeling a bit like I was impersonating a vampire, then pulled it around me more tightly. A third car, the black Mercedes sedan with the vanity plates, pulled up behind Ken's Lexus. A handsome white-haired man in a camel topcoat got out of the car.

"What's going on here?" he asked.

"The police got a report last night that someone was vandalizing the fabric store," said a woman in a pink terry-cloth robe with the letter *B* monogrammed in maroon. "I heard they've been keeping a watch on the place since the call came in and caught her this morning."

"Caught her red-handed! A squatter. Still inside the store!" said another like-attired woman with a plastic cap on her head.

"I'm not vandalizing it. I live here," I said through the metal gate. I fed my fingers through the openings and gripped the joints. "Tell them," I said to Ken. His hair stuck up on one side, like he'd been woken unexpectedly and hadn't had time to use a comb. He shook his head and said something under his breath to the officer.

"Is this how you welcome people to this quiet little town? Sirens and accusations?"

Ken stepped forward. "Poly, calm down."

The uniformed officer set the megaphone on the back of his car and stepped over to me. "Miss, we're just doing our job. We came over to check on the building as soon as we got the call from the Senior Patrol about suspicious activity on this street."

"Someone reported me to the police?" I asked.

"He reported you to me," said the businessman, stepping forward.

"Who are you?"

"Poly, this is Mr. McMichael," said Ken. He looked less official without his crested blazer and tried to stand straighter to compensate. He succeeded only in looking like the head of the math club who was trying to impress Pythagoras. "Mr. Pickers heard somebody breaking into a storefront on this strip. He called Mr. McMichael because he owns this strip."

"Which storefront? Mine? Because he doesn't own *mine*."

I turned my focus from Ken to the businessman, "You don't own *this* property. *I* own this property."

"She's right," Ken said to the officer. "Technically, she's the owner of this building. For now, at least."

"Strike that 'for now' from the record. I own this building. I own everything in this building."

"I'm sorry, Miss . . . Monroe, did you say?" said the officer.

"Yes. Poly Monroe."

He fed his hand through an opening in the gate. "Ms. Monroe, I'm Deputy Sheriff Clark. From the sheriff's office, mobile unit. I'm sorry for the inconvenience. Mr. Pickers called Mr. McMichael this morning and we're a little unclear about which store he was referring to. Sounds like it was a misunderstanding. Are you planning on staying in San Ladrón for any length of time?"

I shook his hand and dropped my voice, ignoring Ken and Mr. McMichael. "I feel a little funny talking to you through a gate. Can you hold on a minute? I'll come out the back."

I closed the door and ran back across the concrete, stopping only briefly at the wrap stand to push my feet into a pair of faded red velvet slippers with Chinese beadwork on the front. They were slightly too long for me but warmed my toes. I wrapped the zebra fur around me tightly and pushed the back door open.

I didn't get far.

In the parking lot behind the store, next to the Dumpster, was a body. Even though a length of blue suede had been pulled over his head and tied around the back of his neck, I recognized his distorted features, his outfit, and his cane. It was the body of Mr. Pickers, head of the Senior Patrol.

His legs splayed out in front of him, one bent at an unnatural angle, the other straight, parallel to his cane. The left foot of his dusty brown loafers had a hole in the sole, showing the bottom of a cranberry sock. His tan jacket was open over a beige button-down shirt and navy-blue work pants. A puddle of blood from the back of his head seeped through the blue suede and pooled by one of the wheels on the Dumpster.

My stomach spun like towels in a dryer, hitting me with a wave of nausea. I coughed twice. I reached out for something for balance, but I was too far away from the building, too far from the Dumpster. I moved backward a few steps, stumbled over a concrete block, then pressed my back up against the door. I fumbled with the knob until the door was open, then closed the door behind me and tried to catch my breath.

"Ms. Monroe?" said Officer Clark. I looked at the front gate. The officer stood by the rusted metal, watching me. "Are you okay?"

"Mr. Pickers—outside—by my Dumpster."

"Mr. Pickers is no threat to you."

"He's—he's dead."

We locked eyes for a few seconds. "Ms. Monroe, stay where you are."

Officer Clark disappeared from my view.

I propped myself on both palms and breathed in, breathed out. Ringing filled my ears, until I realized it was the sound of sirens. I had a brief thought about meeting Officer Clark outside, but felt too dizzy when I stepped away from the counter to act on the impulse. I bowed my head, kept my palms on the white laminate counter, and closed my eyes, trying to block out the noise.

Tires kicked up gravel. Car doors slammed. Voices—lots of voices. Footsteps. I pulled myself together and walked to the back door, opening it to a scene of Officer Clark conferring with a woman in a black pantsuit. Another man snapped photos of the body with a large camera that hung around his neck. The crowd of people who had been gathering in front of the store now gathered in the alley. Another officer faced them, his arms out on both sides, blocking their view.

I looked back at the Dumpster, then turned away, fighting dizziness.

"Why don't we go inside?" said Officer Clark. He held his arm out, palm open, indicating the back door and blocking my view of the body at the same time. I turned to the fabric store and trudged inside, heading straight for the wrap stand.

"What do you think happened here?" he asked.

"I don't know what happened. You woke me up with your sirens."

"When's the last time you went out back?"

"Last night." I thought about it for a second. "I had trash." I looked around the floor of the register area, then at the back door.

"What were you throwing out?"

"Trash," I repeated, then continued. "I got takeout from the bar on the corner. A white plastic bag from last night's dinner, and whatever else was in the trash can. Looked like notes and receipts. A couple of scraps of fabric. I tied it all up in a couple of yards of blue suede and threw it away." I felt the color drain from my face.

Officer Clark went to the back door and pushed it open. I watched his head turn slowly as he scanned the lot. "You find a bag of trash?" he asked someone. I didn't hear an answer, but after a pause he continued. "Can you tell what's inside?"

"A takeout bag from The Broadside. Couple of squeezed-out packets of ketchup. A strip of zebra fur like the one she's wearing," said another voice.

"Any blue suede?"

The technician pointed to the body of Mr. Pickers. Officer Clark's head nodded and then he let the door shut again and returned to me at the wrap stand. "So you went out the back door to throw something out. What happened next?"

"Nothing. I saw—there was a man watching me. I came back inside and called my boyfriend."

"Where's he?" He looked past me to the interior of the store.

"He's in Los Angeles."

"What did you expect him to do?"

Why did everyone think I wanted Carson to do something? "I was unnerved. My car was vandalized yesterday and I wanted to hear a familiar voice."

"Did you report the vandalism?"

"No."

"Why not?"

"I don't know. Nothing was stolen and I already know my insurance won't cover it. It seemed like more of an inconvenience. I thought it was smarter to use the time to see if the mechanic could get it fixed so I could drive home."

"Where's your car now?"

"Charlie's Automotive."

The officer wrote something in a notebook. "So you called your boyfriend. Then what happened?"

"Nothing. We hung up and I went to bed."

"You don't remember anything else?"

"What are you getting at?"

"Ms. Monroe, when you threw your trash out, did you hear anything, see anything, smell anything unusual? Do you remember any other movement out there?"

"No."

"Think about it."

I started to answer, then stopped, realizing what he was asking of me. I closed my eyes and stood for a second, reimagining the scene as it had unfolded. "I opened the door. I was holding the trash. It was cloudy. I coughed twice, then opened the Dumpster and threw my trash inside."

"What do you mean, cloudy?"

"I don't know why I said that. Is it overcast?"

The officer headed to the back door and pushed it open again, looking at the sky. When he didn't close the door, I followed him and looked up. The sky was so uniformly blue it looked like a background someone had Photoshopped onto the otherwise disturbing scene. A construction truck, like the one I'd seen yesterday, drove through the alley. As it disappeared past the row of shrubs that marked off the edge of the property line, a cloud of concrete-colored dust filled the air.

"Cloudy like that?" asked Clark.

"Yes," I said, stifling another cough. "What does it mean?"

"Ms. Monroe, it means if you're thinking of staying here, you better start locking all the doors. And if you're thinking of leaving, I'd advise you to ignore the impulse."

Four

"Do I have to stay at the store?" I asked.

"You can stay wherever you want, but we need your contact information in the event of more questions."

"No—I don't mean that. Do I have to stay here right now? While you're doing this?" I waved my hands in big circles to take in the team processing the crime scene. "Because I'd really rather not."

"We'll be through here in a couple of hours."

I gave the Deputy Sheriff my contact info. He paused, as though he expected me to tell him where I was headed, but when I offered nothing else, he clicked the back of his pen and tucked it into the breast pocket of his uniform.

I collected my messenger bag and cell phone from the apartment upstairs where I'd spent the night, and kept my head down as I left out the back door of the fabric store and headed to the alley. Ken caught up with me as I rounded the corner.

"What are you doing, Poly? Why are you still here at the store?"

"My car was vandalized yesterday. I have to stick around until it's fixed, probably later today."

"You slept in there, didn't you? We have hotels, you know. If you're planning to stay in San Ladrón for any length of time, you might want to find another place to spend your nights."

"As a matter of fact, Charlie offered me her sofa to crash on, but I turned her down."

He turned to face the auto shop and thumbed over his shoulder. "*That* Charlie?"

"Yes, that Charlie."

"I wouldn't get too friendly with her if I were you."

"Why not?"

"She's trouble. Take it from me."

"She seemed perfectly fine yesterday when I asked her to fix my car."

"I'm sure she did. She probably saw *sucker* written across your face. You said your car was vandalized? Don't let her talk you into a bunch of work you don't need."

"Is that why you don't like her? She overcharged you for service on your Lexus? Serves you right for driving a fancy luxury car."

"Be careful who you make friends with, Poly. That's my only piece of advice." He got into his car and drove away before I had a chance to regret insulting his vehicle and passing up the opportunity for a ride.

The annoyance from yesterday, the fear from last night, and the shock of the morning had left me numb. Twenty-four hours ago I was on my way to an appointment with a high school friend who was going to help me navigate the inheritance of the fabric store. The events of the past day were gears to a machine that had been shaken too hard and no longer fit together. I couldn't focus on the bigger decision of selling the store or keeping it. I couldn't process Ken's annoyance. I didn't know what to do so I limited myself to the simplest of decisions. Turn left? Turn Right?

I turned left.

I walked down San Ladrón Avenue, past the gas station on the corner, through the light. Across the street, a few doors down from Charlie's shop, was the visitor's center. Catty-corner from me was a coffee shop named Jitterbug, and directly across the street was a beauty salon and a dentist. This town sure has a lot of salons, I thought. The light turned green and I crossed to the salon but kept walking. I passed a veterinarian, a scrapbook supply store, and a consignment shop before I discovered a small shop called Tea Totalers.

The building was a small white stucco storefront. Faded floral curtains hung inside the windows. A patio of mismatched wrought iron tables and chairs were arranged in front of the door covered with brightly colored seat cushions that didn't quite fit the chairs. A young couple exited the door and the scent of cinnamon exited with them. I waited until they'd reached the sidewalk where I stood before retracing their steps to the door of the shop. I could use a cup of tea, I thought. I could probably use something stronger, but the name of the store suggested I'd have to go somewhere else for that.

A bell chimed as I entered. Customers sat on stools that faced the faded curtains, checking their e-mails on laptops and cell phones. A *Free Wi-Fi* sign hung on the dark wood wall next to a small painting of a rooster. A shelf lined with large glass jars sat below the painting, each jar filled with crushed leaves. Masking tape labels on each jar indicated *Darjeeling*, *Chamomile*, *Earl Grey*, and *Proprietary Blend*. A stout woman in a floral dress that looked as faded as the curtains lifted the lid of the Proprietary Blend and leaned close, inhaling the scent. Even from my position by the door I could smell lemon and ginger wafting from the jar.

"May I help you?" prompted the woman behind the counter. Her hair was pulled back into a soft blond ponytail. An oval-shaped plastic pin with the name *Genevieve* in curly black handwriting pierced the strap of her apron. The outside of the *G* was faded, as if she'd gradually rubbed bits of it off while pinning it on.

I looked around at the other patrons. Everyone else was holding a cup or a mug, so I knew she was talking to me. I stepped forward and scanned the chalkboard menu.

"I'd like a cup of tea, please," I asked. "I smelled cinnamon from the street but I don't see it on the board."

She smiled. "You smelled our cinnamon scones, not our tea."

"Busted. I'd like one of those, then. And a cup of tea, too." I scanned the chalkboard again. "Chamomile, I guess."

Her head tipped to the side. "I don't think so."

"Excuse me?"

"I can read people. At least I can read their tea needs. You're not one of our regulars, so I don't know anything about your life, but you look as if you need something stronger than chamomile. I have just the thing. May I surprise you?"

"Sure," I said, half wondering if she served spiked mugs of Lipton from the back room.

I paid for my food and inquired about the restroom situation. A few minutes and a very necessary detour later, I returned to the restaurant and found a vacant seat under a poster of a black cat. Whoever had decorated the shop had attempted French countryside with dashes of French kitchen and French provincial thrown into the mix. The effort was not entirely successful but charming nonetheless. It succeeded in distracting me from the murder behind Land of a Thousand Fabrics, and a part of me wanted to ask if they had a vacant apartment upstairs so I could take up residency in pseudo-France.

The woman carried a wicker tray to my table. "This is ginger tea. If you don't like it I'll bring you something else, but I think it goes nicely with the cinnamon scone."

"Sounds yummy," I said. I picked up the plate with the scone while she set a small ceramic teapot in the center of the table. Cheerful blue and yellow flowers were painted under the glaze. A small chip in the handle gave evidence that it wasn't brand-new.

"It's nice to have a patron who isn't in a hurry. Are you taking a break from a road trip?" she asked.

"Not exactly." I wondered how much about my situation I should offer up to her. "I had a meeting in the area. It ended earlier than I thought, so now I have some spare time."

"Spare time. I don't remember what that feels like. Too many people rush, rush, rush around. We put up the Wi-Fi signs and doubled our business, but I still think the place was nicer when it was just tea, scones, and people reading books." She turned her head to the side and looked at my messenger bag out of the corner of her eye. "You should tell me now if you have a computer in there so I can stop before I embarrass myself."

"No computer," I said. "Just a wallet and a phone and some paperwork."

She smiled. "I'll let you get to it, then. Stay as long as you like. The morning rush is over and we're going to be slow until lunchtime."

I poured a mug of tea and added a scoop of honey from a jar that sat on the table. The scone delivered on its promise of cinnamon goodness and I considered ordering another. I pulled the file of paperwork that Ken had given me out of my messenger bag and started reading through it as I ate. I had a hard time concentrating. At first I thought it was the legalese, but the general unrest I felt whenever I thought about selling the store told me that wasn't it.

I leaned back and took a sip of tea. I focused on the white

eyelet trim that edged the faded curtain. White eyelet, just like the dress Aunt Millie had made me for my ninth-grade dance.

It was my first grown-up dance. The other girls in my class had taken trips to Los Angeles's shopping centers, returning with garment bags of colorful dresses and matching shoes. The boys talked about renting tuxedos. Aunt Millie asked me to come to the store after school, said she had a surprise for me. When I arrived, she had seven bolts of creamy white eyelet leaning against the side of the cutting station. She'd bought the fabric in Lyon, France, several years earlier. She'd imagined women coming in for custom bridal dresses, but the cost had kept it out of reach of most incomes, especially for a dress that might take upward of ten yards of fabric.

Next to the fabric was a mannequin dressed in an off-the-shoulder cotton dress. It was unlike the styles that were sold in the stores around town. It was from the late thirties. It was moth-eaten in several places, beyond repair. Aunt Millie asked if I wanted to learn how to deconstruct a garment and use it as a pattern for something new. The idea intrigued me. We started the project that day, snipping invisible threads and marking pieces of the collar, bodice, skirt, belt, and interfacing. I spent two hours after school every day for the next two weeks working side by side Aunt Millie on that dress. When it was done, it was perfect.

I wore it to my ninth-grade dance. I'd never forget how it felt to move around the dance floor, the full, multilayered eyelet skirt swishing around my ankles. I'd been taller than most of the boys by that time, and had only been asked to dance twice, but it hadn't mattered. It was the first time I'd helped construct a garment for myself. It was the first time I recognized the transformative power of the luxurious fabrics from my aunt and uncle's store.

I was lost in the memory when a bell sounded over the door to the tea shop.

"Vaughn, so nice to see you this morning," the woman said.

"Hi, Genevieve. What's good today?"

I looked up from the file to see Vaughn McMichael approach the counter. He hadn't noticed me sitting along the side of the store yet. I closed the folder and stuffed it into my messenger bag. Vaughn's back was to me. I stood up and slung the bag over my right shoulder, wiped my mouth of crumbs, and headed to the door. The strap from the messenger bag caught on the scrollwork of the white metal chair and pulled it two feet forward with me. I jerked back and shrugged out from the strap, wrestling it free before stepping away. When I turned to see if anyone had noticed, both Vaughn and Genevieve were staring.

"I'm sorry for the noise. Thank you for the tea. I just realized I'm late." I hustled out the front door to the sidewalk, then turned left and walked three more blocks. I found a wooden bench under a blossoming dogwood tree and collapsed.

My phone vibrated with a call from an unfamiliar number. "Hello?"

"Ms. Monroe? This is Officer Clark."

I exhaled. "Officer Clark," I repeated.

"We're all done. You can go back to the store whenever you want."

"Thank you."

I leaned back against the bench and stared at the clear blue sky. My choices were most unsavory. Return to the fabric store, where a man had been killed, or wander the streets of an unfamiliar town, waiting for news of my car. I chose the lesser of two evils and walked back to the fabric store. Unlike the streets of San Ladrón, I had a connection to the store.

A cardboard carton sat in front of the rusted metal fence. There was a blue bow stuck to the top, the premade kind with the adhesive sticky back that came in a bag of a dozen. When I got closer, I saw an envelope jutting out from under the bow. *Polyester Monroe*, it said.

I opened the envelope and pulled out an invoice from Charlie's Automotive. Written in pen across the center of the page was a message: *Welcome to the neighborhood. Need more time with your car. Let me know if you're short on determination.—C*

I unfolded the flaps of the box and exposed four bottles of 10W40, a handful of rags, and a gallon jug of water. Ken could say whatever he wanted, but based on the evidence in front of me, Charlie was A-okay.

Thanks to the discovery of Mr. Pickers's body, I had new motivation for addressing the "how to enter the store from the front" situation. If I were at home, I would have changed into jeans and a T-shirt before tackling the task of oiling the fence, but I wasn't. After tripping three times and sleeping in my clothes, I was less concerned about getting grease on them and more concerned with what I would change into after the project was done. Stains didn't matter to me much; they were the reason I wore black most of the time.

Working for my boss, Giovanni, on any given day I could be repairing sewing machines, scouring fabric distributors, gluing embellishments onto a dress, or delivering a rolling rack of garments to a vendor on Santee Alley. Only on my first couple of days had I made the mistake of dressing like I thought someone in the fashion industry might dress: heels, skinny jeans, a fitted blazer, and a vintage scarf. After the scarf got chewed up in the serger and the low-rise waistband of my jeans left a welt around my midsection, I adopted a simpler uniform: black, plus black, plus black. My short auburn hair and trademark cranberry lipstick provided the color. My low-maintenance routine allowed me to leave the apartment ten minutes after getting out of bed if necessary.

My wardrobe was funereal but functional. Someday I'd

show off my glamorous side with one of the vintage 1930s dresses I bought from eBay. I told Carson they were inspiration for the dresses I designed at To The Nines, but there was a reason I only bought the ones that would accentuate my figure. My hips had developed somewhere around puberty but the rest of my figure didn't get the memo. I'd been wearing the same bra size since high school. I'd heard that eighty percent of women were wearing the wrong size bra, but when I assessed what God gave me, I couldn't believe I'd advanced any further into the alphabet.

I looked up and down the street. A family of four walked toward me but entered the antiques store to my left. Cars were scattered along the street, but I didn't see a lot of people walking around. A gray-haired man in a wheelchair sat on the corner of the sidewalk across the street. If I was going to do this, then I was going to accept that people would notice. I turned back to the gate, dumped a couple glugs of motor oil onto a faded yellow terry-cloth rag, and set to work on the hinges. It was slow going until I developed a system.

After I oiled every hinge on the gate I gave it a tug. The fence cried out but one joint buckled, then two. I threw more of my weight into the project and placed a foot for leverage along the molding by the front door. It wasn't easy, but after an hour's worth of effort, the hinges gave way and the gate retracted.

It was with a sense of accomplishment and anticipation that I pulled the creaky gate open. I felt a surprising wave of emotion. I knew what I'd find inside—after all, I'd spent the night in the store—but this door hadn't been opened in a long time. Being the one to change that felt empowering. Not an investor or a new tenant but me: a Monroe.

I pushed the key into the lock of the front door and turned it, then pulled the door toward me. Beams of sunshine poured through the doorway, highlighting dust particles that floated through the air. I propped the door open with an empty jug of motor oil and went inside.

At the cutting station I found a broom and dustpan. Starting at the front corner by colorful bolts of cotton, I swept, working at a backward and diagonal pattern the way Aunt Millie had taught me to sweep when I helped out after school and on weekends. Sweat dampened my hairline, creating curly tendrils by the nape of my neck. I was due for a trim, but this wasn't the time to worry about my hair. I set the broom down and pulled a roll of black cotton off the shelf, preparing to tear off enough to tie over my head. At the last minute I changed my mind, going with a length of silver silk instead.

Every four feet or so the dustpan resembled a small furry animal. After three trips to the register to empty the dustpan in the trash, I brought the plastic trash bin with me and made it part of my portable cleaning unit. I found a stash of plastic bags under the register and started filling and lining them against the wall by the back door.

It took the better part of three hours to sweep the floor. I was more thorough because I knew quitting, and emptying the trash, involved me going out back and looking at the Dumpster. I was afraid to stop for food or for break, for fear my motivation would dwindle. I didn't know why cleaning the store was so important to me. If I sold it off, no doubt someone else would come in after I left, gut the place, and start from scratch. The only reason it made sense to clean the store was if I intended to open it for business, and it seemed like too much of a stretch to consider that. My life was in Los Angeles, wrapped up with my job at To The Nines, my boyfriend, Carson, and my boss, Giovanni. My car wouldn't be finished for at least another day, and the deputy sheriff had told me not to leave town yet. Cleaning the store gave me something to do. So for now, I was at a standstill in San Ladrón. I found myself thinking there were worse places to be.

I looked around the store at the inventory. Along the right-hand wall were bolts of once-bright cottons. Paisley, gingham, floral, and solids rested on tipped shelves, sorted by color. A film of dust sat on top of them, but I knew that dust sat only on the top layer of the fabric, and once I cut off half a yard of each, I'd expose an assortment that would make a quilter feel like a kid in a candy store.

Beyond the cottons were tables stacked high with longer bolts of decorator fabric. Each table had a sign in the middle. *France*, *Spain*, *Italy*, *England*, *Germany*. Since the building had been closed tight, no water or humidity had snuck in. A surprising number of the fabrics were still in good condition, though some were coated with similar layers of dust.

I could easily sell Giovanni the bolts of satin, silk, and taffeta. These would be a definite improvement to anything he could get from our regular suppliers. I could sketch out a collection that our team of sewers would produce quickly, that would bring in ten times what he normally charged for a dress. This could be it, I thought. This could be the key to me going from head designer of pageant dresses to something more suited to a graduate from FIDM.

I was running out of steam and needed a break. I gave myself a pep talk: Carry the trash out back, throw it out, and then you're done. I grabbed the tops of several bags of trash and leaned against the back door, pushing it open with my hip. I tossed the bags over the edge of the large metal box, and then screamed when I looked inside.

Vaughn McMichael was inside my Dumpster, rooting through my trash.

Five

"Is this part of the 'run Poly out of town' plan? First some local yahoos vandalize my car, then somebody calls the cops on me, and now dig through my trash looking for dirt?" I said.

"I'm not looking for dirt on you," he said.

"Then do you want to tell me what you're doing in the middle of my Dumpster?"

He bent down, disappearing from view. I approached the edge and set the trash down on the outside before looking in. He stood up, cradling two small kittens to either side of his chest.

"How did you know they were there?" I asked.

"I heard something coming from the trash. I have to be honest—considering what happened here this morning, I wasn't sure what I would find."

"You must have been pretty close to hear them," I said. "Are you sure you weren't here for another reason?"

"Like what?"

"Like looking for evidence from this morning?"

"That's not my job."

"But rescuing kittens is?"

"Today it is." Vaughn dropped his head and looked at the kittens in his hands. I couldn't tell if he was trying to think of an explanation or a cover story.

"Who would put two sweet helpless kittens in the Dumpster? In my Dumpster?" I looked to the left and the right of the parking lot at the alleyways that framed out the block. I don't know what I was looking for, but I saw nothing suspicious. "What about the police? They were here a couple of hours ago. They would have looked in there while they were—while they did their thing."

"I don't know how they got here, but they might not have made it through the night."

"What if you hadn't come along? The trash men would have taken them to—" I stopped, sickened by the idea. "And even if someone found them, they'd be in with my trash. People would assume I'd put helpless little kittens in my trash." My voice shook with emotion.

"Hey, it's okay. They're okay now," Vaughn said. The kittens nestled against his William and Mary sweatshirt. The gray one tried to twist around and stick his head under Vaughn's armpit. He was only mildly successful.

"I feel inadequately prepared for the situation. Care to help me out?"

"Sure." I scooped the gray kitten out of Vaughn's hand and cuddled it to my chest, then took the orange one in my other hand. I wasn't exactly well endowed, but they managed to nestle together over the front center hook on my bra. I stole a quick look at Vaughn, who was staring at them. My face grew hot and I shrugged my shoulders forward and readjusted my arms to block Vaughn's view of my chest.

"They're cold," he said.

"You have a lot of nerve pointing out something like that!"

"I'm talking about the kittens. What do you think I'm talking about?"

"My—the kittens." Even without looking at them I could feel them shivering against me. "Can you get the door? I'm pretty sure I can give them a decent temporary home."

Vaughn jogged past me and held the door open while I walked in. I set the kittens on the wrap stand and found the box that had held the motor oil, now empty. I lined it with several cuttings of faux fur. The zebra was getting low, so I cut a few strips of tiger fur as well, creating a patchwork jungle. I added a few more wads of fur—a leopard print and a long gorilla fur to round things out—and carried the box to the wrap stand. Vaughn set the kittens into the box where they cozied up to each other. I stroked the fur on top of each of them. They closed their eyes and started to purr very softly. We remained quiet, as if speaking would interrupt their peace.

"You've been cleaning," Vaughn said, scanning the store's interior.

I nodded. I wasn't sure what he would make of my efforts, and I wasn't sure I could explain my motivation to do so even if he asked.

"Looks good. I see you got the gate open."

I nodded again.

"How about the back room? Have you been back in there yet?"

"You mean since you pulled me through the window? No."

"It's been a long time since anybody's been back there. A lot of people think there's something valuable hidden in that room."

"What?"

"Your aunt Millie's bracelet."

I'd forgotten about the rumors that the reason for the robbery that resulted in my aunt's murder was her gold charm bracelet. "I always assumed the robbers took it."

"They claim they didn't."

"And you believe them? They're crooks who killed my great-aunt. I don't believe anything they said."

"There were still a lot of unanswered questions even after the police closed the case. We'll probably never know the truth."

"The truth is that a couple of robbers broke into the store to steal whatever was in the register. They found Aunt Millie, killed her, stole the bracelet and money, and left. They probably fenced the bracelet before they got caught, or had it melted down into an unrecognizable lump of gold," I said.

"The robbers have always maintained they didn't kill your great-aunt. They said they were hired to rob the place and were guaranteed that it would be empty. The police never found the bracelet and never recovered the missing money."

"Why do you know so much about this?" I asked.

"Why don't you?" he answered back.

"It was my high school graduation. My family made a big deal about it because I'd gotten confirmation of a full scholarship to the fashion institute. Uncle Marius and Aunt Millie were supposed to come later that night after the store closed, but they never made it." I was silent for a moment, staring at the kittens instead of looking at Vaughn. I'd never told anybody about that night, about how my family had kept the truth from me because they thought they were protecting me, and how sick I'd felt when I learned what had happened. I hadn't been back to the store since then.

"When did you find out?"

"Later. Nobody wanted to talk about it. Uncle Marius stopped sending me birthday presents, and he withdrew from the family. I think it was easier for everyone to try to pretend it didn't happen, but I couldn't." I looked away from

Vaughn, surprised and embarrassed that I'd told him so much. I felt him watching me and focused my attention on the kittens, running my open palm over the orange one's tiny head. He raised his head and bumped his little pink nose into my thumb.

"It must have been hard for you, Poly." Vaughn's voice softened when he said my name. His eyes were wide, framed by lashes that were wasted on a guy. His hair had gotten mussed up when he was in the Dumpster and now flopped over his forehead. I had the urge to push it away from his eyes, but felt it was too intimate of a gesture to act on.

"I think it was harder for my family. This huge tragedy happened and nobody grieved properly because they were trying to protect me so I could have a happy graduation. But I didn't care about the graduation. Ten years went by and, because my uncle kept the store locked up and cut himself off from the rest of the family, I never had a chance to come back to the store, to make peace with Aunt Millie being gone. Nobody would talk about it. I wanted to know the truth, and now I'll never know, aside from a decade of rumors."

"I might be able to help with that."

"How?"

He checked his watch. "It's later than I thought and I have to be somewhere. I know this is last-minute, but can I take you to dinner tonight? I'd like to keep talking about this."

His invitation blindsided me. "I haven't thought far enough ahead to know where I'll be tonight."

"Then let me decide that for you. You'll be at the Waverly House at, say, seven thirty? I'll meet you out front."

He got halfway out the door before I called out to him. "Vaughn, you didn't live here when the murder happened. If you had, I would have known you. So who told you? How do you know so much about that night?"

He looked at the ground and then at me. "Mr. Pickers told me."

Six

"Mr. Pickers told you about my great-aunt's murder? Why were you talking to him about my family? What did he know about it?" I asked.

"Meet me tonight. We've got a lot to talk about." Vaughn turned away from me and let himself out the back door. I wanted to run after him and ask more questions, but I didn't. His invitation to dinner was unexpected, and a part of me felt guilty accepting it while I had a steady boyfriend waiting for me back in Los Angeles. The more I thought about it, the more I questioned his presence at my Dumpster hours after the police had finished processing the crime scene. Had he really heard the barely audible mews of a pair of helpless kittens, or was he responsible for them being there in the first place? Like every other question from that morning, I had no answers. And I couldn't help but confront the other side of the question, too. If he *was* telling the truth, if he knew something that connected Mr. Pickers to the fabric store, then I didn't want to pass up the opportunity.

I said good-bye to the two sleeping kittens and went out the front door, locking it behind me. I didn't bother with the gate. Too much work had gone into removing it and, at least for the next twenty-four hours, it would stay retracted. I looked at the curb where I'd parked my car when I first arrived in San Ladrón. It wasn't there. I crossed the street and went to Charlie's Automotive. The same Van Halen CD was playing in the background. My VW was jacked up, but no feet stuck out from under the car.

"Hello?" I called out. "Charlie? Are you here?"

"Keep your pants on, I'll be right out," said a voice from behind a door that blended in with the wall. A few seconds later a toilet flushed, water ran, and the door opened.

"I see you made good use of my present," she said as she dried her hands on a wad of brown paper towels. "I like that about you. You don't just sit around talking about doing something. You dig in and do it."

"I've been busy." I glanced at my reflection, cringing when I saw the silver silk over my head and the grease stains on my face.

"I noticed. What was up with the three-ring circus this morning?"

"You don't know?"

"I know for the first time in years people are saying 'trouble' and pointing at you instead of saying it about me. What gives? Did you turn up evidence in that unsolved murder?"

A pulse of panic shot through my chest at the thought of my aunt, alone in the store the night it had been robbed and she'd been killed. "No. A man was found murdered behind the store."

"Who found him?"

"I did."

"Seems the circus was in place before you answered the door."

She'd been watching the store. Why? Curiosity? Or was there more to it?

"There was a mix-up. Why did you say my aunt's murder was unsolved? The robbers went to jail."

"They say they didn't do it. That doesn't bother you?"

"That they lied? Criminals lie all the time. No, it doesn't bother me."

"Even if it means the person responsible is still out there?"

I looked down at the tools that were scattered on the floor of her shop. She was giving me an opportunity to talk about my aunt's murder, just like Vaughn. The story had been kept silent in my family despite my desire to know the details. But what if? What if she and Vaughn were right, that the person responsible was still free?

And what if the murder behind the store this morning had something to do with it?

"You're here for your car, right?" Charlie said, pulling me from my thoughts. "I have good news and bad news. Bad news first. You need a new ignition switch. It's not that easy to find an ignition switch for an eighty-three VW Bug. I ordered the part, but best-case scenario, I won't have it until tomorrow, and I'm not a best-case scenario kind of person. You want to hear the good news?"

"Sure."

"I'm going to charge you enough that I can afford to buy you lunch." She smiled. Her thick hair was pulled back into a low ponytail today and hung down well past her shoulder blades. When she smiled, she looked pretty, in an "I could beat you up if I wanted" kind of way. I wondered if that got her many dates.

"Tell you what. I'll take a rain check on lunch if I can get a one-time use of your shower."

"I didn't want to say anything, but you look like you just completed an oil-change marathon." She sniffed the air. "I'm immune to the scent of 10W40, but I find it impressive that you haven't added any other scents."

"Let's just say my twenty-four-hour deodorant is working overtime. Where can I get a couple of personal items?"

"Drugstore just past the intersection."

"How about clothes?"

"I think you're asking the wrong questions."

"Meaning what?"

"You got a building full of fabric and you're asking where to get clothes? I'd think you'd be asking where to get a sewing machine."

"This is temporary. It's not like I'm setting up camp here."

"Keep telling yourself that."

Our conversation was interrupted by the loud rumbling of a car out front. Ken climbed out of his black Lexus. By the sounds of it, he was in need of Charlie's services at least as much as I was. I was surprised to see him, considering his earlier warning about her.

"I need to talk to you. Alone."

I looked at Charlie. She took a step backward and held her hands up. "He's talking to you. I think he's in denial about his muffler situation."

"You're here to see me? About what, the offer? I already told you, I need more time."

"That's not it. Things have gotten more complicated." He looked over my shoulder. I followed his gaze to Charlie, who shook her head and walked away. "There's another offer," he said after she left the room.

"Somebody else wants to buy the fabric store? Who?"

"Came in about two hours ago. I would have called you sooner but I wanted to check him out to see if he was legit. He's some finance guy in Los Angeles. Name's Carson Cole."

"I need to use your phone." I snatched Ken's cell from his hand before he had a chance to say no and dialed Carson's number from memory. I'd cycled through most of the entry-level curse words by the time he answered and was contemplating a couple of new ones.

"It's about time you called me back," Carson said.

"What is wrong with you?"

"I've left about a dozen messages on your phone. What's going on?"

"My phone is dead. I've got about two minutes. You're trying to buy the fabric store from me? Why?"

"You heard about my offer. Good. I was wrong. You saying 'no sale' to McMichael was a stroke of genius. I got together a couple of private investors. They'll sell off the inventory for you, then resell the building to McVic for a profit. I heard he's been in negotiations with a Walmart or a Target or somebody. These are big bucks. Don't sign away the store to him. We can make a lot more from this if we play our cards right."

"We? Our? Us?"

"Poly, this is what I do. And the store, the fabric, that's what you do. It's the perfect project to bring us closer together. You should talk to your boss. I bet Giovanni would be interested in the fabrics even if they are dry-rotted. He'll get you to design some kind of appliqué to hide the flaws."

"You didn't tell Giovanni about the store, did you?"

"You sound annoyed."

"I'm tired and cranky and I need a shower and I have to get ready for dinner."

"Your car's not done yet? You took it to a licensed mechanic, right?"

"I forgot this isn't my cell phone. I better go."

"Wait," he said as I was pulling the phone away from my head. I could have hung up, but I didn't. I felt bad about snapping at Carson. There was no way he could have known how I felt about the fabric store since being back inside of it. When I'd left our apartment yesterday, I'd expected to drive an hour to San Ladrón, sign some paperwork and maybe have lunch with Ken, and drive home. I hadn't expected the nostalgic pull of memories that made me think twice about selling. I turned away from Ken and dropped my voice. "A lot has happened since I got here yesterday, and to tell you the truth, I'm tempted to cancel my dinner plans so I can go to sleep early."

"Who are you going to dinner with?"

I paused for a second. "Vaughn McMichael. The son of the man who wants to buy the fabric store."

"Ooh, they're good. You know what they're doing, right? They're trying to soften you up, gain an edge. Whatever you do, don't cancel."

"I don't think it's like that." I thought back over how I'd felt when Vaughn was at the store earlier, when I'd found him in my Dumpster with the kittens. I blushed recalling how I'd reacted when I'd thought he was staring at my chest.

"Why else would he want to take you to dinner?" Carson said.

I bristled. "Don't worry, I won't agree to anything that will jeopardize our future."

"Remember that. But this could be good for us. Act like you like him. That'll keep him from figuring out what we're planning."

"Aren't you the least bit jealous that I'm going to dinner with another man?"

"It's pretty obvious he's interested in your property, not mine." He chuckled.

"I have to go."

I hung up and handed the phone back to Ken. He wiped it against the side of his pants like he needed to rid it of my cooties, then he pushed it into the back pocket of his pants.

"What was that about?" he asked.

"My boyfriend has taken an interest in the store."

"Is he in the fabric business?"

"No. He's in the business business. He's your new offer."

"Your boyfriend has the kind of capital to match Mr. McMichael's offer?" I looked closely at Ken and could practically see the dollar signs in his eyes. "You think he'd want to buy property in San Ladrón?"

"He knows people." I shook my head to myself. How could Carson be so quick to tap his contacts when he thought there was a good deal on the table, but so slow when it came to understanding how I felt about it?

"Relationships are tough, Poly. It'll work itself out," Ken said. "I see your car's still up on the rack. Do you need a ride anywhere?"

I looked inside Charlie's shop. My yellow Bug was four feet in the air. Before I had a chance to ask Ken to drive me to the drugstore, Charlie appeared behind me.

"Yo—Polyester. Think fast." She tossed a set of keys to me. I accidentally knocked them farther out of reach, and Ken snagged them from the air. He looked at them briefly then dropped them into my open palm.

"White Camaro. Out back. You can drive stick, right?"

"Sure," I answered. I'd learned to drive on a stick shift, but it had been a long time. I hoped it was like riding a bike.

"It might look like a throwback to the greatest decade ever, but it's wired with an alarm. Customized. LoJack, too, and Lockdown. The gas gauge is broken, and I can't really say if that's going to matter to you or not. You might want to fill her up at the Circle K on the corner before you go too far."

It took four stalls and restarts for me to get the feel for the muscle car's clutch. I drove to the gas station down the block and spent the better part of a hundred dollar bill to fill the tank. Genevieve's tea shop was down the next block. I parked the car in front of the store and went inside.

This time the store smelled like butterscotch. The line by the register was two people deep and I made it a third. I closed my eyes and inhaled the scent. By the time it was my turn I was willing to spend whatever it cost to get a piece of the mystery baked goods to go.

"I wasn't sure if I'd see you again," said Genevieve. She counted out a stack of one-dollar bills and tucked them into the pocket of her faded apron.

"Did I tell you I was leaving?" I asked. "I don't remember saying that."

"You're the fabric woman everybody's been talking about, right? Gabardine?" She cocked her head to the side.

"Polyester. Poly. Poly Monroe," I said. I glanced over my shoulder to see if I was holding up the line, but no one had entered the shop after me. "Do I want to know what people are saying?" I asked.

"I'm sure you can imagine." She studied me. "Okay, maybe you can't, but no reason to lose sleep over it. People around here like to talk."

"People everywhere like to talk," I added.

"Yes, but around here people make talking practically an Olympic sport." She smiled. "What can I get you?"

"For starters, whatever it is that smells like butterscotch. I'll take one—two of them, and a cup of whatever tea you think would go best with it."

"Two blondies and a special cup of tea coming right up. You can sit anywhere. I'll find you." Her smile held a hint of sadness that I attributed to the empty store.

"I'm not staying this time."

"You're leaving town already?"

"I'm not leaving San Ladrón yet, but I have to pick up a couple of items, so I'll need my order to go."

"You've been bit by the rush-rush bug." She totaled my sale, and wrapped two golden blondies in white wax paper, nestled them into a small white cardboard box, and folded it shut. She sealed it with a tan sticker that had a picture of the Eiffel Tower on it.

"How soon are you going to drink the tea?" she asked.

"As soon as it's cooled down enough to swallow."

"Perfect." She reached for a cardboard cup and fitted a corrugated sleeve over the bottom, then filled it with hot water. From an index card–sized box to the left of the register, she flipped through small white envelopes, pulling out one about a third of the way through a stack. She tapped the contents onto a square of cheesecloth, clamped a small metal ring around the top, and dropped it into the cup.

"Give it at least five minutes to steep. More if you're looking for a caffeine boost."

"What was that?"

"Those are my special blends. I like to experiment. Tell me what you think."

I raised the cup to my nose. "If the smell is any indication, I'm hooked."

"It's a nice complement to the blondies. There's a hint of dried sour cherry in there. Anything else I can help you with today?"

"Only one. Can you give me directions to the closest shopping center?"

I jugged the box and the tea cup on my way to the car and ate one blondie before I pulled away from the curb. I followed Genevieve's directions down Bonita Avenue until I passed two miles of small ranch houses and a senior center, and came to a strip mall anchored with a drugstore. I picked up two plastic bowls for the cats, eyeliner, mascara, underwear, and a strawberry-scented lip gloss for me, and left.

I moved on to a clothing store called Secrets in the Closet. They stocked both new and secondhand clothing, and after a quick scan of the interior to determine the layout, I assembled a makeshift wardrobe of black clothes and checked out. I finished at the grocery store, where I picked up several gallons of water, bowls, cat food, and a litter box.

I drove back to the fabric store and set up food, water, and litter box stations next to the dividing wall. The kittens followed their noses to the corner where I stood with a can of Fancy Feast half-opened. I pulled the metal lid off and forked the wet cat food into a bowl. They bumped shoulders and heads trying to get at the food, until I picked one up and moved him to the opposite side of the bowl. For the next couple of minutes, all I could hear was the sound of them snorting and lapping at the food, until the tabby looked up and licked his mouth. The bowl was empty. I ran my hand over each of their heads, and left.

It was over an hour before I returned the Camaro to Charlie. I found her sitting at a desk, studying a handwritten register of business.

"Does your offer of a shower still stand?" I asked.

"Sort of. I have an unexpected meeting tonight and I can't have you showing up with me. If you're adventurous, you can use the shower here. Sometimes I get caught late and can't make it home, so I installed it. It's pretty bare-bones for the high-maintenance salon crowd around San Ladrón, but it works for me."

I followed her through the garage to a door in the back corner. How bad could it be? I wondered to myself. She led me to a small room, about eight feet square. After I followed her through she kicked a rubber stopper out from under the door. Wedged into the corner was a shower unit shaped like a hexagon. The back three walls were molded out of white laminate; the front were panels of textured Lucite. Someone—presumably Charlie—had lined the Lucite with sheets of contact paper so the unit wasn't see-through.

"Like I said, it's pretty bare-bones. I got the shower unit on clearance. The quality is questionable, but I reinforced all the joints with caulk. The drain's so-so, so don't worry if it backs up a little. There's shampoo and conditioner and soap in the caddy. Your biggest problem is going to be the hot water. It runs out after four minutes. After that you're auditioning for a spot in the polar bear club. The door sometimes sticks, too, but if you put your weight into it, it'll pop right open. Clean towels on the bench. Dirty towels go in the basket underneath it. There are two doors, but I'm locking the one that leads to the shop. You can leave out the door over there." She pointed to a door that separated us from outside. "Got it?"

I scanned the small room. The interior walls of the shed had been whitewashed. Framed pages from a vintage calendar, featuring watercolors of women posing behind robes, blankets, and nightgowns, hung on three of the walls. The ground had been covered with a grid of gray plastic squares that snapped together. I'd seen them advertised somewhere—Sears, Home Depot, Lowe's—for use inside a garage. Along one wall was a white picnic bench with a round wicker basket underneath it. A terry-cloth robe hung from a hook next to the bench.

"Who assembled this place?" I asked her.

"Who do you think?" she answered, hands on her hips.

"I like it." From the look on her face, an angry twist that softened into a smile, I realized she thought I was judging her. "You don't let a lot of people back here, do you?"

"I keep this place secret. People think they've figured me out, but that's because they don't want to look past the obvious things they already know. My business is my business. Professional *and* personal."

"So why are you letting me back here?"

"You're different from the people around here." She pulled the door open and turned back around. "Have fun tonight, Polyester," she called, then left.

I threw the flimsy interior lock—a metal hook that fed

into a loop—on the inside of the door, because it was the only privacy measure available. I stripped down and turned on the water. Four minutes, I thought to myself. I hoped it was long enough to rid myself of the motor oil and grime I'd picked up in the past twenty-four hours.

The jet blast of water was strong, pounding against my shoulders, head, and body. It felt good against my sore, tired muscles, and I was tempted to test Charlie's four-minute estimation. It was around seven o'clock when I'd gotten back to the auto shop and that left only half an hour for me to get ready and get to the Waverly House for my dinner meeting with Vaughn. I had no intention of being late.

I washed and conditioned my hair and lathered up my body with the lemon-scented bar of soap in the caddy. The scent was invigorating. Water swirled around my feet, backing up by the drain like Charlie had predicted. It, too, felt good, soaking my feet like a pedicure bath might have done. Charlie had a good thing back here in her private quarters. No wonder she didn't tell people about it.

As I rinsed the lather from my torso, a pulse of cold water alerted me that my four minutes were almost up. I tipped my head back and pushed my hair away from my face one last time, then tried to turn off the water.

The knob came off in my hand. Cold water replaced hot and pelted me. I pushed against the door. It didn't budge. I put more of my weight into it and pushed as hard as I could against it. Again, no luck.

That's when I realized the water pooling at my feet was halfway up my calves.

Seven

The spray of water turned cold against my skin, making it harder and harder to move. I grabbed the interior handle on the shower and shook it, trying to loosen it up. Nothing worked.

The water level rose to my hips. I turned around and pressed my back against the door, leveraging my foot under the place where the water knob had been. With all my might, I pushed. Nothing.

I didn't know much about the chemical principles of caulk, but I was starting to think something more threatening was at play. I screamed for help and slapped my palms against the interior of the shower unit.

As the water climbed past my midsection, I gave up my efforts to open the door and looked for a new way out. There was no top on the shower unit. I stood on my tiptoes, thankful for my five-foot-nine height, and peeked over the top of the door. Steam interfered with my line of vision, but not enough to see that the door to the shed was now open.

I was running out of options. As I repositioned my feet in the water, now up to my chest, I realized the buildup of water pressure might be my answer. The makeshift shower rocked slightly and I knew the only way out was to try to climb out the top. I moved my body from one wall to another, grabbed ahold of the top of the unit, and pulled myself up, seeking traction with my bare feet on the walls. The unit tipped precariously and crashed to the ground.

A seal of caulk broke open on impact and water gushed out across the gray plastic flooring. I crawled out of the top of the unit, shivering from the now-icy-cold water. My ribs hurt from slamming into the ground. I gasped for breath. My air had never been cut off, but the fear of drowning in a two-foot-square shower had been enough to start me hyperventilating.

I pulled a plush white towel from the folding chair and covered with it, unable to do much more than that in my cold state. It wasn't enough. I reached into the basket where the dirty towels were and pulled out two more, wedging them around my feet. My teeth chattered like a windup set of teeth from a gag store. When I pressed them together to make them stop, my jaw jumped with the same movement.

A male voice sounded from the doorway. "What's going on in there? Charlie, is that you?"

"N-n-n-n-no. It's P-p-p-p-poly M-m-m-m-monroe."

I curled myself into a ball and wrapped my arms around my legs. The towels, sizeable bath sheets, only slightly helped. Water from the broken spout sprayed the interior of the shed, dousing everything. I crawled to the wall where a spigot was hidden under a bench. With a cold, shaking hand, I grabbed the knob and turned it several times to the left. The spray of water transitioned to a trickle, and then nothing.

I leaned against the bench and stuck my legs out in front of me. The calendar pages on the walls were tipped at angles and spotted with drops. The plastic walls of the shower lay in a pile on the floor, bent and cracked. I spied something under the wreckage. It was the triangle-shaped rubber door stopper that Charlie had moved away from the front door before she'd left. What was it doing by the busted shower unit? I tried to stand, but fell down, tripping over my own feet. At least this time I had more than a lack of coordination to blame.

I wrapped a towel around my torso and tucked the edge under my arm, then wrapped a second one around my waist and a third around my shoulders.

Vic McMichael entered the room. He was dressed formally in a tuxedo and bow tie with a black topcoat over it. A white scarf, almost the same shade as his hair, was draped around his neck. Even though my towels were fancy Egyptian cotton, I was painfully underdressed.

"H-h-h-how d-d-d-d-did you know I was in h-h-h-h-here?" I asked.

"Someone heard you scream. Do you need an ambulance?"

"No, I'm okay. Just c-c-c-c-cold."

He looked at the shower unit, lying on its side, and scanned the walls of the shed.

"Get dressed. I'm calling the police," he said, and left.

The clothes that I'd laid out were too wet to wear. Reluctantly I redressed in the dirty clothes I'd arrived in. They were stained and scented with motor oil, but they were dry, and that was all that mattered. I pulled the terry-cloth robe over my black turtleneck and jeans and knotted the belt around at my waist. After running fingers through my hair, I put everything I had brought with me into a plastic shopping bag and stumbled out of the shower/shed.

For the second time that day I was greeted with the red and blue pulse of police lights. A row of senior citizens stood by the sidewalk, staring at me. I wondered if one of them had overheard my scream and called Mr. McMichael?

"Ms. Monroe, do you want to tell me what happened here?" asked Officer Clark, who I'd met that morning. The polite note to his voice suggested we were still on good terms.

"Charlie said I could use her shower. She said the door sometimes stuck but I couldn't get it open. The knob came off in my hand when I tried to turn off the water and the water started backing up in the drain. I didn't know what else to do to get out of there except to tip the unit."

"Sounds a little far-fetched," said one of the seniors. I scanned the row of faces but couldn't identify the speaker. I wasn't sure it mattered much. I turned my attention back to the deputy sheriff.

"Can we talk somewhere more private?" I asked. "Like maybe downtown?"

"We are downtown," he said.

"No, I mean your headquarters. The police station."

"We don't have a police station. We have a mobile sheriff's unit. I'm the sheriff."

"Okay, can we go to the sheriff's office?"

He looked at the crowd and back at me. "You'll have to ride in the back of the car."

"Does the car have a heater?"

"Yes."

"Then I'm okay with that."

I didn't bother making conversation from the backseat. It was a short ride, a couple of blocks, from Charlie's Automotive to the sheriff's mobile unit. It was across the street from the Waverly House, where I had been expected for dinner. Maybe when I was done, I'd go across the street and see if Vaughn was still there. I caught my reflection in the back windows of the police cruiser and decided maybe I wouldn't.

Officer Clark led the way to a small office with a worn wooden desk and a gray filing cabinet. A second chair with a torn black leather cushion faced the desk. Clark took the chair behind the desk, leaving me one option. Before I sat down, I asked, "Is there a restroom I can use?"

"Sure. Through this door, down the hall, on the right."

"Thank you."

I followed his directions. The police station was the last place I'd expected to spend my evening, but at the moment I welcomed the facilities and the sink. The mirrors, not so much. I saw the complete picture that had only been hinted on in the car windows. My face was pale, my lips so faint they were borderline blue. I bit down on the lower lip while I ran hot water over my hands. After turning off the faucet, I finger-combed my hair into a side part and tucked the sides behind my ears. Attempts at vanity were worthless. I looked as exhausted as I felt. No way was I was going to the Waverly House after this.

I retraced my steps back to Officer Clark's desk. "Deputy sheriff, I don't know if this is allowed or not, but can I make a phone call?"

"You're not under arrest."

"I didn't mean 'one phone call' like that. I mean, can I use a phone here to make a call? My cell phone is dead."

"What kind of cell do you have?"

"iPhone."

He pulled a wooden drawer filled with power cords out of the desk and set it in front of me, then turned the phone around so it faced me, too. "We probably have a charger in here for your phone. In the meantime, dial nine first, and then dial your number."

I rooted through the drawer for the right charger, and then found an outlet to the right of me. After plugging it in, I dialed information from the desk phone. The call was answered after five rings. "Waverly House, how may I help you?"

"Do you have a Mr. Vaughn McMichael dining with you tonight?" I asked.

"Yes, we do."

"Would it be possible to give him a message?"

"I can get him if you'd like. He's waiting for the other half of his party."

"I'm the other half of his party and I'm not going to make it. Something came up."

"I see. Would you like to speak to him yourself?"

"No, thank you. Please tell him I apologized and said it couldn't be helped."

"Your name, miss?"

"Poly Monroe," I said.

"I'll give him the message."

She wished me a nice evening and hung up first. I placed the black receiver back on the cradle and wondered if I should have given more details or spoken to Vaughn.

Deputy Sheriff Clark stood in the doorway with two chipped white mugs. Steam rolled from the tops of them. "Coffee or hot chocolate?"

"You actually have hot chocolate?"

"Mrs. Pickers gave us a jar every year for Christmas. Never knew anybody to buy cocoa in a ten-gallon drum before."

"There's a *Mrs.* Pickers?" I asked.

"There was. She passed away a few years ago. Funny old couple, the Pickers. They were always arguing. I think he started the Senior Patrol to get a break from her."

He smiled to himself, obviously touched by a memory

he chose not to share. He looked back at me and held out the mug. "Give me a sec to get another cocoa. I was sure you were going to take the coffee."

I curled my fingers around the hot mug and breathed in the comforting scent of the cocoa before taking a sip. It almost didn't seem real that an hour ago I was in the middle of a near-death experience in a two-foot-square shower behind an auto shop and now I was sipping hot chocolate with a cop.

Deputy Sheriff Clark returned with his own mug of steaming hot chocolate. His had tiny marshmallows on top. "Do you want to tell me what happened back there?" he asked, leaning back in his chair.

I took another sip and set the mug on the edge of the desk. "Charlie said I could use her shower. She said the door sticks sometimes, and it did. The water backed up. It was waist-high when I tipped it over to get out."

"You could have hurt yourself with a stunt like that."

"It wasn't a stunt." I studied the sheriff's face. I wasn't sure what to make of his choice of words. "The shower was next to the bench. I knew if I could tip the unit into the bench, it would soften the fall to the ground. Plus, I had all of that water in there to cushion me. And I held on to the edge of the box so my body didn't hit the ground when the unit did."

He leaned back in the chair, testing the springs. His chocolate sat on the desk in front of him, untouched, his marshmallows melting and pooling into a foamy layer of white across the top of the mug.

"So, Charlie told you the shower door sticks sometimes. And it did."

"Yes, but I think it was more than stuck. I think someone trapped me. It should have opened when I pushed on it, and when I looked over the top of it, the door was open."

"I thought you said it stuck?"

"The door to the gardening shed. The front door."

"Maybe it blew open?"

"No. I locked it before I got undressed."

"Locked it how?"

"It had one of those flimsy metal hook-and-circle latches." I put the index finger and thumb of my left hand together in an "okay" sign and hooked my right index finger into it to demonstrate the mechanism. "It would be easy enough to open if someone wanted to get in. I think someone came in and jammed the doorstop under the shower unit door so it wouldn't open."

"Did you look at the shower after you tipped it?"

"No. I was freezing. The water turned cold after about four minutes and I was in there for more than that."

"How do you know about the cold water?"

"Charlie told me that, too."

"So by your account you were stuck in the shower, the water turned ice-cold, and you figured the only way out was to tip it and climb out the top?"

"You don't believe me?"

He continued. "Who else knew you were in that shower besides Charlie?"

"Nobody."

"Do you think she did this?"

"No. Why would she do that kind of damage to her own property?"

"Then explain why you think someone was out to get you instead of her."

"You think someone thought I was her?"

"You seem pretty convinced that this was about you."

"Aren't you?"

"I'm convinced that the situation makes you look like a victim, much like the vandalism to your car that kept you in our town. Tell me this, Ms. Monroe, why would somebody do these things to you?"

"Maybe someone wanted to send me a message saying I'm not welcome here." I was getting angry. The jovial Deputy Sheriff Clark had faked me out with a complimentary phone charger and a mug of hot chocolate and now he was making me feel foolish. "I didn't make this up. What would have happened if nobody came along?"

"Ms. Monroe, even if the drain was clogged, it's not possible that the unit would have filled with water. There are breakaway seals at the corners that would have burst under the pressure. The door would have fallen off, probably in a matter of seconds from when you decided to tip the thing. You probably hurt yourself more by what you did than if you'd stayed calm. And if anyone's to blame for the damage to Charlie's property, it's you."

I didn't like what Officer Clark was insinuating. "I didn't make this up," I maintained.

"It's understandable that you're under a lot of stress. A death in the family can do that. We didn't make things easier when we showed up at the fabric store this morning, and the discovery of a body on your property, well, those are circumstances anybody would find hard to take." He tapped the recorder sitting by his desk. "I have your statement from tonight and I'll type it up and start a file on it. In the meantime, I suggest you get a hot meal and a good night's sleep."

I wasn't inclined to panicking, but the deputy sheriff's matter-of-fact tone, the rational explanation of events, and the routine manner in which he was treating me made me wonder if maybe I was tired, if maybe I'd made more out of my brush with death than there was. I glanced at the clock on the wall. It was quarter to nine but it felt like it was after midnight.

"Ms. Monroe, here's my card. Call me if you need me."

I unplugged my cell phone and held the cord out to the deputy sheriff.

He waved it away. "Keep it. We got a ton of them lying around here. You need anything else? A ride somewhere?"

"No, I can walk." I stood up and pushed the chair in under the front of the desk. "There is one thing you can give me. Mr. McMichael's phone number?"

"You're going to sell to him?"

"I haven't decided about that yet. I wanted to say thank you."

"For what?"

"For showing up when he did. He's the one who found me." Deputy Sheriff Clark stared at me blankly.

"He's the one who called you," I added.

"I don't know what you're talking about. My call came in from the Senior Patrol."

Eight

"But Mr. Pickers is—" I cut myself off before finishing my sentence.

"Mr. Pickers wasn't the only member of the Senior Patrol."

"Why would the Senior Patrol be behind Charlie's auto shop? It's not like someone could have seen me from the street."

The deputy sheriff leaned back in his chair and took another drink from his mug. "Maybe you're right. Maybe the Senior Patrol thinks it's a good idea to keep an eye on you."

"Why? Because I'm not from around here? Or because I don't want to sell the store?"

"Maybe because their founding member was found murdered on your property and a piece of fabric from your store was tied around his head."

"I didn't have anything to do with that."

Deputy Sheriff Clark held my stare for a couple of beats while my proclamation hung in the air, unchallenged. The longer I waited for him to speak, the more aware I became of the possibility that he didn't believe me. I fought the urge to repeat myself for fear too much protesting would add to his all but stated suspicion of guilt.

"May I leave, Sheriff?"

He nodded once. I thanked him for the hot chocolate and headed back to the fabric store.

Something wasn't right. It had started yesterday, when my car was vandalized. In less than twenty-four hours the police had shown up assuming I was squatting on the property, I'd found the body of a neighborhood patroller in my new backyard, and I'd been trapped in Charlie's shower unit. Worst of all, I was being treated like I'd staged things to make me look like a victim, too. Coupled with Sheriff Clark's request that I not leave town, I suspected the recent acts of vandalism did more to incriminate than exonerate me. If the people of San Ladrón wanted to turn gossip into an Olympic sport, I was providing ample gear for the playing field.

It was dark as I crossed the street. I looked to the left, past the hair salon and the consignment shop, to the tea store. The faded floral curtains were drawn, but a faint glow came from the windows. I wondered how late a tea shop stayed open in a town like San Ladrón, and whether or not Genevieve's friendliness would go the way of the deputy sheriff's if I stayed much longer.

I crossed San Ladrón Avenue, and then crossed Bonita, heading back to Charlie's. The rest of the businesses on the street were dark, long past closing time. The last thing I wanted was to return to Charlie's garage, but I knew I owed her some kind of explanation. I tore a sheet of paper out of the notebook in my bag and scribbled a quick note in pencil. *I'm sorry about the shower. Call me and I'll explain.* I thought about including a line about ignoring gossip, but from what I already knew about Charlie, that probably went without saying. I folded the note in half and stuck it in the crack between her door and the molding, right above the knob.

I returned to the fabric store and entered through the front, this time pulling the gate shut behind me. Safety first, I thought. Freak accident or not, I was alone, a stranger in a small, insular community. Whether or not anybody wanted to come out and say it, it seemed they weren't welcoming me with open arms. At least one thing was certain: The Senior Patrol was keeping an eye on me. The fact offered little solace.

Once inside, I found the kittens back in their box. The orange one stretched a paw out and yawned. I scooped each up and kissed their heads, then set them on top of the cutting table. The tabby had clear blue eyes and a tiny pink nose. The other was his twin except in shades of gray, as if someone had printed a photo from a printer that was low on toner.

I left them on top of the cutting station and stripped off the motor oil–stained clothes I'd been wearing. They were destined for the trash. I would have loved to bundle up in flannel pajamas and a thick terry-cloth robe, but my shopping priorities earlier that day had been less about warmth and more about style. I pulled the black silk nightgown over my head and slipped my arms into the sleeves of a matching duster. Not warm enough. I tore the tags off of the black sweatshirt and zipped myself into it. Next I withdrew the other damp purchases from the shopping bag. With a length of ribbon from the wall of trims and buttons, I created a makeshift clothesline and hung the rest of my purchases: a pair of black pants, a pair of black skinny jeans, one black tube skirt, one black turtleneck, one black tunic. Surrounded by the most exotic fabrics in the most unusual colors, my wardrobe of cheap black garments looked as though the life had been sucked out of them. I remembered what Charlie had said earlier when I'd asked her where I could get some clothes. *You're asking the wrong questions.* Maybe she was right. Maybe I was.

I flipped to a blank page at the back of Aunt Millie's sales ledger, found a stubby pencil in the drawer of the wrap stand, and scribbled *Mr. Pickers/Senior Patrol/fabric store/connection?* I chewed on the eraser of the pencil as I stared at the page. Why had the murderer tied the blue suede around Mr. Pickers's head? To incriminate me, or to send a message that the murder was connected to the store? I didn't know enough about any of the things I'd written down to know what to make of them, and it was frustrating. Somebody around here had to have answers, and I was going to find them.

I flipped a few pages forward to another blank page and doodled a random circular pattern that matched my swirling thoughts. Before long, I sketched around it, a shoulder, a sleeve, a dress.

Drawing clothes came easily to me, easier than it was to create a pattern and turn the sketch into a real live garment. I simply pictured one element and built a dress around it. That's one of the reasons I was the concept designer at To The Nines. I had the ideas needed to conceive our collection each season, even if the collection was a batch of brightly colored dresses with gaudy embellishments, perfect for beauty pageants and proms. Someone else took my sketches to make patterns so the sewing team could turn them into reality.

People had always liked to watch me sketch, to tweak a line here, add a feather or a brooch, color it in with accents of gold, silver, or an array of brightly imagined stones. When I first imagined a concept, I escaped into a fantasy world of art deco inspiration. I could close my eyes and see the world that existed in the movies I loved from the thirties, then add them to my drawing.

As much as people were impressed with my talent, I was equally impressed when the sewing team blocked out a pattern on a bust form with flexible tape or draped a mannequin with fabric and turned it into what it was that I'd drawn. It was Giovanni who dumbed down my designs, claiming that they would cost too much in production. "That's nice, but this isn't the postwar thirties. Use half as much fabric and lose the buttons. Zippers are cheaper."

Once, when I picked up a bolt of blue sateen from our supplier, he told me to get a bigger discount because of a defect to the fabric. I hung the bolt on a fabric roller and pulled five yards out. When I asked him to show me the defect, he took a needle to the fabric, lifted a thread from the center, and pulled it across the width of the garment. "There's your defect. Now go get that discount." When I refused, he sent me home without pay. I didn't return for a week, and five dresses in the blue fabric were in various stages of completion on our small army of bust forms when I finally did go back. I covered the visible flaw with a carefully placed trim of tiny blue sequins that cost twice as much as the fabric, paying the invoice the day we received it. Giovanni never said a word, and I never really knew which one of us won the battle of wills.

Tonight, I lost myself in the sketch. Though I only had the blunt pencil to work with, I imagined a woman with brilliant platinum hair parted on the side, in a gold gown with a sweetheart neckline, embellished on the shoulders with spirals of matte gold and silver sequins. The gown, fitted at the waist, accentuated an hourglass figure: snug around the hips, cascading to the floor in a pool of fabric. It was the kind of dress that would give a store like Land of a Thousand Fabrics a great reputation again, for having the kind of materials you couldn't find at the smaller fabric stores. It was the kind of dress that would have looked good on me if I lived the kind of life that let me dress up in fancy clothes instead of worrying about the damage a glue gun could do to cashmere.

Giovanni would never approve such a gown. He could cut four cocktail dresses from the same amount of fabric, and the amount of time it would take to hand-sew the sequins on in the elaborate decoration I'd designed would shut the workroom down for a week. It was a special dress, inspired by the ones hanging in the back of my closet in Los Angeles that had never been worn.

A sound by the back door tore me away from the sketch. The kittens, standing at the edge of the table, both looked up as well. One of them let out a tiny squeak. I ran to them, scooping each up under her belly, and set them inside the nest of fur. I moved the box to the floor inside the register stand and crouched next to it.

There was a light tapping on the back door, then a voice. "Poly, are you in there? It's Vaughn McMichael. I just heard about tonight." There was a stretch of silence. "If you're in there, can you open the door and let me in? I feel a little silly talking to a door."

I giggled under my breath, but waited another moment.

"I don't suppose it matters or not, but I have food," he said. "And wine. And I can't be sure, but the Senior Patrol might be in the neighborhood and I'm not sure how my standing here is going to look on their report."

At the mention of the Senior Patrol I straightened up. I pushed the ledger back into the drawer of the wrap stand and walked to the back door, lifting the bar lock that slid into place and unlocking the dead bolt. It took a couple of minutes until I got it all open, but when I did, Vaughn stood on the other side of the door, a take-out bag from the Waverly House in one hand, a shopping bag from the grocery store in the other, and a flat blue box, wrapped in soft ivory paper with a white ribbon around it, tucked under his arm. His eyes dropped to my body, clothed in the bulky black zip-front hoodie over the slinky black nightgown, and back to my face.

"I wasn't sure if I would find you here, but I didn't know where else to look. May I come in?"

I stepped back and let him pass, then closed and locked the door.

"You're practically moved in, aren't you?" he asked as he looked at the clothes hanging across the store.

"It's been a rough night. I didn't plan to come back here, but I didn't know where else to go."

"I heard."

"Who told you?" I asked, wondering which version he knew.

"Word gets around," he said. "When the hostess came over to tell me you canceled, the couple at the table next to me said they heard somebody named Polyester was taken to the police station."

"That's what people are saying?"

He smiled. "It's true, isn't it?"

"Yes, I guess it is."

"I called Officer Clark. He told me what happened and said you walked back here." He shrugged like it was the most normal turn of events he'd heard. "Now, since you're obviously dressed for dinner," he said, pausing to glance back down at my sweatshirt, "the only thing left is for me to set the table and serve it."

"Trust me. This is a vast improvement over what I was wearing two hours ago. Follow me," I said, turning away from him.

Now, where to eat? I'd spent the previous night in the apartment upstairs and while I knew the polite thing to do would be to invite Vaughn up and eat at a table like civilized people, I wasn't ready to let him into my personal space just yet. But for all the fabric and trim that the store housed, it was short on chairs. I hadn't entirely recovered from the cold-shower incident and had little desire to sit on the concrete floor, even if we covered it with fabric.

I tapped my palm on the top of the cutting table. "How's this?" I asked.

"Looks good to me." He set his bags down and pulled a white eyelet tablecloth from inside one of them, then spread it out over the top of the laminate counter. Next, he pulled out two candleholders and fitted them with long tapers. I found a pack of matches in the drawer under the register and worked my way through half of the pack before one of the matches caught. I lit the tapers while Vaughn set out a small basket of bread, salt and pepper shakers, and a bottle of wine.

"Where did all of this come from?" I asked.

"I asked you to dinner at the Waverly House. Since you couldn't get to the restaurant, I brought the restaurant to you." He withdrew two plates, then three containers that were definitely not disposable. "It's a silly dinner. Truffle mac and cheese, pommes frites, spinach artichoke dip, and calamari."

"No steaks?" I asked with a smile.

"I didn't know if you were a vegetarian and figured I'd play it safe. Besides, the kitchen was closing and this was the best they could do. I hope it's okay."

"It's okay," I said. Understatement of the year, I thought to myself. According to Carson, a person could not live on appetizers alone, though if given the chance I'd prove him wrong.

Vaughn poured red wine into two stemmed glasses and handed me one. I wondered exactly how much influence the McMichael family had in San Ladrón that something like this was doable on short notice?

As we sat across from each other, cross-legged, plates on our laps, eating a meal that might have come from the kids' menu, I realized that this was the first time since I'd arrived that I had dropped my guard and was enjoying myself.

"How are the kittens?" he asked between bites.

"Good. They got dinner before you arrived. I should consider myself lucky. I forgot to eat all day and the only thing here is a few more cans of Fancy Feast."

"You remembered to pick up cat food but nothing for yourself?"

"I thought I was getting dinner."

"Then I'm glad I delivered. Literally."

"So am I."

I set my plate down and spun to the side so I could hop down. Aches in my muscles were starting to announce themselves, from oiling the fence and cleaning the interior of the store, to knocking over the shower unit at Charlie's. I suspected I'd feel ten times worse tomorrow after a stationary night of sleep. I reached into the box and pulled out each of the kittens, then set them on the counter. Immediately they homed in on the scent of food. Vaughn held his plate up, out of reach. Mine was the more vulnerable one, or would have been if it hadn't been empty.

"Have you named them yet?"

"Not yet." I stroked the head of the gray one. He looked up at me and meowed. He closed his eyes tightly and pushed his pink nose upward. "They sure are cute, aren't they?"

The kitten had climbed over Vaughn's calf and rested his paws on his knee, staring up at the plate he held.

"You think you'll take them with you when you go back to Los Angeles?" he asked.

"I haven't thought much about that."

"About what, the kittens, or going back to Los Angeles?"

"Both. I haven't thought much about anything but the store for the past two days."

"Do you like it here?"

"Here, where? The store? The town?"

"Either. Both."

"I don't know much about the town. But the store—I love the store. I was born in here," I volunteered.

"In the store? Seriously?"

"That's how I got my name. The story goes that my mom helped Great-Aunt Millie with the store through her pregnancy with me. I came earlier than anybody expected. She gave birth to me on a bed of polyester so that's what they named me—Polyester."

"So the store is part of you."

"Or I'm a part of the store. I don't know if it's because it's my family, or because I was born here, or because every year on my birthday Aunt Millie and Uncle Marius sent me five yards of one of their exotic fabrics, but I feel like it's in my blood." I dropped my head for a moment as I realized I was explaining the very reason I'd turned down his father's offer on the store. "Now that the store is mine, I don't want to walk away from it too hastily."

"You feel a connection to San Ladrón and the store because of your family."

"That's right."

"It's the same with me. I moved back to San Ladrón because of my father. He had a heart attack a couple of years ago. That's the only time in my life when he needed me. I would never have met you if it weren't for him," Vaughn interjected unexpectedly.

"But your dad wants me gone."

"He doesn't want you gone. He wants you to sell the store. Those are very different things."

"Not to me, they're not."

"I bet if I told him how I—" The light of the candles flickered over his face. He didn't finish his thought.

"How you what?" I said.

I looked at the empty plates, the open bottle of wine, the candles, and the ivory box with the white satin bow. I didn't know how I'd missed it when he first arrived, but suddenly Vaughn's intentions seemed clear.

"Your father knew about what happened to me tonight. He was there. Maybe he even had something to do with it."

"My dad wouldn't hurt you to get what he wants."

"But he's not above using you, is he? Are you going to tell him how you wined and dined me and made subtle suggestions under candlelight and wooed me with presents?" I gestured toward the gift box. "I bet he'd be proud of you— like you're a chip of the old block."

"You think that's why I'm here?"

I set down my utensils and shook my head. "I can't believe I didn't see through you when you invited me to dinner." I moved the gray kitten from my lap and jumped down from the wrap stand. "I know I said I didn't know what I was going to do, but I was wrong. You can tell your father I'm not selling. I'm going to stay in San Ladrón and reopen the store."

Vaughn stared at me for a second or two, a pained expression on his face. He hopped down from the cutting station, too. "I wouldn't mind if you did stay, Poly, but don't do it to spite my family. My coming here tonight has nothing to do with what my dad wants. You said you wanted answers. I want answers, too. Look inside the box. And if you want to talk, call me." He walked to the back door, easily undid the locks, and left.

Nine

I stormed after Vaughn and threw the dead bolt and the bar lock into place, then turned around and leaned against the door. I did want to talk to somebody. And I wanted answers, too, to an ever-increasing number of questions. In the wake of the shower incident, I'd forgotten the reason Vaughn claimed to have invited me to dinner in the first place. He said my family wasn't the only one affected by Great-Aunt Millie's murder.

According to my half-charged cell phone, it was after eleven, and my body screamed with pain from the day's events. I blew out each of the candles, and carried the box of kittens upstairs with me, the ivory box Vaughn had brought now wedged under my left arm. After unlocking the apartment, I set the box on the floor by the sofa where I'd slept last night and sat down, pulling the blanket up over my legs. I slid the ribbon off of the box. I didn't know what to expect, but it most definitely wasn't the scrapbook inside.

And when I flipped the cover open and read the headline on the first page, I knew I wouldn't be sleeping any time soon.

SAN LADRÓN ROCKED BY MURDER

Under the headline was a picture of Aunt Millie, and next to it was a picture of Land of a Thousand Fabrics. The paper was dated ten years earlier.

The city of San Ladrón was rocked by the murder of a longtime resident. The victim, Millie Monroe, was the wife of Marius Monroe and half owner of Land of a Thousand Fabrics on Bonita Avenue. The murder was the unfortunate end to a robbery at the store late Thursday night. Two suspects are being held without bail.

I flipped the page. The next article was dated about a week later.

THIRD PARTY SUSPECTED IN MURDER PLOT?

Last week's account of a robbery gone wrong that ended in the murder of San Ladrón resident Millie Monroe might be more complicated than originally thought. Robbers Joe and Pete Esterhaus, arrested hours after the body was discovered in Land of a Thousand Fabrics on Bonita Avenue, confessed to the robbery but maintained their innocence of the murder. In a statement by Joe Esterhaus, "We were hired to rob the place by some rich guy. He guaranteed the place would be empty and it was." Police responded to an anonymous tip and discovered the body of Millie Monroe in the back of the store.

The cash register had been emptied of all monies. It was the third day of a weekend sale and according to the registry, the take had been just over four thousand dollars. Residents of San Ladrón and neighboring cities had flocked to the store to buy from the owner's wide assortment of international fabrics at a great discount.

I pulled the blanket further up my torso to counter the chill that snaked down my spine. The news clippings continued. They ranged in legitimacy from bona fide newspaper articles to letters addressed to the editor. The words blurred in front of my eyes but I couldn't stop reading. *Has anyone considered real estate a motive for murder?* asked one letter. *Who would benefit from Millie's death?* asked another. *Owner Closes Store but Refuses to Sell*, said the next page. *Millionaire Asked to Front Reward Money, Refuses* followed by *Is there a murderer at large in San Ladrón?*

The next headline was more to the point.

IS VIC MCMICHAEL CAPABLE OF MURDER?

Vaughn had hinted at the fact that my great aunt Millie's murder had impacted his family, too. And where my family wouldn't talk about it, he had done the opposite: cut out every piece of noteworthy news and archived it in a scrapbook. I flipped the book shut, and then opened the back cover. The page was blank. I flipped from the back forward four pages until I found the last entry, a headline with no copy.

SAN LADRÓN DEVELOPER HOSPITALIZED
AFTER HEART ATTACK

The date on the top of the newspaper was six months after Aunt Millie's murder.

I shut the scrapbook and lay back on the fur. Vaughn had moved back to San Ladrón because of his father's heart attack. I'd come back because of the store. But the store's past and the store's future were tied together in something that involved us both, or our families, at least. And now there had been another murder at the store.

Ten years after the fact. I didn't care what anybody said. I didn't care that they treated me as though I were the problem. I knew Mr. Pickers's murder wasn't a coincidence. I knew it had something to do with me inheriting the store. But what? I didn't remember anybody in my family ever talking about him. So what did he have to do with the store?

I opened the scrapbook and read the last article.

WITNESS STATEMENT CONFUSES INVESTIGATION

Local banker and longtime San Ladrón resident Tom Pickers's claim to have seen a figure leaving Land of a Thousand Fabrics the night of the robbery has left the police in search of a monster. Pickers, 63, is a thirty-year employee of The San Ladrón Savings and Trust. Two months after Millie Monroe's death, Pickers came forward with information about the robbery at the family-owned fabric store. He reported to the police that "Millie Monroe called me earlier that night. She wanted me to pick up the register take from the weekend sale instead of keeping it for the next morning. We made arrangements for me to pick it up after the store closed. I was late getting to the store. I saw someone leave by the back door. He was distorted, like a monster. I hid in the shadows and then ran. The next morning I went back to the store, but it was too late."

The date on the newspaper was two months after Aunt Millie's murder. I wondered why Mr. Pickers had waited so long before going to the police. Had his fear over what he'd seen kept him quiet, or had he known more than he told?

And how had that factored into his murder behind the store yesterday? I kept reading.

Tom Pickers has lived a quiet life in San Ladrón since the death of his wife. His statement has been disputed by residents who claim he was not of sound mind the night of the crime. Despite criticism, he has signed a statement that describes what he saw.

I closed my eyes and images of his body filled my mind. His cranberry socks, his navy-blue work pants, and beige shirt. The blue suede fabric over his head, the blood that seeped through it. I opened my eyes to make the image go away. The monster, if there was one, was the person who killed him. My return to San Ladrón had triggered something in the community. The vandalism to my car, the report that I was squatting on the property, the shower incident—all were connected by one thing, and it wasn't the store. It was me.

I thought about Mr. Pickers. He had started the Senior Patrol ten years ago, just about the time of the robbery. He'd been watching over the store. I saw him the night I arrived when Ken and I stood on the street—and I knew. Whoever had it in for me had it in for Mr. Pickers, too. Mr. Pickers knew something. And even though nobody believed him at the time, there was a chance my arrival had stirred it all up.

Maybe there was another reason Mr. McMichael wanted the property so badly. While Uncle Marius had closed the store but kept it as it was when Millie was alive, Mr. McMichael wanted it gone forever, obliterated from his memories. If our goals seemed at odds before, today they were flat-out polar opposites.

The next morning I woke up with a stiff neck, sore shoulders, and a noticeable bruising around my midsection. It was eight thirty, and as inappropriate as it would have been, I half wished Charlie would show up and offer to buy me a drink.

I climbed from the sofa and stretched my arms as high as I could, then shook out each leg. I quickly scrubbed my fingers over my short hair then tucked the flyaway tendrils behind my ears. I ran downstairs to the fabric store and pulled a couple of new clothing items from where they hung, then dressed in the new black leggings and midthigh black jersey tunic with a shiny black vinyl square set in the middle of the front. I'd found it on the clearance bar yesterday and considered myself lucky that my tastes were ahead of the San Ladrón fashion curve. I did what I could with a tube of mascara and the strawberry lip gloss then pulled my black riding boots on over the leggings. After opening a second can of cat food for the kittens, I glanced at the remaining mess from last night's impromptu Waverly House delivery and then left.

I didn't get far. Parked in the lot behind the building was Carson's vintage Mercedes. With Carson standing next to the driver's-side door.

"What are you doing here?" I asked.

"I figured I should come, check out my investment." He stepped away from the car and walked past me to the back door. "This run-down building? This is it?"

I crossed my arms over my chest. "What, no kiss? Aren't you happy to see me?"

He turned back and leaned forward, lips puckered, expecting me to reciprocate. Instead, I turned my head and his kiss landed on my cheek.

"Okay, you're mad at me. Nothing new there. What's going on, Poly?"

"Nothing's going on. I just can't believe you drove all the way up here to check on me."

"It's thirty miles. Not that big of a deal. And you were a little too noncommittal on the phone last night. I figured if this real estate deal really is our get-rich-quick scheme, I better come up here and get involved before you blow it."

"There's nothing to blow. There's no deal. I'm not selling."

"Nice, you're quitting your job now? Moving to this quaint little town? What did they do, slip a Mickey into your hot chocolate?"

"How do you know about the hot chocolate?" I asked.

"I was kidding. Did somebody really give you hot chocolate? I shouldn't be surprised. Where's your car?"

"At the shop."

"Still? You really are a sucker, Poly."

Carson dropped into step next to me. We were close to the same height, which made it easy to keep pace with each other. It also made it hard to make a good argument defending a pair of shoes over two inches high. Carson slung an arm around my shoulder. We took an awkward few steps until he dropped his arm to my waist. I altered my walk slightly so we were out of sync, making him lose touch with me altogether. It was a passive-aggressive move on my part and I knew it, but while I didn't like him invading my space, I didn't feel like getting into a fight about it, either.

"Why don't we go to the hotel? I can unpack and you can show me the town."

"There is no hotel. I mean, there's probably a hotel somewhere, but I'm not staying at one."

"You're crashing on somebody's sofa?"

"Not exactly."

"Poly, where have you been sleeping?"

"At the store. That reminds me, I have to call someone about turning on the water."

"I didn't want to say anything, but no wonder you look so bad." He ran a hand over his hair, holding it back from his forehead, until he let go and it bounced down into place. The man had more hair than I did.

"Who says I look bad?"

"When's the last time you took a shower?"

"Last night." I looked across the street at Charlie's Auto-motive. The *Closed* sign was still in the window. I needed to talk to her about last night's incident and find out when she planned to be done with my car, but not while Carson was hanging out with me. There was regular complicated, and there was capital-*C* Complicated. "Why don't you work out a hotel room and meet up with me later? There are a couple of things I have to take care of this morning. We'll get more done if we split up."

"You sure you don't want to come with me? It's been a long time since we've been alone in a hotel room. I could help you get cleaned up. Could be fun."

"Later," I said, only half paying attention to him. "Meet me back at the store at, what time is it?" I patted my pockets for my phone before realizing I'd left it charging at the store.

"It's nine thirty."

"Okay, meet me at the store at three." I turned around and jogged down the alley, twisting my ankle on a piece of wood. In an awkward couple of steps I regained my balance and walked the rest of the way with his laughter ringing in my ears.

Last night, it was candlelight that illuminated the area, and today, it struck me that somebody needed to return the borrowed items to the Waverly House. I stuck my phone in my small cross-body handbag and set it by the door while I set about packing up the candelabras, the plates, the cloth napkins, and the silverware. It easily fit into one bag instead of the two Vaughn had shown up with now that the food was gone. I put both hands down on the counter and thought about last night. For someone I had just met, someone who had a very different agenda from my own, it had been remarkably easy to spend time with him.

He was the only person I'd ever met who was okay with me talking about Aunt Millie's murder. And more than okay, he had a vested interest in finding out the truth. Where my family moved from San Ladrón months after the tragedy, he had moved back. Where Uncle Marius's mourning split us up, his dad's health brought his family together.

I was embarrassed by my outburst. After reading the scrapbook he had brought for me to read, I was beginning to believe he really had wanted to talk. If nothing else, I wanted to call him to apologize and say thank you. I opened the drawer below the cash register and pushed the tape measure and chalk to the side in search of his business card, the one he'd given me that first day in the store. I found it easily in the mostly empty drawer and keyed his number into my phone. As it rang, I opened the sales log and idly flipped through the pages.

I hung up the phone when I realized that pages had been torn from the back of the ledger.

Ten

I had sketched in that sales ledger just last night, and I knew it had been intact. And there had been only one person in the store since then. Vaughn.

My mind buzzed like a switch had been thrown and electric current flowed through it. I'd taken notes in that ledger just the night before. What had I written? *Mr. Pickers/Senior Patrol/fabric store/connection?* It meant nothing to me at the time. But it must have meant something to Vaughn. And if there was something in there that pertained to his father, he would have had good reason to remove the pages. I kicked myself for thinking for a second that Vaughn and I were looking for the same answers. We might both be playing the information game, but most likely for opposing teams.

I put the ledger back under the cash wrap and carried the Waverly House belongings out back. The historic residence was about three blocks away, not far by a long shot, but being loaded down with borrowed dinner items made it a more difficult journey.

I arrived in front of the historic Victorian mansion a couple minutes later. Last night, I'd noticed the outline of the house, trimmed in tiny white lights, making it look like a gingerbread house. In the daylight I could take in the magnificence—both in size and in color—of the restored landmark. Two floors topped with peaked gables, a round turret on the left corner, and at least two dozen windows that faced the street. The siding had been painted Wedgwood blue and the trim in white, like a vintage cameo. I knew Victorian style was colorful and I appreciated the subtle sophistication of the building, true to its heritage but in no way loud or garish. The building stood like a queen might have: tall and majestic, anchoring the corner of the town.

I took a deep breath and walked up the small flight of stairs that led to the front door. The interior was dark, lit only by hanging bronze chandeliers that matched the style of the exterior but shed little light. A hostess stood outside the restaurant flipping through pages of a guest book.

"Excuse me. This is going to sound odd, but I have some of your kitchen items that were borrowed last night—"

The woman looked up. She had a round, cherubic face set off by bright blue eyes and pink cheeks. Her curly red hair was pulled back from her face, though a few tendrils had escaped and framed her forehead and cheeks.

"Who are you?" she asked rather abruptly.

"Poly Monroe. I just want to return these things—"

"Wait right here."

Before I could protest, or rather, while I was in the middle of protesting, she went down the hallway and into the last door on the left. A busboy appeared inside the restaurant and I flagged him over. He seemed nervous, as though he thought he'd get in trouble for talking to me.

"Hi, I just want to return this stuff. It was borrowed last night. Can you put it in the kitchen, or wherever it goes?"

He shook his head rapidly and moved away from the velvet rope that separated us. Just as I was about to set the bags down and leave, I was addressed very formally.

"Ms. Monroe?" said a tall, thin woman in an ivory sweater, black-and-white skirt, and rust-colored double-faced wool jacket. I guessed her to be in her seventies. A pair of eyeglasses hung from a silver chain around her neck, and her dark gray hair, streaked with white, was swept away from her face into layers that ended above the collar of her shirt. "Ms. Polyester Monroe?"

"Yes, I'm Poly Monroe. I want to return these items—" I started for the fourth time.

"You're Helen and John's daughter?" she asked.

"Yes. I'm sorry if this is a problem, but someone borrowed these things for me last night—"

She turned to the young redhead who stood by the hostess desk. "Sandra, Vaughn borrowed these things from us last night. He phoned me earlier today and said Ms. Monroe would be returning them. Please return them to the kitchen."

At the mention of Vaughn's name, the redhead turned red. The older woman took the bags from me and handed them to the hostess. She did a poor job of concealing her curiosity over the contents of the bags. The gray-haired woman waited until Sandra was well out of earshot before she turned to me.

"Ms. Monroe, would you come with me?" She stood sideways and held one hand out toward me, palm side up, and another in front of her, indicating a direction. There was nothing threatening about her, though I felt a little as though I were about to get lectured on the inappropriateness of borrowing kitchen supplies from an establishment as formal as the Waverly House.

I took a tentative step in her direction and she smiled.

She led the way down the hallway, back to the last door on the left. She held the door open and again gestured her open palm toward one of the beige needlepoint chairs in front of the oak table that served as a desk. After sitting down, I was surprised that she sat in the chair opposite me instead of taking the more expected leather chair behind the table.

"I didn't mean to cause any trouble," I offered.

"There's no trouble. Everything was arranged with our permission."

"Then why am I here?"

She leaned back in her chair and crossed her legs, exposing her ankles and low-heeled black patent leather shoes. "I would have known you anywhere. You look just like her."

"Like who?" I asked.

"Like Millie."

"You knew my great-aunt?" I asked, sitting forward.

"I did. There was a time when she and I were very good friends. I do miss her, still." She held out a hand for me to shake. "I'm Adelaide Brooks. I thought you might be interested in talking about her."

"Absolutely, I would love to."

The door opened and a man in a white shirt and black pants entered, carrying a silver tray that held a small ceramic pot, two cups and saucers, tea, lemon wedges, and a pitcher of milk. He set it on the desk and the woman thanked him. "Tea?"

"I would love some."

She poured a cup of hot water for me and held out a selection of packets. I chose the first one that had *zing* in the title. I added a bit of milk, something I'd once seen in a movie, and neglected the lemon. She smiled at my actions then did the same thing. I didn't know if I'd impressed her with my preference, or if my actions were so far off that she wanted to make me comfortable by not making it obvious.

"I imagine it's been an emotional couple of days for you. May I ask what the fabric store is like after all these years?"

"I think a healthy layer of dust preserved the place. I spent yesterday afternoon cleaning it after I got the front gate open."

"If you intend to sell the property, your efforts were unnecessary."

"You're probably right."

"Do you intend to sell the property?"

"I don't know what I intend to do. I don't intend to make a quick decision, I know that much. And whatever happens, I don't want the fabric store remembered as the scene of a homicide. Not again."

"It's possible that Mr. Pickers was the victim of a random act of violence, just like your great-aunt was."

"You don't believe that, do you?"

"There are reasons I should. Very strong reasons." Adelaide Brooks studied me for a moment.

"What have you been told about that night?" she asked after we'd each took a sip.

"Nothing. Well, *almost* nothing." I took another sip, and set the cup on the saucer that rested on my lap. "The store was robbed. The robbers claimed they were hired and told that the store would be empty. But she was there. They killed her and took the weekend's cash from the register. Four thousand dollars. My great-aunt died over four thousand dollars." My voice dropped to a whisper when I said the last part.

"My dear, that is the account that some people believe, so I can't fault you for thinking of it as the truth. But there is more to the story of Millie's murder." She took another sip, then cradled her cup on the small saucer that rested on the desk in front of her.

"Millie had a bracelet that she wore almost all the time. An heirloom charm bracelet that Marius brought back from the war. It had a thick chain filled with charms the size of silver dollars—many of them made of gold. Those not made of gold were made from coins of the time, coins worth their own small fortune to collectors. He said the bracelet came from a wealthy family in Europe, a gift for him helping them hide when the Germans came into their mansion. He dressed in the uniform of a German soldier and posed as one of the enemy, pretending to search the house. It was a risky move on his part, and it saved the lives of several people. They showed their gratitude with a gift, the bracelet that had been in their family since the fifteenth century."

"I remember the bracelet. I used to play with it when I was little. It tinkled when Aunt Millie moved. We always knew where she was because of the sound it made. And even when she worked, she wouldn't take it off. It had little gold spools, a tiny pair of scissors, even a sewing machine. When I was little I used to say the bracelet matched her."

"That bracelet was worth a lot of money when Marius brought it stateside, and it has only increased in value."

"But the robbers stole it."

"I'm not so sure of that," she said. She hooked one finger through the loop on the side of the floral teacup in her lap and studied me carefully.

I folded my hands in my lap and looked at them. I could tell there was more to her story, and I waited for her to go on. As the silence grew, from polite to awkward, I felt the need to say something, anything.

"Ms. Brooks, I appreciate the tea, and I appreciate everything you have told me. But I'm afraid I can't take the word of the criminals as easily as you can. Two men were arrested for robbing the store. They confessed to being there. They probably stole the bracelet right before they killed my aunt. She was a fighter, I believe that. But the two men who were arrested are probably the two who did it."

"What about Mr. Pickers's murder?"

"What does Mr. Pickers's murder have to do with anything? He wasn't part of my family."

She stood up and walked around to the back of the desk, slid the top center drawer open, and pulled out a small key on a pink ribbon. She leaned over and opened the bottom drawer of the desk and extracted a small jewelry box. She inserted the key in the box and opened the lid.

A faint scent of roses wafted from the box and the melody of a song, vaguely familiar but not entirely recognizable, played as the small figure of a woman twirled on a pedestal inside. Ms. Brooks lifted the corner of the faded green velvet lining and reached under it, extracting a sizeable gold coin trimmed in an elaborate braid of tarnished metal. A loop dangled from one side, as though it had once been worn as part of a piece of jewelry, perhaps a valuable charm bracelet like the one my great-aunt used to wear. She set the coin in front of me and studied me. I didn't pick it up. After a few seconds of eye contact I looked away, uncomfortable under the heat of her stare.

"Ms. Monroe, do you know what that is?" she asked.

"I think I do," I said. "How did you get it?"

"Someone I once cared for very deeply gave it to me. He asked me to put it in a safe place and never speak of it."

"This is from her bracelet, isn't it?" I whispered. Chills tickled my neck and ran down my back like a snowman was playing piano on my spine.

"I believe that it is."

"And you never told anybody you had this?"

"I never believed it would do any good."

"But—"

"Ms. Monroe, I don't believe the person who gave me that coin was the murderer. I believe someone who has never been caught has been living with the crime. The murder yesterday all but proves it. I believe the time for secrets has come and gone, and that while it's important to honor the past, it's imperative to protect the future. When I heard that Marius had left the store to you, I hoped you would take an interest in it, and it seems you have. But you will never be entirely free to live in this town, to pursue any kind of a future from what lies between those four walls, if you don't first pursue the questions that surround your family."

I picked up the coin and turned it over, then pressed it into my palm and squeezed my hand shut. I closed my eyes and wished for an answer, a sign, a feeling that Aunt Millie was there with me. But she wasn't. I was alone in the office of a strange woman who wanted to fill my head with town gossip that should probably have stayed quiet. I opened my fist and set the coin on the desk.

"But what does Mr. Pickers's murder have to do with my family?"

"Mr. Pickers wasn't related to you, but he's a part of your family history," she said.

My eyes darted to the left for a split second then back to her face.

"Millie had made arrangements for Tom Pickers to come by the store and pick up the deposit for the bank. In order to make things easy for everyone, she accumulated the cash from Friday and Saturday. He was to pick it up the weekend take on Sunday and deposit it on Monday."

"I remember when she made the plans. It was because it was my graduation weekend. She and Uncle Marius were going to close up the store and come to Los Angeles Sunday night. They couldn't be at my graduation because of the sale."

She sat straighter in her chair and looked directly at me.

"My dear, Tom Pickers didn't make it to the store that night. The money was never found."

"What else can you tell me about Mr. Pickers?"

"There's not much I can tell you that doesn't come from the rumor mill."

"I don't want rumors. I want facts. Did you know him?"

"Not very well."

"But somebody must have, right?"

"Ms. Monroe, thank you for taking time to talk with me today. If nothing else, you've given me a chance to talk about something that I've long kept secret." She gestured toward the coin. "Take it. It might lead you to some answers."

I looked at the coin but didn't pick it up. Just because Adelaide seemed to be done talking to me didn't mean I was done asking questions. "No other parts of the bracelet ever turned up?" I asked as I stood.

"No."

"And where was this found?"

"In your store."

"By the police?"

"By my ex-husband."

"Who is your ex-husband?" I asked.

"My dear, I'm sorry, I thought you knew who I was."

I felt my face change, my forehead pulling tight and my lips pinching together. She stood up and looked at me, eye to eye.

"I'm Vaughn's mother."

Eleven

"I thought Vaughn told you," Adelaide Brooks said. "Isn't that why you're here?" Confusion clouded her soft gray eyes.

"I came by to return a few things that he borrowed last night. I didn't want anyone to think I was planning on keeping them."

"But surely he told you that I arranged for him to bring the Waverly House to you when you couldn't come to the Waverly House. Didn't he?"

They were the same words Vaughn had used. I took a deep breath and exhaled. "I'm sure he would have explained it if I hadn't asked him to leave." I expected her to ask about my actions, but she didn't. I felt like I owed her more, some kind of explanation for being rude to her son. "I'm afraid I got the wrong impression. I thought he was there because he wanted something from me."

"And what did you think he wanted?" As she asked the

question she stood straighter, as though her motherly instincts were prepared to defend her son's intentions.

"It's not like that, Ms. Brooks. Mr. McMichael wants to buy my great-uncle's store. I got the impression that Vaughn was there to, um, improve negotiations."

She studied me for an uncomfortable few seconds then smiled, showing a row of very straight teeth. "My dear, the McMichael men are charming, and at least one of them likes to believe he gets what he wants. I am proof that he might get it but he doesn't always keep it. I like to think I've taught the other one a little about that with my actions."

"When did you and Mr. McMichael divorce?"

She gently closed her eyes. "It feels like it was a lifetime ago."

"When did he find the charm? Before or . . ."

"I don't know. At the time I cherished it as a memento of a lost friend. As time has passed, I've wondered how he came to have it in the first place." She looked down at her hands and then back up at me. "Ms. Monroe, I like you, and I applaud your loyalty to your family's past. I wish you would keep the store, but I know that's not very likely. In the meantime, enjoy your time in San Ladrón. Get to know what Marius and Millie loved about our small town. And if there is anything you need while you're here, don't hesitate to ask."

"Thank you."

I held out my hand and she took it, resting her other hand on top of it and patting gently. It was when she smiled that I saw the resemblance between her and Vaughn, a familiar curve of the lips and the appearance of dimples. I hadn't taken notice, but I seriously doubted that Mr. McMichael had dimples.

"A word of advice. Don't get lost following ghosts and shadows. Identify what is truly important to you. Make that your priority and everything else of import will find a way to support it. Those who don't care about your goals will only distract you and tear you down. Life is too short to do battle with people who want to destroy your dreams." Her eyes grew misty, but she blinked several times, halting the tears before they fell.

"Adelaide, why do people suspect your ex-husband? I read some of the newspaper articles, but there must be more to it than the newspapers said."

"It all came down to Mr. Pickers. There was a very public argument between the two men shortly after the murder, and then Mr. Pickers came forward and made his statement. My ex-husband became very active in his pursuit to buy the fabric store. People questioned his timing and motives."

"What was the argument about?"

"Mr. Pickers suspected Vaughn's father of being involved."

"Why?"

"Tom Pickers was the only person who claimed to see something that night."

"He claimed to have seen a monster."

"Yes, he did. He also claimed to have seen my ex-husband's car." She dropped her eyes. "The men who were arrested claimed that they'd been hired to rob the store. When Tom said he saw Vic's car in the neighborhood, a lot of people put two and two together and assumed he was the one who'd orchestrated the whole thing."

"Was he?"

"I don't know. Vic told the police he had business in the neighborhood. A lot of people owe him their jobs and their livelihoods, and several people backed up his story. Still, Tom Pickers's suspicion was contagious. Vic is a free man, but the court of public opinion convicted him a long time ago. My ex-husband has many friends in San Ladrón. A few enemies, too. He's learned to tolerate both."

Ms. Brooks dropped my hand and opened the door to her office for me. I got about five feet down the hall when she called out my name.

"Ms. Monroe, you forgot this." She caught up with me and pressed the charm from the bracelet into my hand. "You're the only rightful owner, as far as I can see. Cherish it. Millie would have wanted you to."

"I still have questions," I said as my hand closed around the oversized gold charm for the second time.

"You need to seek out the answers elsewhere. But remember, keep the bracelet in mind. Find the bracelet, and you'll find the answers to more than one question." Her eyes welled up a second time, and I suspected she'd have a more difficult time of blinking back the tears. I thanked her and said good-bye, then left, walking past the hostess station and out the front door.

I walked down the main street of San Ladrón, not sure where I was going to go next. I passed the visitor's center and the municipal building, two dentists' offices and three hair salons. As I waited for the light to change so I could cross the street, I realized I was standing in front of the Senior Center. Before I had a chance to think things through, I followed a gravel path to the front door, passing a cast iron statue of an early San Ladrón settler on the way.

The front lobby of the Senior Center reminded me of the admissions office of FIDM. To my left was a cork bulletin board covered in notices about the neighborhood. I approached the bulletin board and scanned the notices. A bright yellow sheet of paper was thumbtacked to the right and announced the upcoming Senior Patrol meeting on Thursday. Under *agenda* it said: *new neighborhood watch routes have been posted by water fountain.* I pushed away the corners of the flyers that covered this one and looked for an indication of when it had been posted. Before or after Mr. Pickers's murder? Were the new routes being assigned because his territory was now unaccounted for? Or did they regularly reassign territories?

A hand-drawn map was on the middle of the bright

yellow sheet of paper, indicating where the next meeting would be held. There was a star on the page a few streets north of San Ladrón Avenue. I hadn't explored much in that direction, but it was within walking distance. I unpinned the page and folded it down to pocket-sized, shoving it into the vinyl pocket in the center of my tunic.

I wandered farther down the center hallway. Rooms sat on my left and right, like a school, though the interiors of each room were carpeted and furnished with brightly colored sofas and white laminate furniture. Instead of paintings, quilts had been hung on the walls, bringing a collection of hues to each area.

A few ladies sat in the first room I passed. They looked up at me, and returned to their individual projects. Knitting, needlepoint. I stuck my head in.

"Excuse me, is there a water fountain here?" I asked.

"Down the hall, next to the exit," the lady with the needlepoint said without looking up.

I thanked her and picked up the pace. When I reached the water fountain, I found a clear plastic bin attached to the wall. Inside were sheets of paper with the Senior Patrol assignments on them. I pulled one sheet from the bin. Next to Bonita Avenue East, Tom Pickers's name was crossed off and the word *Open* had been written. I flipped through the rest of the copies. They were all the same.

A small wastepaper basket sat to the right of the water fountain. It hadn't been emptied recently and was close to overflowing. Under an empty juice bottle and a plastic takeout cup was a sheaf of papers that looked like those in the bin on the wall. I wondered if whoever had put the new ones announcing the opening on my street had thrown the old ones away, and if so, was there anything else in there I could learn from?

I looked back down the hallway. I heard movement in one of the rooms, but didn't know which one. Before I had a chance to be spotted, I knelt down and picked up the handles of the trash can liner. I stood up quickly and yanked it out of the metal bin. The bag stuck. I shook it until the bin fell from the plastic and clattered to the floor. I quickly dropped down and righted the bin. When I looked up, a woman stared at me from inside one of the rooms.

"Sorry for the noise," I said quickly. I turned around and left out the back door.

I carried the trash down the three concrete stairs, then wound around the pebble path back past the iron statue. It was just after noon. I walked through the grounds, which had patches of dry grass, to the sidewalk. To my left was a Circle K. Across the street was a shopping center with a coffee shop, a dollar store, and a couple of restaurants. I was on foot, with a bag of trash that I had every intention of going through when I had some privacy. Tea Totalers was to my right. It was an easy decision.

One bell rang over my head as I pushed the door open. Genevieve was stacking magazines on a bookshelf under the poster of the black cat. "Looks like I got me a repeat customer," she said in a bad impersonation of John Wayne.

"I considered disguising myself before walking in so you wouldn't think I was developing a dependency issue."

"In this business? I wish more people were like you. Do you have time to sit today, or are you on the go?"

I scanned the interior of the store. The surrounding empty seats, bad for Genevieve's business, were good for my need for solitude. "I have a little time," I said. "Do you have any more of those blondies?"

"You wouldn't like lunch?"

"I didn't realize you served lunch."

"I'm trying to branch out, expand my menu. Today I have avocado and crab soup and radish crostini. I'd love a taste tester. . . ."

"That's your experimental menu? I was expecting ham and cheese."

"Ham and cheese, good idea. Maybe I'll try that tomorrow."

Genevieve disappeared into the back, behind a curtain of blue and white check, and I carried my bag of trash to the powder room.

I locked the door behind me and, after considering the options, moved the braided rug to the door and sat on it. I opened the bag and picked through the trash, transferring bottles, cups, and Styrofoam take-out containers to the small wicker wastepaper basket in the corner. Something red and sticky coated my fingers. At the bottom of the bag I found a half-empty packet of duck sauce stuck to a bar tab from The Broadside. Something was written on the back of the receipt. I turned it over and saw the name *Tommy Pickers* underlined twice. When I looked back at the receipt, I realized it was dated for the day I'd arrived in San Ladrón.

Twelve

I rinsed my hands and looked around for paper towels or a hand drier. There were none. I dried my hands on my leggings. Was this Mr. Pickers's bar tab, or had someone who frequented The Broadside had a reason to make note of his name? I didn't know. I'd seen Mr. Pickers Friday night. Ken and I had been in front of the store. The old man could have been going to the bar, or coming from the bar. Either way, why was his name on this piece of paper I'd found at the Senior Center? Why had it been buried under an avalanche of trash, where it might never have been found?

There was a tap on the door. "You okay in there?" asked Genevieve.

"I'll be out in a sec," I called through the door. I pushed the rest of the trash into her basket and wrapped the sticky receipt in toilet paper, then pushed it into the vinyl pocket on my tunic. I opened the door and found her in front of me, holding a wicker tray by two handles. On the tray was a small teapot, a mug with no handles, a cup filled with green soup, and three small pieces of French bread coated in something creamy and white, topped with thin slices of white radishes outlined in pink.

"Follow me," she said. We reached a small table and she set the tray on the wooden surface. "There's sweet butter on the crostini under the radishes, and fleur de sel sprinkled on top. Let me know what you think."

"You haven't tried any of this?"

"I've tried too much of this," she said, and glanced down at her tummy. "I may be biased. I figure if the recipe came from France, it must be good." She filled the mug with tea and set it on the table, followed by the soup and the plate of crostini.

"Genevieve, did you know Mr. Pickers?" I asked.

"Not well. Why?"

"I was just wondering about him." I bit into the crostini and let the sweet butter melt in my mouth. "Mr. Pickers was head of the Senior Patrol and he kept watch over the stretch of Bonita that my store is on. I feel like maybe I should know something about him since he was—he won't be someone else is going to be assigned to my street instead."

"Around here, nobody gets assigned to anything. The Senior Patrol is made up of volunteers. They had a meeting here once, but it was a short meeting after they realized I only served tea."

"They wanted dinner?"

"They wanted booze. I think they started meeting at The Broadside Tavern after that."

I stiffened at the mention of the bar. "The Broadside is across the street from the fabric store."

"Close. Across the street and down a couple of store-fronts."

"Who runs it?"

"Why do you want to know?"

Our conversation was interrupted by the shrill ring of my phone. I pulled it out of my pocket. It was Charlie. "I have to take this," I said.

Genevieve nodded and went back to the counter.

Charlie didn't waste time on small talk. "You're not in a hurry to leave town, are you?"

"Why?"

"Your car's going to take a few more days to fix. Whoever did the damage took the job seriously. Those wires are a mess."

"So what's it going to be? This afternoon? Tonight?"

"I finally found a guy who has your ignition switch, so it's going to take at least another day. Maybe two." She paused. "I'm going to pick it up now. Wanna come?"

"Sure. I'm at Tea Totalers."

Genevieve looked up from the register at the mention of her store.

"Be there in twenty," Charlie said.

I set the phone back on the table and took a sip of my soup. Genevieve approached the table. "Everything okay?"

"Not sure," I said.

She pulled a chair away from the table and sat across from me. "Why were you asking me about The Broadside? Are you planning on going in there and asking questions about the Senior Patrol?"

"Maybe," I said.

"I don't think it's going to do you any good." Her chin tipped up and she looked down her nose at me. I fought the urge to fidget. "Mr. Pickers was a drinker. There was a whole stretch of bars down there and he used to hang out at them. Rumor has it he lost a lot of money betting on billiards at The Broadside and never paid. Can't imagine that made him too popular. Course, you don't hang out at that bar because you want to be popular."

"I went there my first day here."

She looked at me funny. "You're a braver woman than I am. Tough crowd hangs there. I'd be afraid to walk in by myself."

"I wasn't by myself," I said. I hesitated for a second. "I was with Charlie, the mechanic." I cut my eyes to my phone for a second, and then back to my food.

Genevieve wiped her hands on her apron. "I like Charlie. She likes to act tough herself, but underneath the motor oil she's just a woman on her own, trying to make a living."

"How do you know so much about everybody?"

"My husband and I thought this tea shop would be our livelihood, but the store hasn't taken off the way we projected. Now I run the store alone. He had to go back to his day job of driving a truck, and when the economy crashed a couple of years ago, he picked up a taxi route in addition to the truck. We had to make ends meet, and as bad as that stretch of nightlife was for San Ladrón, it was good for a cab driver."

"Could your husband tell me anything else about Mr. Pickers?"

She looked up at me and smiled a tender smile. "You'd do better asking Duke. He owns the place but he doesn't advertise it. You can usually find him there during happy hour. Midfifties, gray hair, voice kinda raspy like he smokes too much. He's a good guy. The kind people look up to, or would if they could figure out how."

"Genevieve, yesterday you said something about people from San Ladrón turning gossip into an Olympic sport. Was it hard for you to move here, being an outsider?"

"Oh gosh, no. I moved here a couple of years ago after I got married. My husband is from here. We met a few years ago at the World Tea Expo. After we married, it was either live in California or Arizona. Not a hard decision for me."

"So people accepted you? They were friendly?"

She laughed. "You mean your membership application

to San Ladrón's social circle was rejected already? That was fast." She stood up and pushed the chair under the table. "Sometimes it feels like a private club around here, but I had a ready-made membership card in the form of a marriage license. Still, people aren't rushing to support my tea shop the way they do other local restaurants. I'm not complaining—well, I guess I am, a little, but I shouldn't. There's a lot of people who have it worse," she added.

"Maybe you should throw some kind of party here. An open house. Invite everybody you know and everybody you don't. People should be lining up to drink your proprietary tea blend and eat your blondies and scones. And if this is any indication of what you can do for lunch, forgeddaboudit," I finished, in my best Tony Soprano. If she criticized my impersonation, I figured I could blame her for introducing accents to begin with.

"If only it were that easy."

"Think about it. If people start to associate Tea Totalers with getting together, they might start planning to meet up with each other here, and that would be good for business, right?"

She picked up a piece of my crostini and bit into it. After several crunches she swallowed and dabbed at the corner of her mouth with a paper napkin. "I don't think I'm ready for that. People would laugh at me. Why come here when they can go to the places they've been going their whole lives?"

"You have to give people a reason to change their habits. Otherwise they're going to keep doing whatever it is they always do. It's easier than trying something new." I thought about my relationship with Carson, with the routine we'd fallen into. Maybe that was the problem. Maybe somewhere along the line we stopped trying.

"I like the way you think, Poly. Maybe instead of worrying about these fuddy-duddies who've lived here forever, we should start our own club. Outsiders. Only people who've lived here for less than a decade can join." She stood up and carried the wicker tray to the counter. I took a bite out of the last crostini and finished off the last of the avocado soup. It was better than the last ten meals I'd had in Los Angeles.

I ducked my head under the long strap of my messenger bag and approached the counter. "I should get going," I said. "How much was lunch?"

"Lunch is on the house."

"Genevieve, that's not the way to run a business."

"I insist," she said. "But it'll be fourteen dollars for the tea," she added with a smile.

I paid her and left. When I reached the sidewalk, I saw Charlie's Camaro idling at the traffic light to my right. I wondered if what Genevieve had said was right, if Charlie played into her tough-girl image to protect her privacy and ward off gossip. I called her name and waved. When the light changed, she turned left, drove past me, then hung a U-turn in the middle of the street and pulled up to the curb next to me.

She leaned across the passenger side and jutted her chin in my direction. "Hop in," she said.

It was after one. I had arranged to meet up with Carson in two hours but on the off chance that he had returned to the store early, I didn't care to know about it. My mind was abuzz with information and I half wanted silence to think about what it all meant, but I needed to talk to Charlie about the shower incident. I climbed into the passenger side and buckled the seat belt. She U-turned again and headed north, to a section of town I hadn't yet explored.

"I'm sorry about your shower," I said. "When did you find out?"

"This morning. I was out all night."

"How bad is the damage?"

"I should be asking you the same thing."

"I'm okay," I said, then realized I kind of wasn't. "I have a couple of bruises around my ribs, but they'll heal. I finally got warm after spending an hour at the police station."

"Sheriff's office," she corrected.

"Whatever."

"What exactly happened?"

"It's kind of a blur. The shower felt really good, but you said I had four minutes. When the water started to turn cold I tried to turn it off but the knob came off and I couldn't. Then the door wouldn't open, but you said it stuck, so I kept trying to unstick it."

"I thought you'd know the difference between stuck and sabotaged."

"Who else knew I was back there?" I asked.

"Nobody. Why?"

"Because somebody trapped me in there. And if they didn't know I was in there, maybe they thought they were trapping you."

Charlie took a sudden left turn and my body slammed against the inside of the door. I didn't know what kind of a life she lived or whether or not something like this had ever happened to her before. All I knew was that I wanted to talk to somebody about some of the things that I'd experienced since arriving in San Ladrón, and I didn't have a lot of options.

She swung the Camaro into a U-turn midstreet and pulled up to a small building with a pile of tires stacked alongside the right exterior wall. "Wait here," she said. She went inside while I sat in the car. I touched my fingertips to the bruises on my ribs and my shoulder and winced. Better to sit completely still and pretend the bruises weren't there.

Charlie returned a few minutes later. She tossed a brown paper bag on the seat behind me and started back.

"You've lived here awhile, right?" I asked her.

"Nope . . . Moved here a couple of years ago. Thinking

about moving out again. I don't think I'm the type to stick around any one place, and this town might be over for me."

"Do you know the McMichaels?"

"Who doesn't?" she replied. "Old man McMichael owns most of this town and tries to buy what he doesn't own. I'm not interested in selling the shop, so I'm not one of his favorites, but what's he going to do with that little stretch of real estate? It's small potatoes to him, so he leaves me alone. Not like your situation."

"So you know he wants the store?"

"Polyester, everybody knows he wants the store. And a lot of people want him to have the store."

There was an endearing, no-bullshit quality to Charlie's manner and calling me by my full name fit. Usually when people called me Polyester it was in jest, a way to mock me. I didn't get the feeling Charlie was doing it to get a reaction, so I didn't mind.

"Why do a lot of people want him to get Uncle Marius's store? It can't be solely because he's going to put a megastore there, right? There are antiques stores and small businesses all along that street. If he knocked them all down, those stores would go out of business. A lot of nostalgia and collectibles would go back into a lot of attics."

"Who said he's going to knock it all down? He could turn the whole block into an antique mall. Take the plot behind you and level it and start hosting a monthly flea market. The Rose Bowl brings a lot of people to Pasadena. There's no reason he couldn't do that for San Ladrón—bring people here and put us on the map."

"That's a good idea. Is he considering that?"

"I doubt it, but he should."

I leaned back against the torn interior of the muscle car and let the wind slap my face. Maybe if I knew what Mr. McMichael wanted to do with the store, it would be different. Maybe I'd consider selling and going home. Maybe

Carson had been right and I would never fit in to this small town. Maybe—

"You okay over there?"

"Yes, why?"

"You keep saying 'maybe.' Maybe what?"

I didn't realize I'd been thinking out loud. "What do you think about Vaughn?" I asked, changing the subject.

"My first impression? Spoiled little rich kid."

"That's what I thought, too."

She took a hard left and again I swayed against the door to the car. "Turns out he's not. He's done good by people around here, people who would have lost their properties when the housing market went south a couple of years back."

"How do you know that?"

"I was one of them. Got behind on the payments on the shop. Business was slow. I thought I was going to have to sell it. But when I went to the bank, they said the payments had been made for me. By him."

"Why would he do that?" I asked. It was a generous move. Almost too generous. If I had been Charlie, I would have been suspicious. I was curious to find out why she wasn't.

"He said it was a loan, that he respected what I was trying to do by owning my own business and not asking for special treatment. I tried to fight the gesture because I didn't want to owe him anything, but he was persistent. Turns out his loan was what I needed to get through a tough couple of months. We worked out an arrangement." She paused and took her eyes from the road for a second to look at me and wiggled her eyebrows, like *arrangement* had a secondary meaning. "In the meantime, business picked up and I paid him back. He still asks for the occasional favor, and I'm happy to oblige. It's the least I can do."

I looked out the window again. She was being purposely vague, I guessed, because she liked having an audience for her story. I didn't want to admit that it bothered me that that "arrangement" might have involved something more than the exchange of money. It shouldn't bother me. A couple of times when Giovanni couldn't make the payroll expenses, I had to rely on Carson to float me through my debts. There had definitely been a price to pay for that. And even I had to admit that I didn't know much about Vaughn McMichael. He could be playboy of the year on the San Ladrón calendar for all I knew, and Charlie could be one of a number of women who liked him. If he was the son of a real estate tycoon who owned half of the town, then he surely had more to offer than those light-green-flecked-with-gold eyes, the angular cut of his jaw, and the broad shoulders that filled out his William and Mary sweatshirt.

". . . besides, there aren't a lot of people around San Ladrón who can offer him what I can," she finished. I silently cursed myself for tuning her out, but wondered for the briefest of seconds if this was part of Charlie's thing, baiting me to see how much dirt I really wanted.

We sat at a red light. She stared at me while waiting for the light to change. Based on our conversation, I wasn't sure anything I said would be kept between us girls. The last thing I wanted was for Vaughn to find out that I'd been asking about him.

"How about Adelaide Brooks? What do you think of her?" I asked. The light turned green but Charlie didn't notice.

"I don't want to talk about her," she said. The driver behind us honked his horn, two short taps, and Charlie found the gas pedal.

"It's good to be in a position of power," I said, when it became clear that she wasn't going to talk about Adelaide. "If you and Vaughn have a good thing, do what you have to do to keep it going."

She threw her head back and laughed a long, throaty laugh. I fought the urge to ask what was so funny.

"I like you, Polyester. I hope you stick around."

"Until you finish fixing my car I don't have much of a choice."

"That means I'm in a position of power over you, too. Good to know. I'll try not to let it go to my head."

She pulled the Camaro onto Bonita Avenue and accelerated. The tires screeched and the truck rocked to the left then right until she straightened it out. She pulled the car up to the front of the fabric store and I discovered I had bigger concerns than Charlie's power over me.

Carson and Vaughn stood in front of the gate.

Thirteen

"Somebody's popular," she said. "The new guy. Is he with you?"

"Sort of," I said.

"Cute, in a small-tipper kind of way." She flicked an eyebrow and pursed her cherry-red lips. I smiled a friendly smile but didn't comment.

"He's a finance guy. He's here to take me home."

"Finance guy. He probably smelled the money McMichael offered you. You sure he's not here to talk you into selling?"

I turned away from the scene of the two men and looked at Charlie. "Why would you say that?"

"Testing your resolve, that's all. Got your keys?" she asked.

"Yes."

"You want my advice? Don't give them to him."

I hopped out of the car. Charlie peeled away from the

curb before the door was shut. I wondered why she hadn't hung around, considering she knew Vaughn. There could be a thousand reasons, starting with the secret nature of their relationship and the very public presence of us on the street.

I approached the guys.

"You should have told me I have competition," said Carson.

"Nothing happened."

"I hope not. My offer's a lot more lucrative than his."

"Your offer?" I asked.

Vaughn looked down at the toes of his white Stan Smiths, but not fast enough to hide the smile tugging at the corners of his mouth.

"The investors I told you about. What did you think I meant?" He looked back and forth between us. "You and him? He's only interested in one thing." He laughed his banker laugh, the empty one he saved for clients and his boss. I had come to hate it.

"What are you doing here?" I asked Carson.

"You told me to meet you here at three. I've been waiting for an hour."

"It's only three thirty."

"I got bored. There's not a lot to do in this town. But you're so predictable I figured you'd be late. I already got us a room and the good news is it's ready for check-in. Let's go."

"I need to get a couple of things from the store."

"I parked the car in the back. I'll meet you here in two minutes."

I waited until Carson had disappeared around the side of the curb before making eye contact with Vaughn. I didn't know why he hadn't left, and I didn't know what I was going to say. Within the past twenty-four hours I'd learned that his father was suspected in the murder of my great-aunt, I'd learned about the bracelet from his mother, and his relationship with Charlie had put me on alert. I couldn't justify the nice guy he appeared to be now with the act of taking the note from the ledger. And since I wasn't sure why he was there in the first place, I didn't know if he really *was* a nice guy.

"He's your boyfriend?" Vaughn asked.

I looked back at the vacant street corner for a few seconds, then faced Vaughn and nodded.

"Did you tell him your plan to reopen the store?"

"I told him I wasn't selling."

"So he came to help you out?"

"In his own way." My vague comment solicited raised eyebrows from Vaughn. "He found another buyer for the store. He thinks that's the way to get me to go home."

"I thought you said he knows you don't want to sell."

"He means well. He doesn't understand why I feel the way I feel."

Carson's car appeared at the other end of the block. He pulled out and swung it up against the curb on the opposite side of the street.

"He also doesn't understand that I really am his competition."

"No, that I think he does understand. He's known from the beginning that your father wants to buy the store."

Vaughn turned his attention from Carson to me. "That's not what I meant."

His words hung in the air for a few seconds. I looked at him, gauging what his words meant. After a few awkward seconds of eye contact, he smiled a crooked smile, one dimple appearing on his cheek. I expected him to look away first, but he didn't flinch.

Carson tapped the horn twice, an unnecessary gesture since Vaughn and I were the only two people on the street. I pointed at the gate and held up my index finger to indicate that I wasn't done yet. He rolled down the window.

"Hurry up," he called.

I unlocked the gate and yanked on it forcefully, the hinges giving way more easily than they had the day before. Next I unlocked the front door and entered. My bag of personal items was by the cutting station next to the box with the kittens.

The kittens. I couldn't leave them in the store alone.

I threaded the plastic shopping bag over my left arm and hoisted the cardboard box against my hip. I carried them with me out the front door, set the box on the sidewalk, and relocked the store.

"How are they?" asked Vaughn. We looked down into the box at the same time and our heads bonked against each other.

"Ow," I said. I stood up and rubbed my forehead. He did the same. "They're okay. They're starting to meow."

"You sure the hotel will take them?"

"I'm not leaving them here."

"Let me watch them for the night."

Carson tapped the horn again. I looked at the car, then back at Vaughn. "I don't trust you enough to let you watch them."

"You know, I don't think you're as predictable as your boyfriend thinks."

I picked up the box and carried it to the car. I didn't turn around to see the look on Vaughn's face as we drove away.

"So what's the deal with that guy? Did you give him reason to believe you were going to sell to him?"

"No, Carson, I didn't. I made it very clear that I don't want to sell to anybody."

"Good girl. He seems like the persistent type, but I know he's only working for his dad. The real battle will be when I see his dad later today."

"You're going to see Mr. McMichael today? What for?"

"If you want to win a battle, you have to know your

competition. I figured as long as I was here I might as well see what this guy's all about."

"But it's Sunday."

"Business doesn't stop because of the weekend. The man works round the clock. Who knows? Maybe McVic will be impressed by me and I'll become his protégé. What's in the box?"

"Just some stuff from the store."

I stared out the window, letting the conversation drop. Two days away from Carson had been unexpectedly nice. No conversations about my job or our future. None of his high fives over interest rates or the stock market. Carson and I had fallen into a rut in Los Angeles. Tacos on Tuesday. Wings on Wednesday. Sex on Saturday. Our routine was dictated by the day of the week, and I felt like I was on the verge of a meltdown. But it was only Sunday, and the way our life had been structured, meltdowns weren't acceptable until Monday.

When I'd gotten the call that Great-Uncle Marius had passed away and left the store to me, I'd been a little bit in shock. Carson had been the one to schedule the initial meeting with Ken and arrange for me to come to sign the paperwork. I'd been thankful for his knowledge at the time, his efficiency. The reading of the will, the handling of my family's belongings, it all felt so impersonal, and it was nice to have someone step in and manage the process so I didn't have to. It was the first time in years I was happy that Carson functioned like a machine in matters of the heart. I had grown accustomed to his little quirks in Los Angeles, but outside of our element, I wanted him to shed those quirks, like taking a vacation from himself.

That's what this time in San Ladrón felt like. A vacation from myself. Adopting two stray kittens I already knew I couldn't have in my LA apartment, refusing to sell the store, making new friends like Genevieve and Charlie, it all felt right, like I had somehow awakened from a very boring dream. Or maybe, this was the dream and I was about to wake up. It surprised me to realize I didn't want to wake up, to return to my reality. I was *this close* to buying something other than black. That's how I knew my world was changing.

Carson pulled the car under the carport in front of a Best Western. "You want to wait in the car? I'll pick up the keys."

"Fine," I said.

I waited until Carson entered the lobby of the hotel before reaching into the box and rubbing each kitten between their ears. They turned their pink noses toward me and squeezed their eyes shut. The gray one sounded like a tiny engine. I didn't know what I was going to do with them when I went back to LA, but I didn't want to think about that yet.

A tap on the window startled me and I jumped. Carson stood outside. I lowered the window. "Take the keys and pull the car around to the side that faces the trees. We're in unit five on the first floor."

"You know I don't like to stay on the lower level," I said.

"This is San Ladrón, not Los Angeles. It's probably the safest town in California. Nobody's going to break into our room while we're sleeping."

"Can't you go inside and ask for a different room?"

He leaned in the open window and lowered his voice. "That's exactly my plan, but we have to find something wrong with the room before I can go back in and renegotiate. If I ask for another room and they have it, we're done. If I find some kind of problem with the room they gave us, they'll have to either figure it out or give us a discount. Trust me, Poly. I know what I'm doing."

His face was inches from mine, and if he had been so inclined he could have leaned forward and kissed me.

"Are those cats?" he said instead.

I looked into the box where the two kittens were climbing over each other, trying to get me to pet them again.

"No, Carson, they're bullfrogs."

He stood up and looked at the office, then strode around the car and climbed into the driver's side, slamming the door behind him. Without any additional words he pulled forward, swung the car to unit five, and parked. Before I had a chance to explain he got out of the car, slammed the door again, and popped the trunk. I counted the seconds that passed until he slammed the trunk and entered the hotel room. He slammed that door, too.

I waited a solid five minutes in the car, expecting him to come out and see what was taking me so long. I didn't want to be sitting in a car in a Best Western parking lot. I wanted to go to The Broadside Tavern and find out about Mr. Pickers. I went from mildly annoyed to angry in those five minutes. By five minutes and fifteen seconds, I knew what to do. I got out of the car and went into the hotel room.

Carson's jacket was on the bed and the door to the bathroom was closed. I crossed the room and rooted around through his pockets until I found the keys to the car.

It was time Carson learned what Vaughn had already recognized. I wasn't as predictable as he thought.

Fourteen

I pulled onto the side street and turned onto Bonita Avenue, heading the only direction I knew. It was close to four. An orange neon sign flickered in the window of a bar down the road from the fabric store. In the past two days, the *O* and the *A* had burned out and advertised The Brdside instead. Instead of turning into the alley that ran behind my store, I drove past the bar, turned onto a side street, and parked in the gravel lot by the back door between a pickup truck and a motorcycle.

"Wish me luck," I said to the kittens. I cracked the windows and locked the doors, heading inside.

I pushed against the unmarked wooden doors and they gave under the pressure, swinging in like I was entering a saloon. The interior was dark and it took a couple of blinks for my eyes to adjust to the light.

The bar lined the right side of the room. Three men sat

at bar stools at the far end. One stared at the TV screen mounted on the wall, his hand cupped around the base of a half-empty glass of beer. The other two glanced at me, then resumed their conversation.

The door swung shut behind me, hitting the backs of my heels. I jumped a few steps forward and put a hand out on the bar to steady myself. Something brushed against my calf and I twisted to look. A large black Labrador moved past me and two burly men followed. I recognized them as the men who had come to Charlie's shop the day my car was vandalized. One wore a black-and-red checkered shirt with a faded denim vest and jeans. The other had a T-shirt with the sleeves torn off, exposing an assortment of colorful tattoos featuring women and anchors. As the second one passed me, I read *Ahoy* on his bicep. They made no secret of the fact that they recognized me, too. Ahoy grabbed a peanut from a barrel in the corner, cracked it, and threw the shell on the floor. He tossed the nut into his mouth and followed the black lab to the pool tables. The man in the wheelchair I'd seen out front the day I cleaned the gate sat behind the felt table, watching me.

I scanned the rest of the interior, realizing how impulsive my entry had been. The man who stared at the TV screen finished his beer, stood up, and moved behind the counter.

"You want something?" He poured fresh beers for the other men and filled a red plastic basket with shelled peanuts from the wooden barrel."

"Is Duke here?"

"You don't know?

"Know what?"

"If Duke's here."

I turned away from him and looked around the room again, my eyes resting on the pool game. Colorful balls were scattered on the green felt. "Excuse me," I said to the bartender, and walked past a Ms. Pac-Man machine to the wheelchair bound man.

"You get lost on your way out?" he asked.

"No, I came here to talk to you."

"Lucky me." He maneuvered the wheels of his chair back and forth in short bursts until he was facing me. "Most people don't come here for the conversation."

I dropped into one of the vacant chairs and looked directly at him. He fit the description I'd been given to a T. I wondered why Genevieve hadn't mentioned the chair, then remembered her words: *He's a good guy. The kind people look up to, or would if they could figure out how.* "You're Duke?" He nodded.

"I'm Poly." I hesitated, not sure if a spontaneous meeting in a dark corner of a bar required me to add my last name.

"I know who you are. What I don't know is why you're here."

"I'm here to talk to you about Tom Pickers."

Behind Duke, Ahoy made his next shot, interrupting the otherwise silent bar with the sharp snap of billiard against billiard. It was followed by a number of balls falling into pockets and rolling down their chambers.

"Like I said, people don't come here for the conversation," Duke said. He backed away about a foot, and then rolled past me to an office to the left of the bar.

I stood up from my chair and tapped my fingers on the black vinyl pocket on the outside of my tunic. I wasn't sure if I should follow him or get the heck out of there. Ahoy set his cue stick on the felt and approached me. "What do you want to know about Tom Pickers? Maybe I could tell you a thing or two," he said. His eyes dropped to my throat, then my chest, then lower.

My heart raced. I clenched my teeth and felt the pulse of a nerve ending through my molar all the way up to my temple. I stepped backward, one step, then two, until I knew

I had a clear path to the bar and out the front door. I could leave Carson's car until tomorrow.

But the kittens. I couldn't leave the kittens.

The back door opened and a burst of blinding sunlight flooded the interior. Charlie held her hand over her eyes and looked at me.

"Yo—Polyester. I thought I saw you come in here."

Her sudden appearance threw me off, but at the moment, she was the familiar face I needed. She leaned over the bar, her cropped Metallica T-shirt exposing her flat tummy and a silver belly button ring right above the waistband of her jeans.

"Can I get a couple of beers and some quarters for the Jukebox?" she asked the bartender. He finished drying a glass and nodded. I weaved my way through torn vinyl chairs on casters until I stood next to the barstool she occupied.

"This was a bad idea," I said to her.

"You came here for information, right?" she said in a low voice. "So don't leave until you get it." She looked over my shoulder. When I turned to follow her gaze, Duke was by the end of the bar. He tipped his head toward the office and I followed.

Duke's office wasn't much bigger than a closet. A desk covered in magazines, envelopes, pens, notepads, and a couple of Post-its took up the majority of the interior. He backed his wheelchair up to the cabinets behind him, pushed his hands against the armrests until he was up, and transferred his lean frame into the chair behind the desk. I took a seat opposite him.

"You didn't wait for your beer," he said.

Without thinking, I looked at the door. He pulled two mismatched mugs from the bottom drawer of his desk, turned around and lifted a mostly full pot from a Mr. Coffee machine. After setting one mug in front of me, he pushed a

carousel filled with powdered creamer and colorful sweet-
ener options across the desk. I shook my head and left the
coffee black.

"You must have been talking to Genevieve," he said after
doctoring his own mug. "I can't think of another person
around here who would send you to me with questions about
Tom Pickers."

"What can you tell me about him?"

"Back in the day, Tom Pickers caused me a lot of trouble."

"He's why—" I didn't finish my sentence, but I didn't
have to. Duke glanced at his chair and let me know he knew
what I thought.

"No, that's a different story for a different day. Truth is
Tom Pickers was a victim of circumstance just like me." He
slugged his coffee. "Used to come in here nights, I think to
get away from his wife. Lots of guys do. It's one of the
reasons I've been in business for thirty years."

"How old are you?" I asked, immediately embarrassed
at the question.

"Fifty-seven. Yep, you did the math right. I was probably
about your age when I opened the bar. Owning a bar wasn't
a lifelong dream or anything. It was something I could do
after the accident. And at the time, that's what I needed. A
job I could do." He glanced at the chair and a flicker of anger
crossed his face. "Pickers was a regular, and in this business,
your regulars pay the bills. But when his wife died, he lost
control. Started drinking more and more. Got here early,
closed the place down. Took to playing pool, making bets
he couldn't cover. Every night. He came here because he
didn't have anyplace else to go. The whole town started
talking about him behind his back, but truth is I felt sorry
for him."

"With all due respect, there's a moral line in there. His
misery benefited you."

"It might have if he'd paid his tab, but he didn't. And I

didn't do anything about it, not at first. San Ladrón was changing at that time. Lots of people moving away, leaving California. Crime was on the rise. Business was tough. I got behind on the rent. Tom Pickers worked at the bank and did what he could to help me out, but the bank cracked down. Gave me thirty days to pay or lose the bar. I couldn't afford to lose the bar. It was the only thing I had."

"When was this?"

"About ten years ago."

Duke's clear blue eyes studied me closely. The coincidence of ten years lacked the impact it might otherwise have had. I didn't speak, didn't interrupt. After a few seconds, Duke continued.

"I told him I needed the money he owed me. His tab shouldn't have been public knowledge, but a couple of people found out. That's the problem with a small town like this—can't keep a secret. People are always going to know your business. Pickers got beat up shortly after that. When he wasn't here by four thirty the next day, I thought he'd skipped town. I was wrong. He came in close to midnight, drunk. He ran up his tab, argued his way into a high-stakes game of pool, and started a fight. I had to throw him out. Didn't see him for a couple of days. When the news broke about the robbery at the store, I wasn't the only person who suspected he might have been involved. He was right there, he could have—but he didn't."

"He was supposed to be there but he wasn't. That was the problem. He was supposed to go to the fabric store, pick up the cash take from the weekend, and deposit it in the bank the next day."

"I heard that story, too. No, Tommy was there alright. Can't say how clear his vision was, but he was there. I think that's why he took so long to make a statement. He didn't trust what he saw because he knew he wasn't in his right mind."

"He said he saw a monster."

"Yep, that's what he said."

"Why didn't he call the police? If he was scared, why just walk away?"

"Lots of people wondered that very question, but nobody'll ever know the answer to it now. Tommy was alienated after that. Some thought he went nuts, others thought he had something to do with it."

"Were you one of those people?"

"It occurred to me."

"What happened next?"

"I got the money to pay the back rent and life went on. Tommy came in a few months later and wanted to talk." Duke picked up a staple remover from the corner of his desk and tapped the end on the surface. His head was tipped to the side and I could almost see him struggling with ten-year-old memories. "Tommy had a lot of guilt over what happened that night. Said he couldn't let anything like that happen again and apologized for the way things went down. I told him no hard feelings, but I thought it best if he didn't come back to the bar. Wiped his tab clean and wished him luck. Couple of months go by and I hear he's doing better."

"Has he been back? Since then?"

"No. He got himself together, sobered up. That's when he started up the Senior Patrol."

I thought about the receipt in the pocket of my tunic. "Are you sure he hasn't been back here? The night before he was murdered?"

Duke leaned forward. "Just what is it you're trying to ask me?"

I reached into my pocket and pulled out the wad of toilet paper. I unfolded it on the desk in front of Duke. The paper stuck to the receipt where the duck sauce smudge was, but the printing on the piece of paper was still legible. "I found this at the Senior Center. It has Mr. Pickers's name on the back. I saw him on the street that night and I figured maybe he was on his way here."

Duke picked up the receipt and held it in front of him. I suspected he knew what this was from, but he worked at keeping his expression unreadable. "You found this at the Senior Center?" he repeated. "When?"

"Today. Is that his tab?"

"Nope." He held the paper out to me. "Probably somebody scribbled his name on a piece of scrap paper. I don't think it means much of anything," he said.

Before he had a chance to change his mind, I took the slip of paper and folded it back up.

"Why do you think Mr. Pickers would choose this stretch of town to keep watch over?" I asked.

"That's a funny thing. Once Tommy chose this street, nobody could talk him out of it. He was a stubborn old coot. You would have thought he'd want to avoid it at all costs. I always thought he was trying to figure out what he saw that night."

"What do you think he saw?"

"Not my place to say." Duke finished off his coffee. "Whole town knows we had a rift. If you asked around, you might have heard a different version of events, but it wouldn't have been that far from the truth. Long time ago I learned even if you keep your mouth shut you can't control what people are going to say. I admire you for coming to me instead of listening to gossip."

"Thank you for talking to me about him," I said. I stood up. "I wasn't sure what to expect when I came in here."

"That's funny. Most people who walk into a bar know exactly what to expect."

"A priest and a rabbi?" I asked with a smile.

"Something like that."

Duke stayed behind in his office after I left. I found

Charlie shooting darts and doing shots with the bartender. She was lining up her next throw when she saw me.

"You all done?" she asked.

"I think so."

"Cool. Let me settle the bill and we can get out of here." She tossed the dart in her hand at the board and it landed in the bull's-eye. "That should cover a couple of beers, right?" she said to the bartender.

I hustled to the door, not sure I wanted to stick around and find out how and why Charlie had shown up when she did. The sun was mid-descent and the sky was a watercolor of orange and pink hues. The scent of honeysuckles filled the air. I climbed into Carson's car and peeked in the box at the kittens. They were curled up practically on top of each other, their heads tucked on their paws like a kitten version of yin and yang. I resisted the urge to pet them, knowing it would interrupt their sleep.

I was startled by a sharp rap on the window. I looked up, expecting to see Charlie. Instead, the man in the red-and-black checkered shirt stood next to the car, holding his cue stick in both hands. I rolled the window down about three inches and hit the locks at the same time.

"I don't know what you think you're going to gain by asking questions, but you might want to mind your own business," he said.

"I am minding my own business," I said.

"Pickers owed people money. How's that your business?"

"Those debts are a decade old. If Duke can wipe the slate clean, maybe you should, too. Besides, he was killed at the fabric store. That's my business."

"Not for long, it's not, Polyester."

Heat snaked its way down the base of my neck at the mention of my name. I hadn't introduced myself to this man. He either knew who I was when I entered the bar, or he'd been paying attention while I talked to Duke.

"Take my advice and go back to where you came from. Maybe Duke was willing to forgive and forget but a lot of other people aren't. Pickers wasn't no saint. He owed a lot of people money and didn't make good. The old man got what he deserved."

Fifteen

My heart pounded like a bass drum marking time for a parade. I threw the car into gear and backed out of the alley. I turned left, drove three blocks, then turned right and headed to the fabric store via the alley. I parked the car in the back and carried the box of kittens inside. Carson was going to be mad, but I didn't care. I had a lot to think about and I didn't need him clouding my judgment.

My visit with Duke had given me some background info about Mr. Pickers. Discovering his dark days and his subsequent new leaf would have been enough, but it wasn't. The man at Duke's wearing the flannel shirt had given me the impression that Mr. Pickers's debts ran deeper than those to Duke. Who else had Mr. Pickers owed money to? Were they new debts? And had they factored into his murder? Or had the whole story been fabricated for my benefit to distract me from the connection between Mr. Pickers and my great-aunt? I reached my hand into my pocket and pulled out the

charm Adelaide Brooks had given me. What if the rest of
the bracelet really was still in the store? Did that mean the
men who had been arrested for the crime had been telling
the truth? Was someone else responsible for that crime—
someone who was scared that their secret would come out
if I reopened the store?

I cut a length of quarter-inch-wide black faille ribbon and
fed it through the loop on the end of the charm. I tied it into
a knot, slipped it over my head, and tucked it under the
neckline of the black tunic.

I collected an assortment of envelopes and grocery store
circulars that had been shoved through the gate of the fabric
store, set them inside the carton with the kittens, and climbed
the stairs to the apartment. This time I wasn't running for
my life from an unidentified threat in the alley and I wasn't
distracted by a scrapbook filled with news of my great-aunt's
murder. I wanted to take my time, to really see the place.

I set the carton on the floor and scooped out the kittens,
letting them sniff the hardwood floor and swat at the fringe
on the end of the carpet. There was no place they could go,
and it seemed the perfect time to let cats give in to their
natural curiosity. As they walked tentatively into the living
room, I wandered down the hallway and looked into the
rooms. There was a bathroom. A guest room. And my aunt
and uncle's bedroom.

Like the living room, white sheets had been thrown over
the furniture. Upon closer inspection I realized they weren't
sheets but yards and yards of a thin gauzy cotton. I gathered
the fabric in my hands, exposing an ivory damask bedspread
with tiny pink and blue flowers woven into the print. Small
rectangular pillows, white velvet with pale blue flower buds
that seemed to be growing from within them, were nestled
on the bed by the headboard. I picked one up and flipped it
over in my hands. The nap on the white velvet had crushed
into an abstract pattern on the underside. I rubbed my

fingertips over the fabric a few times, trying to smooth it out, and set it back on the bed.

The walls matched the ivory spread and the molding, stained the same dark wood as the floor, drew my eye to the ceiling. A large oak headboard stood behind the bed, flanked on either side with small white decorative columns. A piece of marble covered each of the columns, creating makeshift tabletops. On one side rested a white lamp with a white milk-glass shade. The other held a newspaper, a book, and a pair of glasses.

It pained me to think that Uncle Marius had left so abruptly that he hadn't even taken his glasses with him. I wondered if he knew at the time that he would never come back into the store or the apartment, or if he'd ever thought to ask someone to bring him some of his belongings. But if he had thought of it, who would he ask? Not my parents. He had shut them out, like the rest of the family. I knew Mom and Dad had volunteered to help him. I had overheard them talking about it one night after my graduation. But Uncle Marius hadn't returned their calls.

Thinking about it now, after all those years, I knew my parents wouldn't have let it go at that. Uncle Marius was family, my grandfather's brother. My dad's father had died during my childhood and I didn't remember having a relationship with him, but Uncle Marius and Aunt Millie were different. They had always been there for my family, for me, until one day they weren't.

I wandered into the kitchen. The counters were spotless, as was the sink. An empty turquoise CorningWare dish sat in the sink, clean. The sight of it triggered a memory from my childhood. I knew that piece of CorningWare, and I knew who it had belonged to. Not Uncle Marius. My parents.

I checked my phone; it was a couple of minutes after four. I called my parents in Burbank and my mom answered.

"Mom, it's Poly. Do you have time to talk?"

"Of course. Is everything okay? Are you at work?"

"I'm still in San Ladrón."

"I didn't realize you were taking vacation time. How long did your boss give you?"

I weighed the pros and cons of telling Mom that I hadn't actually taken vacation. As of tomorrow, eight AM, Giovanni expected me back at work, and I was fairly certain I wasn't going to be there. I didn't know how I was going to get around that other than faking the flu, and I wasn't ready to deal with the guilt of confessing that to my mother.

"A couple of days," I said. "Mom, when's the last time you were in the fabric store? Or the apartment?"

"Oh, geez. It's been a while. Longer than I remember. Why?"

"I'm there now and the furniture has all been covered up. Do you know who did that?"

She hesitated. "I didn't realize Marius had asked anybody to do that. I don't know why, but I always thought of that beautiful turn-of-the-century furniture collecting a decade's worth of dust."

"Would Dad know?"

"I doubt it. Marius pulled away from us after Millie's death. It was a shame, really, that he didn't turn to family to comfort him, but I think we were all too tied to his memories of her."

"Mom, I know you and Dad didn't just leave him alone. Our CorningWare bowl is in the sink, and that afghan you were knitting when I was at the Fashion Institute is draped over the back of a rocking chair in the living room. There's no way those things would be here if you'd cut all ties."

The silence on the other end of the phone was enough to confirm my suspicions. My parents, who always claimed that the murder had torn the family apart, had kept in touch with my uncle and I had never known it. I was hurt, because Uncle Marius had been a part of my life, too, and nobody had bothered to let me know what was going on.

"Poly, listen to me. Your uncle Marius was destroyed when Aunt Millie was murdered. He didn't want to talk to anybody about it, but he didn't want to move on. One day your father and I went to see him, unannounced. We found him in the bedroom, sitting in front of her closet, staring at her clothes. He was a wreck. He hadn't been eating. We took him to a hospital, where your father stayed in the waiting room while they made sure he was okay. When he was released, we thought we'd help him leave the apartment behind and find a new place to live, but he didn't. Several months later a letter arrived from him, thanking us for helping him through a hard time. He wrote that he knew it was time for him to move on, but that he knew he couldn't go back. He told us that he had made arrangements for the apartment and the store, and asked that we keep him informed about your life. He apologized to us in advance for dropping out of our lives but asked that we respect his wishes."

"So he told you? He told you what he was doing and you never told me?" I asked. Tears stung my eyes. It was such a huge thing, them keeping a secret of this magnitude from me, refusing to talk about Uncle Marius and Aunt Millie every time I tried to bring them up.

"Poly, I'm so sorry. Maybe we should have told you, but Marius asked us not to. He knew he was retreating into a solitary life; it was the only way he could imagine going on living. But you were the one person he kept tabs on. We wrote him letters frequently, telling him about your job, your apartment, and your boyfriend. I sent him sketches from the first collection you designed for To The Nines."

"But how do you know he ever got anything? Why would he not react?"

"Every time I sent something, a week later I received a blank thank-you note postmarked in San Ladrón. He never signed them, but he was the only person who could have sent them."

I wandered back to the bedroom and sat on the ivory damask bedspread. It was what I wanted to know, only it was information that came so much later than I wished. My uncle hadn't shut me out of his life. Those ten years, he'd been keeping track of me. Just like I felt a connection to him, he felt a connection to me. Leaving me the store was more than a bequest, it was an apology.

"Mom, what do you think he expected me to do with the store?"

"None of us know the answer to that, Poly. But it's yours now, and it's up to you to decide what happens to it."

I ended the call, then opened the closet at the end of the bed and exposed several dark suits hanging on heavy wooden hangers. I could tell from the style of them that they had been bought in the fifties. The narrow lapels, the long rise, the narrow legs. Uncle Marius's suits, from before he left. Next to them were my great-aunt Millie's dresses. I remembered her glamour almost as much as I remembered her. No matter what she did, whether she was running the store, or going out to buy groceries, she was always dressed beyond what the occasion called for. When I was little, I used to play dress-up in her closet, sometimes even wearing one of her long silken nightgowns to the dinner table with a feather boa over my shoulders. There was a picture of that in a family photo album, somewhere. At the time, I was ten years old. I didn't know what was so funny, but I had loved the attention those fabulous clothes had given me.

It had been a long time since I stopped and thought about the impact Great-Aunt Millie had on me when I was growing up. Not only the time I spent in the store, but being around her, in her silks, cashmeres, wool challis, and feathers. She always loved feathers. And rhinestones. And gold. She taught me that you didn't have to buy the newest fashions to have style. She showed me a closet of clothes she'd made from fabrics in the store. Styles from decades earlier, copied from old vintage dresses she found during her travels around the world. Even though they were far from what had been featured in fashion magazines in the fifties, Millie had made them her own. I suspected she was the center of attention at any party she attended.

She wouldn't have recognized me in the uniform of black that got me through my life, but she would have been the one person to understand what I was trying to do with my job as senior concept designer at To The Nines. She'd take a look at the sketches and recognize designs of the twenties and thirties, clothes suited more for a Mae West movie than a bare-bones dress shop in downtown Los Angeles. I wondered about the girls who came into the store looking for their prom dress or homecoming gown. Giovanni kept our overhead low with cheap materials, but he took a healthy markup on the inventory. When a particular dress didn't sell, he could call someone related to the pageant circuit and move the stock at a discount.

I ran the back of my hand over delicate fabrics in Aunt Millie's closet, then gently fingered the beadwork on her many gowns. Uncle Marius and Aunt Millie used to tell me stories about the lifestyle they led before my parents were born, and these clothes were the kind that would have been worn by someone in a high social circle. I wished I could see them, that I could have been a fly on the wall of that social life. But just like everything else about the store and the town, it was different now. I could pull from the past and use it in the present if I wanted. If I did reopen the store, I could let my family's legacy continue in a new way.

I moved to the kitchen table and flipped through the stack of mail that had accumulated over the past few days. Most of the envelopes were addressed to *Resident*. One catalog of home products advertised a sale on fans and air conditioners. A folded-over grocery store flyer and discount furniture ads rounded out the stack. I carried it all to the garbage. I guess the news was getting out: the store was no longer vacant.

A document-sized white envelope slipped from between the grocery store ads and fell by my feet. I picked it up and scanned the official-looking printed address: *Attn: Carson Cole, c/o Land of a Thousand Fabrics.* That was a first. I checked the return address. *McMichael Development and Investments.*

I stood rooted to the spot. My hands shook as I plunged my index finger under the end of the envelope and tore through it. I reached inside and pulled out a letter typed on crisp white stationery. It was addressed to Carson, and confirmed his meeting with Mr. McMichael today at five o'clock.

I threw the stack of paper to the floor. Sheets scattered across the tile, some floating under the table, others getting lost by the dishwasher. Carson had told me about his meeting with Mr. McMichael, but I hadn't thought he'd go through with it once he knew how I felt. As soon as the paper left my hand I knew throwing things wasn't the answer. I dropped to my hands and knees and corralled the pages back together. I typed the address into the GPS on my phone and studied the directions.

Without a car, Carson couldn't make his appointment, but I could. It was time for me to pay Mr. McMichael a visit and tell him face-to-face what I thought of his offer.

Sixteen

I returned to the closet and pushed the evening clothes out of the way. I found a black sheath dress and jacket in a plastic garment bag. It was clearly from another era, but it would have to do.

I changed out of my tunic and leggings and into the outfit. The jacket had a jeweled collar and laid perfectly over the neckline of the dress. Both garments were the same length. I left the buttons, round shiny black balls, unbuttoned down the front. I felt along the top shelf of the closet for a pair of shoes and knocked over a box of memorabilia. I scooped up the mess and set it on the bed. Aunt Millie's feet were bigger than mine, but I lined the bottoms of a pair of black crocodile pumps with a piece of foam from the batting section of the store, then secured each foot with black ribbon tied over the instep. The heels were low enough that I felt stable.

I left the store and followed the directions to McMichael Development and Investments. I missed the turn onto the highway and ended up turning around in the parking lot of Gnarly Waves, a water park that was closed for the winter. Instead of doubling back, I followed the winding roads alongside of the reservoir until I saw Parkhurst Airfield. My GPS told me McMichael Development and Investments was across the street.

I'd expected a multifloor office building with shiny chrome elevator doors and judgmental doormen. What I found instead was a two-story office building, beige siding with dark brown trim. Jacaranda trees lined the property, spilling bright purple blossoms over the parking lot and the yard. The parking lot sat off to the side, only a handful of cars occupying the numerous spaces. I parked by the doors and went inside.

"May I help you?" asked the uniformed man behind the marble counter.

"I'm here to see Vic McMichael."

"Sign in here." He pushed a leather guest book toward me. I considered writing a fake name, but didn't see the point. I wasn't trying to hide my identity. I was trying to head off a hostile takeover.

"Down the hall, second office on the left."

I followed the directions and let myself into the room. A fortysomething receptionist sat behind a modest desk. A small silver bud vase sat next to her phone and an array of photos sat to the other side by the Tiffany lamp. I wondered if she'd been called in to work on a Sunday because of Carson's appointment and considered apologizing.

"Mr. McMichael is expecting you. Go right in." She gestured toward a wooden door with *Vic McMichael* embossed on a brass nameplate on the outside. I grabbed the knob and turned, boosting my confidence with one last deep breath before entering.

Vic McMichael sat behind a desk that made his secretary's look like the Fisher-Price model. Every white hair on his head was in place. Small rimless glasses sat on his face, barely noticeable except for the steel arms that ran from the lenses to his ears. He wore a navy-blue suit, light blue shirt with white collar, and a navy and red diagonally striped tie. It was from one of the Ivy League colleges, I thought. Or it might have been the standard-issue tie for businessmen around the world. I wasn't sure which.

Before he had a chance to offer me a drink from the assortment of bottles that sat on a cart to the side of his desk, I spoke up. "Why do you want to take the store from me?"

"Ms. Monroe, have a seat."

Before blurting out an immature response about standing preferences, I thought about something Carson had told me once when I asked why he wasn't afraid of anyone in his business meetings. *Act like you're scared and they'll treat you like you don't belong. Act like you do and the next thing you know, you're having a rational conversation. It's only after you enter the conversation phase that you start to get stuff done.* While I may have blown a decent chance at normal with my outburst, I figured there's no time like the present for a do-over.

Tentatively, I sat, more because sitting was the appropriate behavior in his mostly wood office, while stamping my foot and refusing was childlike. I scanned Mr. McMichael's desk for clues to his personality. I found those clues in the framed pictures on the bookcase behind his desk. I recognized Vaughn in a couple of the photos, and a younger version of Mr. McMichael in others. At first it was hard to tell their images apart. In his youth, Mr. McMichael looked just like his son did today. The only thing missing were the dimples. But they were there, on the face of the attractive brunette who stood next to him in the photo: Adelaide Brooks.

"Ms. Monroe, I can appreciate that you want to honor what your relatives built. Land of a Thousand Fabrics was the jewel of San Ladrón, once."

"What makes you think it can't be again?"

He studied me. "So it's true. You're thinking of reopening the store? Have you run a business before?"

"I helped my family with the store when I was growing up. I know the ins and outs."

His lips curled into the tiniest hint of a smile. There were no dimples. I didn't like the thought that he considered me a joke.

"That was before I graduated FIDM and learned the other side of the business. I started working for a garment shop in Los Angeles, where my daily responsibilities include selecting fabrics, negotiating business deals, managing the payroll, and generally ensuring quarterly profits." I stopped speaking, more surprised by my outburst now than when I'd entered the office. Aside from the weakness of "generally," did it sound as good as I thought, or did I sound like the lead in a Reese Witherspoon movie?

The smile faded from Mr. McMichael's face. "Ms. Monroe, I had no idea your degree was in business."

It wasn't, but now hardly felt like the time to correct him.

"My son told me you weren't going to sell. At the time, I wasn't aware of your intentions with the store. Now that I know what you have in mind, and that you're aware of the risks, may I offer you my help?"

"With what?"

"First, you'll need to clear the taxes on the store, update the seller's permits. Reestablish the name as a formidable business. Create a buzz. Then there's the condition of the store's interior. I imagine ten years of neglect have created a need for repairs. I deal in flipping businesses regularly. I have construction crews at my disposal and can pull some strings to get you bumped up on their priority list."

My hands, folded in my lap, tightened around each other.

"Modernize your business practices, from your phones to your registers. Cast a critical eye toward your inventory, dumping what has no value and investing in what the home-maker of the new millennium might want. Assuming, that is, that there is a millennial homemaker and he or she is interested in fabric." Again he paused, this time the smile returning. "But I'm sure you thought through all of this."

"And what would you like in return for all of this help?"

"A split. Fifty-fifty ownership. I can have new paperwork drawn up this afternoon and have Mr. Watts deliver it before close of business."

"I understand that you've been buying up the properties along that stretch of Bonita and mine is the only one left. If I agreed to your terms, what would keep you from selling the strip to a developer?"

"That would be a wise business move."

"You don't care about the businesses that would be ruined? The people whose lives would change?"

"Each of those business owners knew the risks involved when they signed their leases." He leaned back in his chair and folded his fingers together. I felt the scrutiny of his stare and I forced myself to maintain eye contact, despite the heat I felt under the collar of my jacket. "These terms don't give me ownership. They merely give you a safety net. If you agree, I can have a construction crew go over the interior by the end of the week."

"Why should I trust you?"

"Because you don't have much of a choice. Reopening a store that's been hanging under a cloud of sadness for ten years is an uphill battle."

"Mr. McMichael, I know reopening the store will be a lot of work. I'm not afraid of hard work." I stood and pushed my chair under the desk. "Just like I'm not afraid of you."

I left Mr. McMichael's office and walked past his secretary without a word. As I waited for the elevator, I considered going back and asking for parking validation. I

caught my reflection in the mirror. I looked like I was playing dress-up. I was in over my head, and a fifty-year-old
power suit wasn't going to make a shred of difference. I
called Carson.

"Where have you been?" he demanded. "I had an
appointment today. Because of you everything's screwed up."

"I kept your appointment."

"I know. When you took the car, I knew I wasn't going
to make it there. I called McVic's office to reschedule. His
secretary told me you'd shown up. I don't know what you
were thinking, but I wish you would have at least asked my
advice. Now we're going to have to figure out damage
control."

"Carson, we can talk about this later. I'm going to swing
by the fabric store and pick up a few things, then I'll meet
you at the hotel."

"There is no hotel, Poly. I refused the room."

"Where are you?"

"I took a taxi to the fabric store but you weren't there. Now
I'm at some silly mom-and-pop coffee shop. This must be the
only town in America that doesn't have a Starbucks."

"You're probably at Jitterbug. I'll meet you there in
fifteen minutes."

I drove to the fabric store, pulled into the alley that ran
behind it to the parking lot, parked by the Dumpster, and
let myself in. I tossed my handbag and keys on the wrap
stand and went upstairs to change clothes. The last thing I
needed was for Carson to criticize my fashion choices for
the meeting with Mr. McMichael.

I stepped out of the dress and jacket and hung them back
in the closet. My outfit from earlier lay on the comforter on
top of the box I'd spilled earlier. I put it back on. One black
outfit for another. I felt as though I was going through the
motions, changing costumes for different acts of my life.
Business Poly. Girlfriend Poly. Worker Bee Poly. I glanced

back into the closet and stared at the beaded shrugs and the shimmery silk gowns. Was there a Party Poly who could wear those? And when?

I climbed onto the bed and stared at the ceiling. I didn't know what to think about my meeting with Mr. McMichael. I'd surprised myself when I'd spoken up about my experience, but it had all been true. If I wanted to, I could do this.

On any given day at To The Nines I could be negotiating with vendors communicating in Korean-to-English in the workroom, helping young girls pick out their prom dresses, or fixing broken equipment in the sewing room. I had even managed a couple of meetings with the bank when Giovanni was suffering from a stomach flu. He'd been planning to go but felt frequent trips to the bathroom would undermine his credibility. My degree wasn't in business, and I knew I'd make mistakes along the way, but also knew I could figure it out if I wanted. And I finally could admit that I did.

The strangest thing about my meeting with Mr. McMichael was that he hadn't acted like we were at war over the property. He'd appeared calm. Almost helpful.

But then he mentioned the construction crews at his disposal. Were these the same men who had threatened me at The Broadside? And why did Mr. McMichael care so much about what I did with the store? Why was he willing to help me in order to gain possession of it? Was he hoping to get in and destroy evidence that he knew still existed?

I felt something tug the side of the comforter and I screamed, pulling my legs up to the middle of the bed and hugging my knees tightly. A soft meow came from the floor. With my heart already pounding in my chest, I peeked over the edge. The gray kitten stared up at me and meowed again.

"How did you get up here?" I asked. I twisted around until I was on my belly on the bed, and scooped him up with one hand and set him next to the box. He was dwarfed by the queen-sized bed. I bent back down, dangling upside down over the side of the bed and looked under the edge of the damask cover for the other kitten. She wasn't there.

To me, it was a small apartment. To a kitten less than six inches long, it was probably like getting lost in Milan. "Wait here," I said to the one on the bed. He stood next to the box and dropped his head to sniff it. "I'll be right back."

I had to find the orange tabby kitten. I couldn't explain it, but since I'd arrived in San Ladrón, I'd felt like I was alone, like there was nobody there to talk to, nobody to keep me company while I figured out what I was going to do. Those kittens had been alone in the Dumpster. The only thing they had was each other. It was up to me to keep them together.

I entered the hallway on bare feet, happy to step onto the plush Oriental carpet runner to keep me from coming in contact with the cool hardwood floor. I gently blew kisses in the air and tapped my thigh, peering around corners and under chairs. After half an hour, I came up empty. Either the kitten had found a very good hiding spot, or she was downstairs in the store.

I jogged down the metal staircase and called out in a soft, comforting voice. She was small, small enough that I might not see her. I hit the switches on the control panel, but nothing happened. Confused, I turned them to off and back to on. There was no longer any electricity.

I cursed under my breath. The electric company must have shut it off when they didn't receive payment from my uncle. Tomorrow, right after I had the water turned on, I'd call them and set up new billing arrangements. But for tonight, I was destined to live in the dark ages.

Upstairs, afternoon light had kept the room illuminated, so I hadn't used any electricity. Down here, the store was dark. I unlocked the front door and pulled it open, letting the waning sunlight improve my vision. The shadow of the metal fence left cross marks on the concrete floor. I moved past the first large square bin of fabric and peered around another corner.

"Where are you, little kitty?" I asked. "It's cold in here and your brother is upstairs waiting for you."

As I made my way through the store, past the makeshift partition and the broken window where I'd gotten stuck the first day, I wondered what it would take for me to go back there. That was the scene of the murder, and if there really were unanswered questions about my great-aunt's death, then there was a chance the answers were back there. The door was partially open, about the width of one very small cat.

I took a deep breath, knowing what I had to do, but not knowing if I was ready to do it. I put a hand on the door and pushed it open, then stepped inside the darkness. My foot crushed pieces of broken glass from the day I'd entered through the window. The flashlight sat a few feet away from the glass. I picked it up and clicked it on and off. Nothing happened. I slapped it against my palm a few times like I'd seen my dad do, but still, nothing. I set it back on the floor. I closed my eyes for a couple of seconds, and reopened them after they'd had a chance to adjust to the lack of light. I kept one hand on the door as if letting go would throw me into an alternate universe.

I heard a car outside the store. I don't know why, but I pulled myself inside the hidden room and pressed my back up against the wooden partition, listening.

"Poly? Are you in there?"

It was Carson's voice. Even though I wasn't in the mood to deal with him, I knew he deserved better than prolonged avoidance. I had no right to take his car and leave him high and dry at the hotel.

"I'm sorry." I stepped out of the back room and looked at the gate.

Carson stood by the gate. He shielded his eyes with one

hand, trying to figure out where I was standing. "What are you doing in there? Have you gone crazy?"

"Give me a second and I'll get your keys. The car is out back."

He fed his fingers through the metal fence and shook it. Metal clanged against metal loudly. "Open this gate and let me in."

"You don't understand. There's a kitten lost in the store somewhere and I have to find him." I scooped his keys up from the wrap stand and took a few steps toward him.

"You know we can't have pets at the apartment. Or are you going to sneak them in and jeopardize our lease?"

"I'm not going to jeopardize anything. I just need a little time to figure out what I'm going to do."

"What's to figure out? I set this whole thing up. It's ready to go. I don't get why you're fighting me on this."

"You don't get it because you don't listen."

"I listen just fine."

"No, you don't. You don't listen to *me*." My statement hung in the air like a mist. In the resulting silence, I heard a sound coming from somewhere inside the hidden room and turned my head. "Did you hear that?" I asked.

"This is no time for your jokes, Poly. Either let me in or give me the keys. I don't really care which."

I swung my right hand back and then forward like I was bowling. I let go of the keys and they slid across the exposed concrete floor, stopping only when they hit the base of the hinged metal gate. Carson bent down and snatched them off the floor.

"Nice move. Are you coming?" he said.

"You can wait five minutes, Carson." I ducked back into the secret room and got down on my hands and knees, crawling across the floor, blowing kisses. Carson called my name behind me, but I ignored him. As I reached the wall that resembled a bookcase with plastic bins of ribbon, buttons, rhinestones, and other fancy trims, I saw the kitten's small orange body, hovering by the corner. He was shivering and scared.

"Poly, this is stupid. I'm leaving."

"I'll be there in a second," I called. "Come here, sweetheart, it's okay," I cooed. He stepped backward. I knew lunging for him would scare him further. Very slowly I moved forward. Behind me, I heard the metal gate shake. Dry dust that had been settled for decades swirled through the air and caught in my throat. The only way Carson would hear me was if I yelled to him, and yelling would scare the kitten more. I ignored him and crept closer, until I could reach a hand out. He leaned forward and sniffed it, then let me run my fingers over his head.

The gate rattled, scaring the small kitten just as my hands were about to close around his small body. He jumped up and back, actions more befitting a cartoon cat than a real one, and disappeared into darkness around the cover of the bins of buttons and ribbon. Trying to find him now, without a flashlight, would have been futile. The cold concrete floor sent a chill through my pants to my skin. I stood up and stepped backward, tripping over my own foot but regaining balance quickly.

The fence rattled again. "Would you knock that off?" I said under my breath. I might not succeed in finding the kitten tonight, but I wasn't going to let him starve. I crossed the store to the cutting station, peeled the metal lid back from a fresh can of cat food and dumped it into the plastic bowl from the drugstore. I filled the water bowl and set them both by the door that separated the secret room from the store. I glanced at the gate, expecting to see the annoyed look on Carson's face that I knew so well.

I screamed at what I saw instead.

Seventeen

Bloodred liquid covered the formerly white fence, dripping from several of the intersections of metal that I'd oiled two days ago, pooling at the bottom. On the sidewalk, the red liquid seeped toward the street, filling in cracks on the sidewalk in the same freakishly ominous color. A matching trail left a slow moving track into the store. I ran to the gate but stopped a few feet short of the door. My stomach lurched and an acidic taste filled my nostrils and mouth. I backed away, slowly, until I was up against the register, then grabbed my phone and keys and left out the back.

The parking lot was empty, Carson's car gone. I stumbled past the series of diagonal yellow lines that marked off the vacant spaces, into the alley and around the corner to the front of the store. The black Mercedes with the *MCM* license plate was parked in the same lot it had been the first day I'd arrived. I ran to it and beat on the dark-tinted windows with an open palm.

"Is this how you negotiate? What are you trying to do? Scare me into selling? Why are you doing it? What are you trying to hide?" I closed my fist and pounded on the door with the outside of it. There was no acknowledgement from inside the car. "I don't care what you do to scare me off, I won't sell. I won't! I don't care what you offer me. You killed Mr. Pickers and I'm going to figure out why! Whatever secret you're trying to protect, I'll find."

Two arms closed around me from behind and lifted me off my feet. I screamed from the pressure against the bruises on my midsection and instinctively put my feet on the door of the black luxury car. The rubber soles of my boots left dusty footprints on the gleaming paint job. I twisted one way, then the other, pushing against the car with my feet until I heard a string of curse words. The arms around me let go and I fell backward, into another person, onto the ground.

I rolled onto my hands and knees and looked at the person who had attacked me. It was Vaughn. He was on his back, staring up at the sky. A cloud of dirt surrounded us. His chest heaved and fell with deep breaths sucked in through his open mouth. His light brown hair was coated in dirt.

"Are you okay?" he asked, turning his focus to me.

I pushed myself backward until I was kneeling, then smacked my hands against each other to knock off small pieces of gravel that were embedded in the fleshy part of my palm. I didn't answer his question.

Vaughn sat up and rested his arms on top of bent knees. "Do you want to tell me why you're beating up on my dad's car?"

"Do you want to tell me why your family has moved on to scare tactics?"

"What are you talking about?"

"The front of the store. Did you do that?"

Vaughn's expression changed into one of concern. His dimples vanished. He turned to the side and used one hand to push him up to a standing position, then extended the hand to me. I got up on my own without his help and walked past him, toward Bonita Avenue. From the sound of the footsteps behind me, I knew he was following.

As soon as I turned the corner, I heard his sharp intake of breath. The gate was covered in red splotches, something that had been thrown on it haphazardly. It didn't look like paint, and it stank in a somewhat familiar way. Words on the sidewalk in front of the store said *Go Home*.

"Who did this?" asked Vaughn.

"As if you don't know," I answered.

"You can't think *I* did it."

"I don't know what to think."

"Did you call the cops?"

"Maybe I did. Are you scared now?"

"Poly, this is vandalism and it needs to be reported. If you didn't call the cops, I will." He reached into his back pocket and pulled out his cell phone. He dialed a number and asked for Deputy Sheriff Clark. I didn't wait around to hear the details of the call.

An audience of strangers filled the opposite side of the street. I recognized a couple of men from the bar where Charlie and I had gone the first night I'd been in San Ladrón and Duke in his wheelchair. Two blond women stood to one side, and a woman with pieces of foil folded around sections of her hair stood next to them. A man with a small dog cowered behind the group.

"What are you all looking at?" I yelled. "Is this funny to you? Let's run the new girl out of town? I don't think it's funny."

I knew I was acting like a crazy person, only I didn't know how to stop. Two hands landed on my upper arms, rubbing up and down on the black knit fabric of my tunic.

I turned my head. Vaughn had moved close, right behind me. My body went rigid, but he didn't stop.

"The police are going to be here in a second," he said softly in my ear. "You're shaking, and I don't blame you, but you need to calm down." He looked up at the bartender from Antonio's Ristorante. "Everybody, drinks are on me. Tony, take care of them."

The bartender nodded at Vaughn and walked back toward the restaurant. Most of the crowd followed. Duke spun his wheelchair around and rolled back to his bar. The woman with the foil on her hair looked confused, like she couldn't decide between the free drinks and the risk to her hair color.

"Tony, deliver a bottle of champagne to Angie's salon, too."

The two blondes and the woman in foil smiled at each other and entered the door next to the restaurant. The man with the dog turned away from us and walked down the street.

"Is that how you stay under the radar? Mr. Big Shot, who can buy his way out of anything?"

"What am I supposed to be buying my way out of?"

"Whatever happened here."

"What *did* happen here?"

"I don't know."

A police car pulled up by the curb next to us. "You need to tell him exactly what you think is going on," Vaughn said.

"Why? So you can come up with a plausible story to cover your guilt?"

Deputy Sheriff Clark got out of the car and looked at the store. He approached the gate and leaned into it, sniffing the red liquid. He turned around, careful not to tarnish the back of his uniform by leaning into the gate, and looked at the splotches on the sidewalk. After scribbling something into a small notebook, he approached us.

"Do either of you know who did this?" he asked.

I looked at Vaughn, then back at the deputy sheriff, as if the answer was obvious.

"She thinks I did it," Vaughn said.

"I want to talk to you. Alone," I said to the deputy sheriff. Vaughn stepped backward and I led Deputy Sheriff Clark past the front gate to a shaded bench, where we sat down.

"Miss Monroe, is what Vaughn said true? You think he did this?"

"I don't know why else he's here. His father has made no secret of the fact that he wants to buy the store from me. I found some things out recently. I don't think Mr. McMichael wants the store for business reasons. I think he's hiding something. Scare tactics might be a way for him to up his game and make me sell."

Deputy Sheriff Clark ignored my statement. "Is there anybody else who might have done this?"

"Like who?"

"Ms. Monroe, a man was murdered behind your store two days ago. Since you arrived you've been at the center of a couple of incidents around town. Maybe that's normal in downtown Los Angeles, but we don't get behavior like this around San Ladrón often, so I'm thinking that somebody is trying to send you a message. A message in ketchup."

I looked at the storefront, dripping in red. I hadn't wanted to think about what the liquid was, but that explained the faint scent and the acidic taste in my mouth. "Ketchup?"

He nodded.

"I want you to give me a list of anybody who you know who might have reason to want to scare you out of town."

"The person at the top of that list is Vaughn McMichael. Or at least his dad is. His son could be doing his dirty work."

"I don't like what's been happening in our town since you arrived. I'm going to get to the bottom of it. Making up accusations to make yourself look innocent isn't going to help your case. The McMichael family is well respected in

San Ladrón. Vic McMichael will only put up with what could be called defamation of character for so long before he fights back."

"What are you saying?" He didn't answer. "What about the other stuff—my car and the shower and the murd—" My breath caught in my throat. "You think I did this to my own store?" I jerked a thumb toward the gate. "Why would I do that?"

"You tell me," he said.

I stood up from the bench to put distance between the deputy sheriff and myself. I looked over my shoulder at the sickening appearance of the storefront and ran a hand through my choppy short hair. Vaughn stood on the sidewalk watching us. I clenched my teeth together and narrowed my eyes. He wouldn't get away with this. I looked back at the deputy sheriff.

"Two nights ago, Vaughn McMichael stole information from inside the store. I don't know why. It was in a ledger of sales info from when the store was open. I'd made some notes on the back pages about Mr. Pickers and the things that had happened since I arrived. I don't know what else was in the ledger, but it looked like my aunt used the book to write down thoughts and plans on blank pages, in addition to the daily sales tallies. I don't know why he took it."

"Have you asked him about it?"

I shook my head.

The deputy sheriff stood up and walked past the front of the store to where Vaughn stood talking on his cell phone. I followed a few steps behind, but couldn't hear them because their voices were low. When I reached the two of them, I stood at an angle, looking back and forth between their faces. Whatever conversation had transpired, it had been short, and it was over.

Deputy Sheriff Clark closed his notebook and put it back

into his breast pocket. "Ms. Monroe, is there anything else you want to tell me?"

I thought about the charm Adelaide Brooks had given me. It meant something, but I didn't know how useful it would be to the deputy sheriff. What did a charm from an old bracelet prove? It meant nothing to anybody but me. For all I knew, it was a red herring, intended to set me off on a completely different trail, away from Mr. Pickers and into the land of family secrets and foggy memories. Until I knew what it meant, I wasn't going to tip my hand.

"No."

"If you think of anything else, I want you to call. Right away. I've made arrangements to stay in the mobile unit, so unless I'm on a call, I'm three blocks away. If anything else happens, I'll know about it."

I didn't like how he said that last part. Made it sound like he was going to keep an eye on me. He held out a hand and I shook it, then he crossed the street to his car and left Vaughn and me alone in front of the store.

"Let's end this right now," Vaughn said.

"Why did you steal information from the store? What were you looking for?"

His face grew red. "If you saw me take the ledger, why didn't you say something? Or ask me?" He rubbed his thumb and forefinger across his forehead a couple of times, shielding his face from me, then looked up again. "I thought I could have it back to you before you noticed it was missing."

"I'm talking about the pages from the sales journal. How exactly were you planning to replace the missing pages?"

"I didn't take any pages. The book's intact. Come with me."

He walked to the black sedan and unlocked the doors with a remote. A turquoise notebook sat on the passenger seat on top of a nondescript flat white box. He hesitated for a second. "Will you get into the car?"

"No."

"You really think I'm the bad guy, don't you?"

"What would you think if you were in my shoes?" I asked.

He tucked his hands into the front pockets of his khaki pants. The collar of his navy-blue sweater was turned up against a second white collar from a polo shirt underneath. The few buttons down the front of his sweater were unbuttoned. One was missing. He didn't impress me as the type to wear a sweater with a missing button and I wondered if it had fallen off when we'd scuffled.

"I guess if I were in your shoes, I'd see exactly what you see, which is too bad, because it couldn't be further from the truth." He reached into the car and pulled out the ledger. "I acted on a spontaneous impulse. I don't normally do that, but it is what it is." He held the notebook out and I took it, but he didn't let go right away. For a few seconds, we stood there like we were playing tug-of-war. When he let go, I pulled the book into my chest and wrapped my arms around it.

"Did you look at the scrapbook?" he asked. The breeze ruffled his hair, pushing a shock of it onto his forehead.

"Yes."

"So you should understand why I'm interested in the store and what becomes of it. What's it going to take for you to believe that?"

"Trust. The one thing you can't buy."

"Why are you so hung up on my family's money? It's insulting."

"Some of us have had to work, Vaughn. My parents worked at the fabric store all the time. I helped out when I was a teenager, and I couldn't even tell anybody until I was sixteen. While you were out on your yacht with your dad, I was learning the difference between jacquard and damask."

"I watched the way my father did business. He bullied people into agreeing to his terms. I didn't want to be like him. I paid for my own education by working two jobs so I wouldn't have a mountain of debt when I graduated. I interned at an investment firm in Richmond—for no pay— for the first six months after graduation. When a job opened up, I interviewed for it like everyone else. So don't tell me I don't know about hard work."

We stood there for a few seconds, locked in a heated glare, until Vaughn looked back into the car. He leaned down and moved the white box to the passenger seat, then climbed in and pulled the door shut without a good bye.

The sun was on its way down past the horizon, throwing the store into a shadow. With the electricity turned off, there was little I was going to be able to see or do inside the store. I carried the turquoise notebook back inside and slid it back into the drawer below the register where it had been for years. I threw my wallet and cell phone into a small cross-chest pouch, locked the front door, and left out the back. It was a short walk through the alley and across the street, until I ended up at Charlie's Automotive.

She stood with her back to me, typing on a computer keyboard. Her long thick hair was clumped into sections, and secured in the back with a green rubber band from an office supply store. Her upper body shielded my view of the computer screen, though I could tell it was black. The cursor bounced from field to field as she tapped the tab key and the up and down arrows.

"Hey," I said, to let her know I was there. She didn't respond. "You wouldn't believe the day I've had," I added. Again, nothing.

I thought back about how we'd left things that morning,

after she had dropped me off in front of the store where Vaughn and Carson stood. Nothing had seemed strange at the time. But ignoring me while I stood a couple of feet away seemed odd. I reached out and tapped her left shoulder, and she jumped.

When she turned around, I saw a thin white cord running between her two ears, connected in front of the second button on her uniform, and running down the length of her shirt to her pocket. She turned back to the computer and closed out the window, then reached up and pulled the earbuds out and shoved them into her pocket.

"You scared me," she said.

"I thought you heard me come in."

"Too much noise out there today. I could have turned up the volume but then the salon next door complains, so I went iPod. Gotta be honest, Eddie doesn't sound the same as he does when he's cranked to ten on the boom box, though."

I didn't waste time asking for an explanation to whatever it was she was talking about. "Can I borrow a bucket and some rags?"

"Not willing to risk another shower?"

"Somebody threw ketchup on the gate to the store. I think it's better to clean it tonight than to wait until tomorrow."

"I heard something happened over there. Ketchup, huh? Looks creepy, like blood." She craned her neck to see past me. "Somebody's testing you. I'm curious. What's it going to be?"

"What's what going to be?"

"You. Are you scared off yet or are you in for the long haul?"

"I don't like being bullied, if that's what you're asking. But everything is still so vague. Is this about selling the store to Mr. McMichael? Then why was Mr. Pickers murdered out back? Are those two things connected or were they two random acts that happened to involve me? And then there's my car, and the shower, and now this." I waved my hand toward the gate outside. "Those attacks are personal. More than just trying to get me to sell the store. It's like somebody doesn't want me to stay in San Ladrón. But why kill Mr. Pickers to get me to leave? How did my showing up have anything to do with him?"

"Why *are* you staying?"

"Because the deputy sheriff told me not to leave."

"He can't do that, you know. The whole 'don't leave town while the investigation is ongoing' thing. Load of bull. You're free to leave whenever you want."

"What if I don't want?"

"Now we're getting to the heart of the matter." She tilted her back and bent her leg so her Converse sneaker was resting on her knee. "You're right, though. The attack on the storefront is personal. You know anybody who would play the personal card?"

Yesterday I would have thought no. But today there was somebody else in the picture. Somebody who had been at the store moments before the attack.

Carson.

"I have to make a phone call." I left the interior of the auto shop and stood on the sidewalk, one finger plugged into my left ear, the other hand pressing my cell to my head. Carson answered on the fourth ring.

"Hey," he said in a soft voice. "I'm sorry about earlier. You have every right to be angry."

"Carson, where are you?"

"I'm stuck in traffic on the one-oh-one."

"You left?"

"I sat at the coffee shop for an hour waiting for you to get my message. When you didn't, I took off."

"What message? The gate? The ketchup? Did you do that?"

There was a pause on the other end of the phone. "What are you talking about?"

"Did you vandalize the store?" I demanded.

"Have you gone nuts?"

"I'm serious, Carson. Did you do that? Throw ketchup on the gate to scare me into running to you for protection?"

"Poly, I wrote you a note and stuck it in the fence in front of the store you're so concerned with. I told you where I'd be and how long I'd wait."

"When?"

"After you tossed the keys to me. What is this about?"

"Someone vandalized the store."

"And you thought it was me? Is that where we are right now?"

"I don't know where we are now, Carson."

"Maybe you should think about it and call me when you do." He disconnected.

I turned to Charlie. "Is my car done yet?"

"Tomorrow."

"Okay, can I borrow your Camaro again?" I asked. "I need to get some stuff to clean the fence."

"You can't borrow the Camaro, but you can take my truck. Keys are on the pegboard. If I'm gone when you get back, you can take a bucket and rags from the back corner."

"Thanks."

I took the keys with me and headed around behind the auto shop. The truck was parked at an angle several yards from where the shower/shed stood. It was the result of either a hasty park job or a backyard that made it so it didn't really matter. I threw the gearshift into reverse, swung it into an arc, then turned around and made an illegal left turn onto the street, tires screeching as I accelerated.

I should have anticipated the flashing blue and red lights in the rearview mirror.

I pulled over to the curb and waited for a gray-haired man in a uniform to adjust his hat and approach the car. He was older and thinner than Deputy Sheriff Clark and his uniform was a better fit.

"License and registration," he said as he stood next to my side of the car. My hands shook as I fiddled with my wallet, trying to get the small piece of plastic out from inside the tight sleeve. Once it was freed, I handed it to him.

"I borrowed this car from a friend. She's right back there in Charlie's Automotive. We're so close that if you want we can go back to her store."

He studied my license. "You're not from San Ladrón."

"No, I live in downtown Los Angeles. Like I said, I borrowed the car from Charlie—"

"Registration, ma'am," he interrupted.

I reached across the seat and yanked on the glove box, the universal storage spot for registration papers. It was locked. "Just a second," I said. The officer had his hands resting by his front pockets, his thumbs hooked into the opening.

I pulled the keys from the ignition and tried each one until I found one that fit the lock. I lowered the glove box slowly and pulled out a wad of papers. "I'm sure it's one of these," I said out the window, then looked back at the stack. Under two still-sealed envelopes from the bank and an old newspaper, I found the registration card. As I held it out to the officer, I noticed something interesting.

The truck was registered to Vic McMichael.

Eighteen

I pulled the piece of paper back toward me so I could look at it again. *Vic McMichael.* Why would Charlie have a truck registered to Vaughn's dad? Was she on their payroll? Was I one of the "favors" she tended to for Vaughn?

"Ma'am?" prompted the officer. Reluctantly I held out the piece of paper and he carried it, along with my license, to his car. I watched in the rearview mirror as he sat down, turned on a small flashlight, and moved it over my license. My mind stung with possibilities of what this might mean.

I'd met Charlie the first day I came to San Ladrón, on Friday. I met her because my car had been tampered with. My bad luck had been her good fortune, or so it seemed at the time. I'd been attacked in her shower, and she was the only person who knew I was in there—at least that's what I thought until Mr. McMichael showed up to help me. But how did he know I was there?

And then there was the ketchup vandalism on the

storefront. The chaos had brought out almost every person who was in a one-block radius—every person but Charlie, who claimed her earbuds had blocked out the commotion. She had appeared outside the Waverly House right as I left, after talking to Vaughn's mom. Was this a gigantic conspiracy from the McMichael family?

Was the McMichael family capable of killing an innocent man in order to get me out of the picture and gain control of the fabric store?

And if that was the case, why?

I didn't want to believe it was all about a piece of real estate. I wanted to believe it was about my great-aunt. But what if it wasn't, and what if someone in San Ladrón was using my connection to my family to distract me from whatever was really going on? What if Mr. Pickers's past had come back to haunt him and his murder had nothing to do with me?

I didn't know who to turn to. I had thought Charlie was my friend, but now I wasn't so sure of her motivations. Anybody from the McMichael family was off the list. I wasn't sure if I should count Adelaide as friend or foe—the information she gave me was interesting, but could have been a carefully planted bit of misdirection. I could have asked Carson to help me search the store while he was still in San Ladrón, but he had already left. Besides, I knew that request would come with a very hefty price that wouldn't guarantee his cooperation.

This time, I was on my own.

The officer returned to the truck with my identification and a small clipboard. "Ms. Monroe, you pulled out of that lot like you were in some kind of hurry."

"I was. I mean, I am."

"You realize that hurry cost you about ten minutes while I ran your license and plates, don't you?"

I nodded.

"How long do you plan to stay in San Ladrón?"

"I don't know."

"Days? Weeks? Months?" he prompted.

His insistence on finding out the length of my stay was off-putting. "I'm due back at work this week," I said, hoping the vague piece of information would serve as an answer.

"I'm giving you a warning. Be careful where you're going. You could have very nearly caused an accident back there by charging ahead. I'll give you a break today, but don't do it again. The next time I won't be in such a giving mood."

I expected a smile to go along with his comment, but there was none. "Thank you, Officer," I said, taking the papers from him. As I waited for him to get back to his car, I looked at the registration again. The address listed was that of Charlie's shop. I put it on top of the envelopes in my lap, then idly flipped through them. Each one was addressed to Charlie's Automotive. Nothing else in there made mention of the name McMichael. If I hadn't been pulled over, needing her registration, I might never have discovered the connection between her and the McMichael family.

I locked the paperwork back into the glove box and slowly pulled the car onto the street while the officer was watching me.

This time I had no idea what direction I was heading.

I ended up at Get Hammered, a hardware store five blocks down the street from the fabric store. Under the name of the store was the slogan, *Tools plus more for the DIY crowd.* A sign out front indicated parking in the rear. I pulled into the alley and parked in the last of the six spaces designated for customers. I wandered the aisles, wondering what it would take to clean the gate, what I could buy to make me feel safe and secure. I didn't think a padlock would make much of a difference and I couldn't see myself with a weapon.

I turned the corner from the hunting supplies and found myself face-to-face with an aisle of inexpensive sewing machines. They were starters, on sale for less than a hundred dollars. Compared to the industrial ones Giovanni had at To The Nines, these looked like toys.

As much as I had loved playing with fabric when I was at FIDM, combining swatches to create interesting color and texture palettes, I'd never completely embraced pattern making and sewing. My highest grades had come when assigned to a team project. I picked out the textiles and sketched a concept, and my partner turned my vision into reality. It was why I was so perfectly suited to my job and why I had such a great relationship with the women in the workroom. Even with the Korean-to-English language barrier, we communicated through fabric and sketches.

I loved every one of those ladies. They'd been raised using sewing machines as easily as they used kitchen supplies. Every once in a while one of them would bring me a wedding dress or special negligee that had been left to them by their parents or grandparents. They knew how much I'd appreciate the craftsmanship that had gone into each of those pieces. A couple of those garments had even been tailored to fit me when Giovanni went out of town. I cherished the garments as much as I cherished the camaraderie of the staff. They represented an appreciation, a feeling of family that Carson didn't understand. I stopped trying to explain it after the first couple of times. Maybe he didn't have to understand it. Even if we were going to build a life together, I needed to have some cherished things that were just for me.

I picked up one of the sewing machine boxes and carried it with me as I looked for the cleaning supply section. The box was awkward. I passed the toy aisle and noticed a red wagon. I set the sewing machine in the wagon and pulled it behind me.

When I reached the cleaning section, I added a bucket, box of construction-grade rags, and two gallons of industrial-strength cleaner. I could have borrowed supplies from Charlie, but after seeing the name on the registration, I wasn't comfortable turning to her for help. The wagon filled quickly. A petite Mexican woman with brown curly hair appeared in the aisle next to me, staring at the contents.

"Is this yours?" she asked.

"Yes. I'm sorry, is it in your way? I didn't realize I needed a cart."

"That's a lot of cleaner."

"I have a big mess to clean up."

"You better be careful with that stuff. It stinks to high heaven and the fumes are a killer. Last year my boys Carlos and Antonio knocked over a pail of bluing. Stained the floor, the wall, and the cat. I got two of them clean, but I was in bed for a week recovering from what the chemicals did to my lungs."

"I shouldn't have to worry about that too much. My mess is outside." I picked up a box of surgical masks, but put them back on the shelf. "Thanks for the warning. Maybe if I do the grunt work tonight the fresh air will counter the stink by morning."

"You can't clean tonight!"

"Why not?"

"I don't know where you live, but we have zoning laws around here. If you're outside making noise with a bucket of smelly chemicals, somebody's going to call the sheriff's office on you."

"The Senior Patrol?"

She smiled warmly. "Most likely."

"I think they've taken a special interest in me."

"Then you better wait until morning. No point making enemies while you're here."

I didn't bother to tell the nice lady that it appeared to be too late for that.

"I'm telling you, wait until tomorrow to do your cleaning," she said.

"From the sound of it, I don't have a choice."

"Where do you live? I can help you if you want."

"No, that won't be necessary," I said quickly.

She pulled a business card out of a zippered pocket on the outside of her oversized black handbag and held it out. *Neato!* it read, with a picture of a curvy Mexican woman in a *Saturday Night Fever* pose, holding a feather duster in her raised hand. Below the picture was the name Maria Lopez. "Cleaning is my business."

"I'm sorry, I didn't know. I'm Poly." I held out my hand to shake hers, a gesture that felt too impersonal for the friendliness this woman was showing me.

She laughed. "Don't apologize. Everybody does something, and I make decent money. It started out me and my sisters, but now we have ten employees," she said proudly. She winked at me. "I get invited into some of the best houses in San Ladrón, and when you're a maid, trust me, you get to see everybody's dirty little secrets."

I took the card to be polite. "No wonder you know about the cleaning products. I just have one question."

"Only one? Shoot."

"How did you clean the cat?"

Her eyebrows drew together for a moment while she made sense of my question, and then she laughed a high-pitched giggle. "I didn't. I changed his name to Peppermint."

Her laughter was contagious, and temporarily I forgot my problems. I pulled my wagon to the hardware section of the store and added a two-thousand-candle-watt flashlight to my purchases. Off to the right of the store were a few shelves stocked with soaps and various paper products. I assumed this was the "plus more" that the sign out front had indicated. I added soap and toilet paper to my pile. Tomorrow was Monday and I planned to bring the apartment utilities out of the dark ages. Earlier in the day, I hadn't taken much time to check out what other things Uncle Marius may have left behind, but I had a feeling whatever it was, it hadn't been designed to sit around for ten years before being used.

By the time I arrived at the checkout line, the stack in the wagon teetered like it was going to fall. I unpacked the items from the wagon and set them on the conveyor belt, then scanned the headlines of celebrity trash magazines and local newspapers while the molasses-slow cashier scanned the items of the man in front of me. That's when I saw it.

VISITOR BRINGS VANDALISM TO SAN LADRÓN

I plucked the newspaper from the stand. A photo of Land of a Thousand Fabrics was under the headline with copy to the left. As I read, my stomach twisted into a knot. The article was about me.

Correction: half of it was about me, half of it was about Mr. Pickers's murder.

"You want the wagon, too?" prompted a voice. I looked up at the cashier. He'd finished with the man in front of me and had moved on to my purchases. Behind me a short line was forming, people looking to see what the holdup was.

"Yes," I said, lifting it so he could scan the barcode. "And the newspaper."

He keyed something into the register and gave me a total. I was low on cash, so I pulled a credit card out of my wallet and swiped it. After the transaction was complete I realized it had been my To The Nines corporate card. Giovanni was going to take issue with that, I expected.

I set my bags back into the wagon and pulled it to Charlie's truck, then loaded them into the back. Before driving home, I carried the newspaper with me to the driver's seat. The outside air was filled with the scent of mesquite. Somebody was having a cookout. For a split second my mouth watered at the thought of a hamburger like the one I'd had from The Broadside, but the thought triggered the memory of the ketchup-stained gate, which sent a wave of unsettling anxiety through me again.

I started the engine. My hands shook as I unfolded the newspaper and I didn't think it was a good idea to drive. This time I read the article in full. It did little to calm me.

VISITOR BRINGS VANDALISM TO SAN LADRÓN

A storefront on Bonita Avenue was the victim of an act of vandalism not usually seen in San Ladrón, and tenants believe they know the cause. "Things were fine until two days ago, when she moved in," said one tenant, who prefers to be anonymous. "Our town was always safe, and our businesses were, too. Now that she's here, everything is changing. I don't feel safe in my own store anymore, and I might need to sell."

The "she" in question is Polyester Monroe, the great niece of former San Ladrón residents Marius and Millie Monroe. Marius passed away last week at the age of eighty-nine, leaving the defunct family business to his relative from Los Angeles. When she arrived in town, so did trouble.

Mr. Pickers, self-appointed head of San Ladrón's Senior Patrol, was found murdered behind the store the day after Ms. Monroe took possession of the property. Mr. Pickers's interest in the storefront has been longstanding. The onetime successful banker lost credibility in the town after making a statement about a "monster in robes" the night of a robbery at the store ten years ago. Shortly thereafter he lost his job, and now, ten years later, he's lost his life.

"Poly is a nice girl who may be in over her head," said Ken Watts, the Realtor who had hoped to transact

*a sale between Poly and another interested party. "She
has emotional connections to the store, which are understandable, but she's not prepared to take ownership of a
store that's been closed for a decade. Maybe nobody is."*

*The store in question is Land of a Thousand Fabrics,
a onetime Mecca of exotic silks, satin, and toile, imported
from countries all over the world. In its prime, Land
brought the glamour of Hollywood to San Ladrón, as
fashion designers and costumers made the trek west of
Los Angeles in search of something they couldn't find in
their own City of Angels. Whether the business would
have survived inevitable changes to fabric, fashion, and
the online availability of items previously exclusive to
them will never be known. The store closed its doors ten
years ago after co-owner Millie Monroe was murdered
in the store during a robbery.*

*Polyester Monroe is the daughter of John and Helen
Monroe, residents of Burbank. None of the family mem-
bers could be reached for comment.*

I read the article a second time, not believing the words
in front of me. Who was this writer? It was attributed to
staff writer. Where did they get their facts? And Ken's com-
ments, though the most compassionate part of the whole
thing, made it sound like I was five years old. The next time
I saw him I was going to punch him in the nose.

I flipped through the call logs on my phone until I reached
his number. It rang five times, and went to voice mail. I
disconnected, then immediately dialed again. This time I
left a message. "Ken, this is Poly Monroe." I lowered the
phone from my head, then re-raised it before hanging up.
"We need to talk," I added.

It was officially dark when I left the store's parking lot.
I drove the truck past Charlie's, slowing as I passed to look
for signs of her. I pulled around the back of Land of a

Thousand Fabrics, unloaded my purchases, and carried them into the store. After reading the article, I wanted more than ever to clean the gate, to get rid of any evidence of the attack. But if the woman with the cleaning business was right, and I was guessing she was, I was looking at an early morning cleanup job, so it was just as well if I turned in early for the night.

I didn't want to leave Charlie's truck behind the store, but the idea of running into her face-to-face tomorrow was an even less desirable option. Had I bothered to get her cell phone number, I would have texted her, a nice generic form of communication. Instead, after putting the bags inside the door, I found a blank piece of paper in the drawer under the register and scribbled a thank-you, locked up, and drove the truck back to her business. I wrapped the keys in the piece of paper, pushed them through the mail slot on her front door, and left.

It was after nine when I reentered the store. The first thing I did was fill the battery chamber of the flashlight with fresh D-cells. Next I checked the bowl of cat food that had been left out by the partition; it was empty. Maybe, armed with the power of two thousand candle watts, I could find the lost kitten before the night was over.

With the flashlight in one hand and as many bags as I could carry in the other, I made my way to the stairs. There, three steps up from the bottom, I found him. He was hunched to the side in a ball, his fur poking up like spikes on a porcupine. He was more than a little dirty, his orange stripes now a shade of gray close to those of his brother. He cowered backward as I reached for him, but he didn't run.

"It's okay, baby, I'll carry you," I said. I set the bag down and carried the flashlight and the kitten up the stairs to the apartment. The gray kitten sat right inside the apartment, staring at us as we entered. He peeped out a meow at the sight of his brother. I laid the flashlight on its side, pointing down the hall, and scooped up the other kitten, carrying them both to the bedroom and setting them on the center of the bed.

"You two, wait here. I have to bring stuff upstairs," I said, wondering when I'd become one of those women who talked to her cats. Whether a future with Carson was in the cards or not, I knew that for him, behavior like this was a deal breaker.

But the reality was Carson's behavior over the past two days had become something of a deal breaker for me. He demonstrated pretty clearly what he thought of my interest in the store. He didn't understand. And it wasn't just that he wanted me to think about my job, because that I could have probably explained away. It was that he didn't care that the store had been left to me by someone in my family, or that I had the chance, the power, the knowledge, and the desire to carry on what my aunt and uncle had started so many years before. He hadn't, for one second, acknowledged that I could do it if I really wanted. I didn't need his business acumen right now. I needed his confidence in me.

The fourth time I returned downstairs with the flashlight, it wasn't to bring anything up with me. It was to collect the notebooks from under the register, to see what kind of sales information had been left behind, and to try to figure out if this was something I could do. Because all of a sudden, saving the store and proving that I could do this seemed like the most important goal of all.

I trained the flashlight beam on the concrete floor as I walked. When I reached the wrap stand, I set the light on its side and tugged on the drawer below the register. It was stuck on something in the back. I jostled it until I managed a narrow opening and fed my hand in to find the obstruction. A straight pin stabbed my thumb and I cried out. I pulled my hand toward me and squeezed my thumb. A drop of blood formed at the center of my fingerprint. I wiped my thumb on my pants and pulled the drawer open with my other hand. The notebooks sat inside. I opened the back cover of the one Vaughn had taken and flipped from the back cover forward, expecting to see evidence of the missing pages.

But the book was intact. I went through it again, this time from the front. The first half of the ledger was filled with logs of purchases, inventory, and sales tallies. On the third to last page were the notes I'd scribbled about Mr. Pickers and the sketch I'd made two nights ago.

I hadn't imagined the missing pages, I knew. I paged through other books from under the register, each time more for verification of my sanity than proof of the destruction of Aunt Millie's notebook. By the time I got through the final book, my sanity was seriously in question. Every book had every page.

Nineteen

I refilled the drawer and set it on top of the wrap stand next to the stack of turquoise cloth notebooks. My eyesight was blurring, but I was too keyed up to relax. Up the stairs I went, into the apartment, to the bed. The kittens were curled up by the pillows, their heads tucked to the side on each of their paws. I didn't know if it was the benefit of blood relation that put them into the exact same pose as they slept or if all cats slept like that. Careful not to disturb them, I picked up the box of memorabilia I'd started flipping through earlier and sank onto the carpet.

With the flashlight on my lap, aimed diagonally toward the ceiling, I flipped through my aunt and uncle's memorabilia. As I reached the bottom of the box, I discovered a collection of envelopes that had been secured with a whisper-pink satin ribbon. Each letter was addressed to Marius Monroe. The return address was Burbank, California. I knew it well; it was the house my parents had moved to after they'd left

Glendora. Before I pulled the first piece of paper from the envelope, I knew what they were. The letters my mother told me she'd sent to my uncle, telling him about my life.

The fact that he'd kept the letters brought tears to my eyes, until confusion distracted me. Uncle Marius didn't live here at that time. He'd moved into the furnished apartment my dad had arranged for him, and he'd left the store closed up. As far as I knew, he'd never come back.

But he must have!

These letters had been stashed at the bottom of the box of photos. That meant he had recently been through the box. Whether a trip down memory lane or a desire to leave a message, he'd taken care to put those letters where they were, and now I'd found them.

I checked the postmarks on the letters from my parents. The earliest one was from my graduation and included a photo of me in my cap and gown. The latest was from six months ago, a page from *Los Angeles Magazine* that listed To The Nines as "best bargain drag attire." I had thought it was funny, but Giovanni had canceled his subscription after that issue ran.

Six months ago. That meant that Great-Uncle Marius had been in the apartment in the past six months. But why? What had brought him back? And was it a one-time trip, or had he come to the store often? How had he gotten in and out without anybody knowing?

My parents would know. I reached for my phone, surprised at the time. It was well past midnight. There was little more I could do tonight. I'd call my parents tomorrow, right after I tackled the fence.

I cleaned myself up as best I could with a washcloth and a bottle of purified water. There was a purplish bruise around my waist from the shower incident at Charlie's. It matched the tiny violets in the wallpaper and was tender to the touch. My shoulders had bruises, too, from falling on top of Vaughn. I was used to bruises on my knees and calves from tripping and falling down. I had small feet for my height, size seven on a five-foot-nine frame, which meant two things: I'd never walk a runway, and I wore a sample-size shoe. Carson had been fascinated by my small feet when we first started dating, giving me foot rubs every Friday night after work. I hadn't discovered his days-of-the-week activities at that point, so until he discovered Fantasy Football, my feet got his undivided attention for a half hour at the end of every workweek.

I patted myself dry with a faded rose-pink terry-cloth towel, changed into the black silk nightgown, and lay down on the bed. Aches and pains announced themselves in muscles I didn't even know I had. I fluffed a pillow and wedged it under my neck and stared at the dark mahogany wood trim that framed out the ceiling of the room. I thought about what it would be like, giving up the life I knew in Los Angeles and reopening the store in San Ladrón.

I had lots of contacts in the Los Angeles fabric district and could build up new inventory, too. And maybe I could even travel to fabric fairs in Paris, Milan, China, and Thailand. What would that cost me? I wondered. How much would I have to make to be able to afford trips like my aunt and uncle had taken, trips to India, Korea, Japan, Spain, France, Romania? Exotic places that in my life at To The Nines I never once dreamed I'd get to? Could it be done?

Most of the fabrics would have to go, but new ones could be brought in. And until I was able to build up the reputation of the store, I could have craft classes on the weekend and teach people how to make curtains, pillows, throw blankets, pot holders. There could be workshops for beginners and for people who already had sewing skills.

The tea shop would be a perfect place to start. Genevieve had told me she wanted her shop to look like a Parisian café. I could help her turn what she had into her dream by reupholstering the seat cushions in toile, replacing the faded curtains with checkered panels that tied onto whitewashed dowel rods. We could frame cuttings from some of the bolts that were damaged and hang them on the wall in whimsical groupings with her roosters and French noir movie posters. She could even throw a grand reopening party: Midnight in Paris. People could get dressed up, have a place to go. It would be the perfect advertisement for her store. I could help her change her life with fabric.

The idea energized me. I slipped my feet into the beaded Chinese slippers and went downstairs. The sewing machine was easy enough to set up. I trained the flashlight beam over the bolts of fabric in the store, occasionally digging through stacks of tubes to locate a particular color. I assembled four different patterns: a butter-yellow and royal-blue toile, two ginghams—one yellow, one blue—and a faded light blue chambray. I added grosgrain ribbon trim to the pile and set to work measuring, cutting, and sewing a set of French-country curtains for Genevieve's store.

Enthusiasm for the project kept me going well into the night. When my vision blurred to the point that repeated blinking did nothing to improve it, I turned off the sewing machine and looked at what I'd accomplished. A pile of curtains sat on the wrap stand. Placemats and napkins in complementing tones sat to the side. I wondered if Genevieve was going to think I was off my rocker when I showed up with a home makeover packed neatly in a red wagon.

Of course she would. Who was I kidding?

I folded up the finished projects and left them on top of the wrap stand. Seconds later I was upstairs between the sheets and the comforter on the bed, the kittens nestled together on my right-hand side. I fell asleep from sheer exhaustion, for the first time forgetting the trouble that had followed me to San Ladrón.

* * *

The next morning I awoke early, eager to get a head start on my day before nosy neighbors would infiltrate my business. The kittens had moved to my pillow during the night and were now pressed against my head. The gray one chewed on a piece of my hair. The orange one was still dirty from the previous night. "You need a bath more than I do," I told him. He looked at me, stretched out a paw, and meowed, as if in agreement.

As I moved from the bed to the bathroom, regretfully aware that the wise thing to do was to put yesterday's outfit back on for the cleaning of the gate, I caught my reflection. My choppy hair stuck up at odd angles. The auburn color was vivid against my pale skin, which glowed next to the black silk nightgown. Even my lips, usually coated in a deep shade of red, had a hint of pink to them that I wasn't used to seeing. I checked the clock, surprised that it was only six thirty. I didn't look that bad for only four hours of sleep. I felt like I'd gone twelve rounds with Rocky Marciano, but I didn't look it. "Take that, San Ladrón," I said to my reflection. "You can beat me up all you want." As long as the bruises stayed hidden, nobody would know I was any worse for wear.

I poured the remaining water into my hands and raked them over my head. After a quick application of tinted moisturizer with a hefty SPF and a slick of strawberry-scented lip balm, I pulled on yesterday's grubby clothes and headed downstairs.

I had expected to be the only person on the street this early, but I wasn't. A group of women in bright yellow T-shirts and jeans were in front of my store, each next to a bucket of sudsy water. They were cleaning the gate. I recognized the woman I'd met at the store yesterday. When she saw me she broke away from her task and smiled a big, toothy grin.

"Good morning!" She called out. "Remember me from last night? Maria Lopez."

"Of course I remember you. What's going on here?" I asked cautiously.

"I read the paper this morning and put two and two together. You're Polyester, aren't you?"

"Poly. I go by Poly."

"It's so cute, you know? That your name is Polyester and you own the fabric store. I told my husband about you after I read the article and he said I should do something to help you. So I got the idea to bring my sisters over to see what we could do."

I wanted to hug her. Instead, I looked at the storefront where the women were busy at work. They'd already cleaned most of the gate. Two women were working on the surrounding stucco surfaces with stiff brushes and another was pouring something on the sidewalk.

"Maria, what do I owe you for this?" In four hours my boss was going to discover that I wasn't showing up for work, and that might have a negative impact on my finances.

"You are a silly woman," she said. "Have you never helped somebody just because you can?"

I thought about Genevieve's tea shop and the fabric makeover I'd imagined the previous night. Maybe she wouldn't think I was crazy. Maybe she'd appreciate the gesture. More than before, I wanted to pay this favor forward.

Maria smiled again, showing most of her teeth. "No cost. But if you have to do *something*, there's a donut shop on the corner."

That time I did hug her.

Another lady came over to us. She was a taller version of Maria, with dark curly hair, olive skin, and bright red lips you wouldn't expect to see on a woman who had gotten up early to scrub the exterior of a building.

"Polyester, this is my sister Juanita," said Maria.

I started to shake her hand, but overcome with their generosity as I was, I hugged her, too. She didn't act surprised, and I wondered how many of their clients hugged them on a regular basis.

"We're almost done with the gate, but the door needs work," Juanita said.

"Can you leave it unlocked before you leave?" said Maria.

"Of course."

The three of us walked to the front of the store together, where I met (and hugged) additional sisters Maricella and Anna respectively. "I don't know what to say, other than thank you."

"You know what says thank you better than almost anything?" said Maria. "Donuts."

I held my hands up. "I'm going, I'm going!"

It wasn't the first piece of goodwill I'd received since being in San Ladrón, but it was a powerful one. One that let me know that I couldn't pretend to categorize this small town quickly or easily. For every Vic McMichael, interested in buying me out, there was an Adelaide Brooks, welcoming me to the neighborhood. For every gossiping resident, there was a Genevieve, inviting me to join her club. For every opportunistic Ken Watts ready to make money from my ownership of the store, there was a Maria Lopez's family-run business, helping me out without expecting to be paid.

I walked toward the hardware store at the end of the block, crossed the street, and kept walking. Like the toucan who follows his nose, I found the donut shop by following the scent trail of sugar and baked goods. A bell chimed over my head as I entered and was immediately enveloped in sweetness that probably added five pounds to my frame.

The shop was empty, except for a large black man behind the counter. He had a stained white apron loosely tied over a plaid shirt and jeans, and was in the process of removing an empty tray from the display case and replacing it with a full one. I would have expected a donut shop to be crazy busy on a Monday morning, but on either side of the shop, booths sat vacant.

I took several deep breaths and closed my eyes, then stepped up to the counter and ordered two dozen assorted donuts from the man.

"You want to pick them or you want me to pick them?" he asked. His voice boomed like a sports announcer's.

In Los Angeles, I had always picked the donuts, leaving nothing to chance. "Surprise me," I said.

He puckered his lips and nodded, very seriously, then took a flat piece of pink cardboard and turned it into a box.

"Big responsibility, letting me choose your donuts. Most people like to choose their own. I think I'll call in some experts."

"You keep the donut expert in the back?"

"I keep two. Carlos! Antonio!" he hollered over his shoulder.

"My mom's cleaning up your mess," said one of the boys.

As soon as I heard the names, I understood why Maria had sent me to the donut shop. "You're Maria's husband?"

"Joe Lopez," he said, and reached over the case of donuts to shake my hand. I almost felt cheated. "My friends call me Big Joe. Boys, this nice lady wants twenty-four of our best donuts. Can I count on you to pick out the best ones?"

Before answering, the boys reached for the donuts covered in chocolate jimmies and put four in the box. Big Joe stepped around from behind the counter and motioned for me to join him at the front of the store away from the boys' hearing.

"Maria told me about you. She said you don't seem like the type of person to bring vandalism to San Ladrón."

"That article wasn't very fair," I said tentatively.

"That article was a piece of crap!" he said. The two boys

looked up at us. "Go back to work, you two," he instructed them. "Maria is a good judge of character and she likes you. So I like you. And every one of those women in front of your store who are helping like you. Don't pay any attention to what the newspaper says. If you need anything while you're here, you call me." He handed me a business card with phone numbers written on the back.

"Why are you being so friendly?" I asked, not because I didn't trust him, but because I wasn't used to this. In the neighborhood where I worked, the only thing that came free was the occasional spit shine on the windshield when I was at lunch, and it was often followed by the request for some spare change.

"Ours is a friendly town, but somebody is trying to make you think it isn't. I won't stand for that."

"Thank you, Joe Lopez," I said.

Whatever trouble I was in, I felt a shift. Like maybe, it really would all be okay. The bell chimed over the front door. Joe stood up straight and wiped his hands on his apron. "Good morning," he said to the customers behind me. When I turned around to face them, I realized my trouble was much deeper than I originally thought.

The new customers were my mom and dad.

Twenty

"We saw the newspaper," my dad said. "You should have called, Poly, if you were in trouble."

"But I did call! I called Mom."

"That is true, John. She called." My mom turned to me. "But you said nothing about vandalism or a murder. I'd say you left some very important details out of that conversation." She crossed her arms over her chest, and I looked to Big Joe for a bit of backup.

"You didn't tell your parents about all that stuff?" he asked. Clearly I was on my own.

"Joe, I'd like to introduce Helen and John Monroe. Mom, Dad, this is Joe Lopez."

"I think we just met your wife at the fabric store. Maria Lopez?" my mother said.

Big Joe nodded. My parents took turns shaking his hand. I looked behind the case for the boys. They were juggling the two large boxes of donuts. Carlos looked like he was dangerously close to dropping them all over the floor. He held his breath as he rounded the corner, walking very slowly, until he arrived in front of me. I took the box and thanked him.

"Are you in trouble?" he asked.

"Why would you ask that?"

"When both of my parents come looking for me, it usually means I'm in trouble."

He looked past me to my parents and I realized what it looked like to an eight-year-old boy. Plus, the reality was, Carlos had nailed it.

"You know what, Carlos? I am in a little bit of trouble."

"Are they going to let you have the donuts? When I'm in trouble I don't get donuts."

Big Joe bent down to Carlos and Antonio's level and chucked both boys under the chin. "How about we take the donuts to Mom and leave Poly here to talk to her parents? Can you help me with that?"

The boys nodded solemnly, but the whole time Carlos stared at me, his dark brown eyes wide with fear for my predicament. "I'll be okay," I told him.

Joe flipped the *Open* sign to *Closed*. "Not much of a crowd ever since that fancy coffee shop opened up down the street. Won't kill us to close for a couple of minutes." He picked up the box. "I'll be back shortly. Help yourself to coffee." The three of them left.

"Poly, after we saw the article, we tried to call. You didn't answer. We drove to the fabric store and found a crowd of women scrubbing the front. Do you want to tell us what's going on?" my dad said. My mom reached a hand up to my hair and flipped the ends between her fingers. I slapped her hand away.

"Maria Lopez and her sisters own a cleaning business. They volunteered to take care of the vandalism from yesterday. I didn't ask them to do it," I said quickly, before they jumped to the incorrect conclusion that I wasn't prepared to take responsibility for what had happened. "Maria sent me here for donuts, and that's when I met Big Joe. They don't like what's been happening, but they don't blame me. See, whatever it says in that article that you read, it's not true. I didn't bring crime to San Ladrón. The crime was already here. Something about the store was the trigger, but that's the only connection."

My mom disappeared behind the counter and filled three white paper cups with coffee, which made it hard to stay mad at her. When she returned, she slid into the booth next to my dad. I felt like they were ganging up on me, but I was determined to be an adult about this.

"Poly, your father and I talked a lot last night, about our decision to keep you in the dark about Marius and Millie. Maybe it wasn't the right thing to do, and we're sorry about that now, but the timing was never right. We're both sorry that it's come to this, but we can't go back in time to change that."

"No, but you can tell me the truth now."

"I told you the truth yesterday."

"You didn't tell me the whole truth. I found the letters." They looked at each other, as though I'd stumped them. "The letters you sent Uncle Marius about me. I found them. There was a box of photos in the closet and in the bottom of the box I found a stack of letters. About me. You told me you sent them to him, but how did they get back into the apartment? You said he never went back."

My mother slid out of the booth and looked at my dad. "I'm going to go help the Lopezes with the store. You and Poly need to talk." She crossed the store and flipped the lock on the back of the door, then left. When I looked back at my dad, he was staring into the cup that he held with both hands.

"You guys lied to me," I said. "My whole life, you lied to me. I don't know what to do with that."

"Poly, why are you still in San Ladrón? Aren't you supposed to be at work today?"

"I'll deal with Giovanni when this is over."

"When what is over?" asked Dad.

"When I find out who killed Mr. Pickers at the store and what it has to do with Aunt Millie."

My dad leaned back against the booth. "Marius and Millie were friends with the McMichaels. Even though Vic and Adelaide were younger by about twenty years, they had a lot in common. From what I understand, Vic admired Marius's business acumen and was in the start-up stages of his own business. Marius taught him a lot, about how they'd started the fabric store when they first came to the States, and about how they kept their contacts all over the world so they could offer something unique. But then Vic came into some money, and their friendship changed. Marius wasn't the mentor anymore. They were more like equals. Vic was a generous man who liked to lavish them with gifts just because he could. The rift happened soon after that. The first time the store had some financial difficulty, Vic offered to buy out the lease. Marius wouldn't hear of it. His pride was pretty severely dented. So Vic went to the bank and worked up a private offer. He thought if he was the owner, Marius and Millie's problems would be over. But when Marius found out, there was a big public fight and the friendship broke off."

"I can see why Uncle Marius was upset, but did he ever tell Mr. McMichael why he was mad? I mean, it's a little weird that Mr. McMichael would be so generous and not have a clue that he was stepping on Uncle Marius's toes."

"Our family sees it that way, sure, but Vic was just being a friend. Marius had done a lot for him, basically taught him all about business and being an entrepreneur, and when Vic inherited his unexpected wealth, he wanted to say thank you. He thought his money was the only way to do that."

"Rich people always think they can say thank you with money," I said, thinking of Vaughn and his elaborate Waverly House dinner. "Money makes a lot of things easier."

"Money also makes a lot of things harder. After the friendship dissolved, Vic and Adelaide were alone. They had no other friends. The strain on their marriage was too much."

"Is that when they divorced?"

"They would have, but Adelaide got pregnant. That boy grew up isolated and alone. I think they sent him off to a private school, then to college on the East Coast. He never grew up like you, like a normal kid. He was wealthy from day one, and had to figure out pretty quickly that some of the friends he made were only interested in him because of his wealth."

"Poor little rich boy," I said.

"Poly, we didn't raise you to pass judgment on other people before getting to know them. From what I've heard, Vaughn McMichael turned out to be a good kid. He didn't have to come back to San Ladrón. He graduated with honors from William and Mary. He landed a respectable job at an investment firm in Richmond, but when his father had a heart attack, he came back here."

"I don't want to talk about Vaughn anymore. I want to talk about Aunt Millie and Uncle Marius. What happened?"

My dad stared out the window at a red car that drove past. He took another drink of his coffee then set it down and pushed it away from him. "They almost lost the store in the eighties. Millie went to Vic McMichael. She asked him for help and didn't tell Marius. Town gossip spread about them after that. About Millie and Vic and about the store going under. Vic made a public offer on the store and that was it. As far as I know, neither of them talked to each other after that. Marius changed the way he did business, cut some of his overhead, and was able to keep the store."

"You said in the eighties. I was alive when some of this was happening?"

"You played a pretty important role, you know. When you were born in the store, Land of a Thousand Fabrics got a lot of press. A little girl named Polyester born in a forty-year-old fabric store? That story brought a bunch of people to see what Marius and Millie had built, and it was just the kind of thing to bring in a new wave of customers and set business back on its heels."

"Is that why Uncle Marius called me his guardian angel?"

"Yes."

"I know you probably don't want to talk about this part, but I have to ask. What happened the night Aunt Millie was murdered?"

"I don't think anybody will ever know the truth about that." My dad stared into his coffee cup again, like it was a crystal ball filled with answers. "Tom Pickers found Marius sitting by Millie's body. Marius was in shock. He couldn't process that she was gone. He'd been sitting next to her all night."

"How do you know this?"

"He came to me, years ago. He said Millie had arranged for him to pick up the cash take from the weekend sale so it wouldn't be sitting around. He'd gone but never made it into the store. He said he'd seen something that scared him and had hid. The next morning he went back to check on the store and heard Marius crying. He called nine-one-one, but it was too late."

"Dad, I heard Mr. Pickers suspected Mr. McMichael was involved in the robbery. That's why he finally came forward and made a statement. People say Vic McMichael hired the robbers and guaranteed that the store would be empty. And the robbers say it was about robbing the store, not about killing anybody. They say they didn't kill anybody. And the only person who saw anything that night—no matter how weird it sounds—is dead, ten years after that night. You don't think there's something off about all of this?"

"I think the robbers were trying to sell a yarn that might lessen their sentence. I think they were after the money and the bracelet and the murder was an accident. I think Tom Pickers had too much to drink, and I think any evidence that says otherwise is probably long gone by now."

I stared out the window. Across the street a steady flow of people frequented a freestanding newsstand. Cars filled Bonita Avenue, backing up when the light changed. Unlike the quiet of the previous weekend, this morning, people were up and out, headed to jobs, I imagined, the same way I had headed into my job every day since Giovanni hired me five years ago. The longer I stayed in San Ladrón, the more I found out about the backstory of the fabric store and the life my great-aunt and -uncle had created there. I knew I didn't want to go back to a job that could barely get me out of bed in the morning.

"Dad, Vic McMichael made me a good offer on the store."

"When?"

"Friday night. The first night I was here. I turned it down. And then Carson showed up with his own offer—well, not *his*, but he got together a bunch of investors in Los Angeles and convinced them to buy the store so they could lock horns with Mr. McMichael."

"He did, did he?"

"I turned down his offer, too. He doesn't understand."

"So you've had two solid offers on the store in the past forty-eight hours."

"Sixty hours is more like it," I corrected.

My dad reached his hand across the table and set it on top of mine. "Tell me this. What is it you're waiting for?"

"A sign, I guess. Something to tell me that it's okay to

leave it all behind in someone else's hands. Because I don't want to. Everything I hear about that store, about what it meant to the family and what Uncle Marius and Aunt Millie went through to keep it, it doesn't seem right to sell it to someone who wants to tear it down."

"What do you think should be done with it?"

"I think it should reopen for business."

"Land of a Thousand Fabrics is a thing of the past. The world has changed since the store's heyday. It won't ever be the same."

It was the same thing Mr. McMichael had said. I hadn't expected my dad to say it, too.

"It doesn't have to be the same. It doesn't even have to be called Land of a Thousand Fabrics. But it could be great again. It could be a place for women to shop for fabric to redecorate or for mothers to bring their daughters to pick out patterns for their prom dresses. I have experience with that, Dad, and you know it. I already have an idea for one shop down the street. And I could run classes on the weekend and get sponsors for craft shows and—"

My dad stared down into his coffee. I studied the bald spot on the top of his head for a second, until he looked back up. "Your mother and I were afraid that something like this would happen."

"What do you mean by that?"

"That store is in your blood. Marius used to say that you were destined to do something that had to do with fabric since you were born in there. You know what he used to sing to you when he rocked you to sleep? 'Material Girl.' He wasn't surprised when you started working for Giovanni. I think he was a little bit proud."

A commotion outside tore my attention from our conversation. On the sidewalk, a small mob approached us, led by Carlos and Antonio, who ran ahead. Carlos clutched a white shoe box to his chest. Behind them, Maria and Joe walked on either side of my mom, with Maria's sisters bringing up the tail of their procession.

"We'll finish talking about this later. Looks like it's time for a shift change." I slid out from the booth and opened the door to the boys who raced in to greet me.

"Poly! We found something!" Carlos said and turned around. "Hurry up, Mom! She's *waiting*!"

I looked at the box in his arms, noting small holes had been punched through the thin cardboard lid. I suspected what was inside—either one or both of the kittens—but Carlos was so proud of his discovery that I remained silent and let him have his moment.

I backed up and held the door open wide as the crowd filed in. My mom's face was flushed pink, a striking contrast to her light gray pixie haircut. Her blue eyes sparkled behind her glasses. "John? You're not going to believe it." She held her arm out to him and he took her hand and stepped to her side. She nodded to Maria.

"What is it?" Dad asked.

"We found pirate gold!" shouted Antonio, who seemed to have kept quiet long enough. His mother shushed him then took the shoe box from Carlos and held it out to me.

"I think this belongs to you."

My hands shook as I took the box from her. I didn't know what to expect when I opened it, but with so many people looking at me, I couldn't ask to look at it later. I raised one leg and balanced the box on my thigh, then removed the lid.

It wasn't a kitten.

"Do you see it?" asked Antonio a second time. He reached up and pulled on my sleeve, knocking the box off balance. It tipped, dumping a charm bracelet that glistened as if it had recently been redipped in gold. I leaned closer. Small charms in the shapes of spools, scissors, thimbles, and one tiny sewing machine were attached to the chain links, next to round coins.

"It's Millie's bracelet," my dad said.

"What does this mean?" I asked.

"It means maybe the robbers were telling the truth."

Twenty-one

Before I could act, the boys dropped to their knees and reached for the bracelet. My mom had tears in her eyes. Clearly, she wasn't going to be the person to tell me how they'd come to find this.

"Maria?" I asked.

"Joe, make sure those boys get every last one of those charms." She put her arm around me and led me to the door. "Let's go outside for a second."

I followed her to the sidewalk. "First, I'm sorry about what my boys did. Ever since they saw *Pirates of the Caribbean*, they think anything gold is pirate treasure."

"They're boys. They're supposed to think that," I said. "How did they find the box? Should I get my dad to hear this?"

"Your mother was there. I'm sure she'll tell him. We had finished cleaning the gate and opened it up so we could go to work on the door. Carlos heard meowing inside the store and when we weren't looking, he went up the stairs and opened the apartment door. I'm sorry."

"Don't be."

"He found two kittens sitting on the other side of the door, and he convinced Antonio that they had to be rescued, so they carried them down to the store without telling us. When you have boys and you don't hear them for five minutes, you know it means they're up to no good, so I went looking for them. They were behind the partition in the store. Carlos tried to put the gray kitten into a box on the shelf to hide it because he didn't want to get in trouble, but the kitten jumped out and knocked the box over. Buttons and ribbon and coins spilled all over the place. The kitten ran to the back, but by that point Carlos thought he'd uncovered hidden treasure."

"He very well might have."

"When I found out what happened, I got your mother. She saw the coins on the floor and almost passed out!" Maria, who had started out as a calm mother of two boys who has seen and had to clean up after everything, had grown excited. Her brown eyes widened to match her boys' and I immediately saw where their sense of adventure came from. "When she told us what they were we knew we had to bring them to you right away. What does it mean?" she finished in a hushed voice.

"I don't know yet."

"I don't think that's true, Poly. I think you know exactly what this means," said my dad from the doorway. I pushed a lock of hair out of my eyes and looked at him. "I think it means you got that sign you were looking for."

Big Joe eased himself behind the counter and poured coffee and hot chocolate for everyone, then disappeared into the back. Within minutes the sweet sugary scent of freshly baked donuts filled the interior of the small shop. The Lopez family mingled with my parents, filling my dad in on the events at the fabric store that morning. Carlos and Antonio were the heroes of the morning, their actions celebrated with crème-filled éclairs. I excused myself and went out front again, needing a moment to process the information.

Adelaide Brooks had told me to focus on the bracelet. She'd said, *Find the bracelet and you'll find the answers.* Only, that wasn't the case. The bracelet had been in the store all the time. What if she wasn't the sweet lady I had taken her for, but was really after the bracelet herself? What if every piece of information she'd fed me, along with that serving of tea, had been carefully chosen to put me on the trail of something I didn't even know still existed and keep me from looking too closely at her family?

And how had she really gotten the charm she'd given me the day we spoke? She'd claimed it had come from her ex-husband, and I'd believed her. But how had that charm gotten separated from the others in the store?

As I stood on the sidewalk, staring across the street at the newsstand, I realized someone was staring back at me. Vaughn. I wondered how long he'd been standing there watching me, and if he knew about the vandalism—that is, if he hadn't been involved in it in the first place. Only, this didn't feel like something he'd do. Whether or not he wanted me around, whether or not he was working for his father, trying to get me to sell the store so they could resell and make a bundle, I couldn't imagine that he'd stoop to ketchup vandalism to make his point. It didn't fit.

Before I could figure out whether or not to acknowledge his presence or turn around and ignore him, I felt a hand on my shoulder. I turned to face my mother. "Your father said you had a good talk."

"It was a start."

"Considering what happened today, we're going to stick around for a bit. Would it be cramping your style if we went back to the apartment?"

"Mom, how exactly would that be cramping my style?"

I asked. "Carson left. He's back in Los Angeles. It's me and two kittens, and I'll go out on a limb and say we'd all welcome the company."

"I wasn't talking about Carson," she said. She looked across the street at Vaughn, still sitting alone. His head was half-hidden behind the newspaper. "That's the McMichael boy, isn't it? Go ask him to join us."

"No, Mom, I'm not going to ask him to join us. This isn't about him, it's about us. It's about family."

"Not all of it," she said. "And this isn't about holding a grudge. I raised you better than that."

"You raised me to have family loyalty. And I do."

"I raised you to be responsible, too." She held my cell phone out. "You left this on the counter charging. You missed several calls from Giovanni—he's your boss, right?"

I took the phone from her and grinded my teeth. How did mothers know how to make a point so well? Did they teach a class on that somewhere?

"I need to return a few phone calls. In private." I spun away from her and stepped off the sidewalk onto a strip of grass that ran between the donut shop and the dentist next door. It was well past morning, now moving somewhere into the lunch hour. I knew she was right and I owed Giovanni a call, but he could wait.

I gently tapped out the numbers 411. After being connected to the local utility office, I bypassed a series of automated cues designed to direct me to the right office, then ended up on the phone with someone named Shirley. I explained the power situation and gave her my address, then sat silent on my end while she presumably either accessed my account or ignored everything I'd said and left me hanging.

"The fabric store? You live up there?"

"Yes, that's me."

"That was tempo for the weekend. We haven't had an account there for years."

"What do you mean 'tempo'?" I asked.

"Temporary service. Turned on by a Realtor, Ken Watts, on Friday morning. He said he was showing the property, asked us to turn on the power for two days."

"Is that normal?" I asked.

"Pretty routine. When you have properties that've been vacant for awhile, nobody's itching to pay the bills, but the Realtors know you can't show a property in the dark. We have agreements with most of the agencies."

"So can I get the power turned back on? Can you transfer the account to me?"

"Did you buy the place?"

"I inherited it."

"Says here it's under the control of Watts Realtor. Until I get word from them, the power's going to have to stay off."

"What if I convince him to turn it back on?"

"That's between you and him. You probably want to try that first, because once I cut his account off, it'll take a couple of days to get it back up and running."

"What about the water?" I asked.

"I can't help you with that. You'll have to talk to the water company."

"Thanks for the information, Shirley." I hung up the phone and thumbed through recent calls until I found Ken's phone number. Big Joe watched me from the window with his arms crossed over his chest. I was being antisocial.

"Ken Watts," he said as an answer.

"Ken, this is Poly. I need a favor. I need you to have the power turned back on at the fabric store until I can have the bills transferred to my name. And the water. Can you get the water turned back on, too?"

"Don't you need to be getting back to Los Angeles yet?"

"Not now." I pushed my hair out of my eyes. "I was going to call you this morning, but I got distracted. You know my aunt's bracelet? The one that's been missing all these years?"

"The one you insist the robbers melted into a lump of gold?"

"Yes, that one. We found it this morning. It's been inside all along."

He whistled. "All this time. I gotta say, I was with you. But that's good news, right? Now you can get some closure and sell the store with no regrets."

"This doesn't mean I'm selling the store." I kicked the toe of my boot against the damp ground. "Can we forget your potential commission and talk like friends? I need the power and the water back on."

"This goes beyond my normal duties," he said.

"Let me put it to you another way: I've been wearing the same clothes for most of the weekend and I'm desperately in need of a shower. If you don't work with me, I'll be forced to come to your office. Without the benefit of regular grooming habits. That's going to cost you a *lot* more than the commission you'll lose by not selling my store to Mr. McMichael. Is that what you want?"

"Your boyfriend said you were stubborn, but I didn't believe him."

"Whatever," I said, careful not to actually agree with him. "I'm good for the money. Can you call them? Now?"

"Fine."

"Thank you, Ken," I said.

He grumbled something I chose not to interpret and hung up. My next call was to Giovanni, who, no doubt, had noticed that I wasn't coming in. I listened to several messages that grew from annoyed to angry, then deleted the whole batch of them and called him back.

"Giovanni, it's Poly."

"Where are you?"

"I'm out of town." I paused for a second, not sure if he was going to ask questions. "Family emergency," I added, to make it sound more dramatic.

"Is this the fabric store your boyfriend wants me to buy? That family emergency?"

"He came to you?"

"Asked me to put up a pretty penny, too. I sure hope the other investor stepped up like I did."

I turned my back on the donut shop and stared out at the cars driving past. "Did he tell you who the other investor was? Did he give you a name?"

"He sure didn't want to. Said the third guy was local and wanted to remain anonymous. I told him I wouldn't even look at his proposal until I knew who I was getting into bed with."

"And?" I held my breath.

"Yeah, he gave me the name. Ken Watts."

Twenty-two

"Ken is the third investor?" I repeated. "He's the agent representing the sale. How can he be an investor, too?"

"That's probably why he wanted to stay anonymous. Not lose his real estate license. If your boyfriend is right about what we stand to make when we sell, I'd probably take the same risk."

"Yes, but I already know you're unethical." My mind spun with possibilities of what this meant. Ken had been the one to tell me about the second offer. Had he come up with the plan when he realized I was willing to play hardball with Mr. McMichael, or had it been Carson's idea and Ken was in the right place at the right time?

"Are you coming back this afternoon?" Giovanni asked. "The seamstresses are waiting for the sketches for our next collection."

I shook off my questions and focused. "That concept wasn't due until Friday."

"I advanced the timetable."

"Why? Even if I hadn't come to San Ladrón I wouldn't have been ready. Not this early. I haven't had a chance to assemble colors or swatches, or to put together an inspiration packet."

"I'm not going to pay these women to sit around all day. Fax me ten sketches and I'll do the rest."

I pictured Giovanni bastardizing my sketches with the cheapest fabrics he could get at the fabric mart. When it didn't work, he'd hand me a hot glue gun and a tray of plastic jewels and instruct me to fix them. I thought of the beautiful bolts of fabric in the store and knew I didn't want to work his way anymore. I could use the store inventory this time. I could write up an invoice and sell him the fabric that I wanted to use.

"Gold," I said.

"What?"

"Gold. Platinum. Copper. Bugle beads and feathers and sequins and fringe. Flapper dresses. That's my concept."

"That crap doesn't sell. I want color. I want blue. Bright blue. And turquoise, teal, peacock. There's your theme: peacock. I'll get you your feathers and you can glue them wherever you want. Just get me sketches."

"We did peacock last year."

"So do it again. People won't remember. Just make sure you put a lot of bright blue in there. I put a bid in on a thousand yards of blue poly satin. We have to move that pronto."

I didn't have the guts to tell Giovanni the only way he'd move a thousand yards of bright blue poly satin was to start selling Superman suits in Santee Alley. "I'll work on sketches soon."

"I want them tomorrow."

"Not tomorrow. What day is it, anyway?"

"It's Monday."

"Best-case scenario I can have something to you by Wednesday."

"If you want to come back to a job, make it a priority," Giovanni said before hanging up.

I kicked the toe of my boot against the side of the donut shop, then placed the sole squarely on one of the panels of aluminum siding and leaned forward, stretching out my hamstrings. It felt good to stretch. I changed feet, putting the left on the building and repeating the stretch. When I finished, I tipped my head to one side then the other, relieving tension in my neck as the joint cracked, then rolled it around and looked straight up at the blue sky. I rolled my shoulders backward twice. I felt like a boxer, limbering up, getting ready for a fight, and in a way I guess I was. My next call was to Carson.

He didn't answer. I waited for his voice mail, figuring I'd take the high road as long as I was alone and nobody could overhear me.

"Carson, it's me. I need to ask you about something—" A repetitive beeping hammered in my ear. I pulled the phone away from my head and looked at the flat screen. The call had been dropped. I moved a few steps to the left and dialed again.

He answered halfway through the third ring. "What do you want, Poly?" he asked. His voice lacked both emotion and warmth and was lower than he usually talked. This was his business side. I'd heard him talk like this before but never to me.

"What happened to hello?" I asked.

"I gave up hello somewhere between you stealing my car and accusing me of vandalism."

"It's been a rough couple of days."

"I came up there to help you out so it wouldn't be so rough on you. That's what being in a relationship is about. Having someone to lean on, to help you. If you had responded to my note, we could have driven home together."

"I couldn't leave last night. Not with everything that's happened."

"I know you're all nostalgic over the store, but this isn't all about you. Think about the other investors. They put up money because they see it as a good risk. We all do. You can take the money we make and open your own store. Something you want. I've never heard you talk about wanting to open a fabric store."

"Speaking of the other investors . . ."

He interrupted me. "Confidentiality clause."

"Don't talk to me like I'm one of your clients." I looked up at the window next to me and saw Big Joe looking back. His brows pulled together with concern. "I just talked to Giovanni and he told me the third investor is Ken."

"I should have known I couldn't trust your boss to keep his mouth shut. *Confidentiality clause* means 'I could lose my job.' Did he tell anybody else? No, don't answer that. I am not going to continue this conversation with you. When you calm down, when you want to have a rational conversation between two adults, then you know where to find me. But as long as you're going to accuse me of something juvenile, we're done."

"You know something? I'm tired of only talking about the things *you* want to talk about at the times *you* want to talk about them. I'm tired of your life being the only one worth anything. I'm tired of living according to your rules of how to get ahead."

"Good-bye, Poly."

"Don't hang up on me!" I yelled into the phone, but it was too late. I threw the phone into a small cluster of landscaping by the corner of the building, regretting the action the second I heard the sound of breaking glass. A small salamander slithered out, startled by the iPhone assault. I kicked at the shrubbery a few times, making sure the salamander didn't leave any friends behind, dropped to my knees, and plunged my hands into the brush to find my broken phone.

"I guess calling you is out of the question," said Vaughn from behind me.

My hand closed around the small rectangle, and I pulled it out of the tangle of exposed roots and fallen leaves. The screen of my phone had cracked on impact with a clay pot cast into the shape of a frog. I shook the phone a few times to bring the display up, but nothing happened. On top of everything else I was going to have to find an Apple store.

The knees of my leggings were wet from the ground, which must have been watered earlier that day. I pointed the phone at Vaughn, and he threw his hands up in the air in surrender and took a step back.

"I'm fresh out of apologies, so if that's what you crossed the street for, you're out of luck," I said.

"It looks like there's a celebration going on inside the donut shop. Good news?"

"To some people," I said. "The Lopez boys found something that belonged to my great-aunt. We all thought it was stolen the night she died."

"So why are you out here?"

"Loose ends," I said. "Life outside of San Ladrón continues, even if we're trapped in a bubble of history here."

"Who's trapped?"

"Everybody I've met since I showed up here is trapped. This whole town is trapped. It's like a time warp, like the circuits of time malfunctioned ten years ago and left a whole bunch of people in the dark."

"I keep trying to tell you I understand how that feels. I've been looking for answers, too."

"Why don't you send Charlie out for answers? She's the one who does your dirty work, right?"

"Charlie's and my relationship is nobody's business but ours."

"Oh, come on, Vaughn. Maybe you two can keep it a secret from the rest of the town, but I figured it out in three days. She might pretend to have something against your father, but she's on the McMichael payroll."

All of the color drained from his face. Half circles, purplish in tone, stood out against his pale skin. He pushed his hair back from his forehead several times in a nervous gesture, and when he finished it stood up like a pompadour.

"You don't know what you're talking about."

"I saw his name on her registration card. Why else would he buy her a car?"

"Because she's family. Charlie is my sister."

Twenty-three

"Charlie is your sister?" I asked. "I don't believe you."

"It's not common knowledge around San Ladrón, because she doesn't want it to be. I found out when I came back to help out my father. A couple of businesses were struggling and it was my job to approach the owners about selling. Many of them did, and that's when he bought up so much of the property around here. Charlie's auto shop was one of the businesses that was having trouble making the rent."

"I know. She told me."

"She was so protective of her business, of what she'd built. She refused help. Dad could have bought her out if he'd wanted to, but I didn't want that to happen. I made the back payments for her and told her to consider it a loan. She was so angry she accused me of working for him, trying to make up for giving her up, and said it was too little too late. I didn't know what she was talking about until she finally told me she'd been given up for adoption. That's when I learned I had a sister."

"Why would she keep it a secret?"

"Pride and hurt. I'm not going to tell you her story. That's her story to tell. But Charlie is a proud woman. She never asked for a penny. She paid back the loan within months and she's never been behind on a payment since."

I thought about Mr. McMichael appearing behind Charlie's Automotive the night the shower was sabotaged. Is that why he was there? He was a father looking for an opportunity to reconnect with his daughter? Or maybe they weren't as estranged as she pretended. Maybe she told him I was in the shower and he was responsible for my being trapped, not for my rescue.

"Charlie deserves to know that you know. Let's go find her at the shop."

"I'm not going anywhere with anybody," I said instinctively. "This building is filled with people who know I'm out here and they'll wonder what happened to me if I suddenly go missing."

As if on cue, the sound of laughter rang out from the front entrance of the store. My mom and dad peeked around the side of the building and waved. "Poly, we're going back to the store to try to find those kittens," my dad said.

"I'm taking this with me." My mom held up the white shoe box with the bracelet. "See you later?"

"Mom, Dad, I don't think you should leave yet," I said, pulling my eyebrows in and tipping my head slightly to the right to indicate that something was amiss.

"Is there something wrong with your eye?" my dad asked.

"She wants us to leave her alone, John," my mom said to my dad. Whatever intuition I suspected she had learned back in mom school had either left her temporarily or was on the fritz.

"Seriously, wait up for me," I said, jogging toward them. Right as I passed Vaughn I tripped over something and fell face down on the wet ground. Moisture seeped through the knees of my already filthy leggings.

"Let me help you up," Vaughn said. He held out a hand, but I ignored it. He put his hands under my arms and helped me, even though I tried to shake him off. Our heads were close together. "I don't care if you're rude to me, and I don't care if you have it in for my father, but if you have any integrity, you'll keep Charlie's background a secret," he whispered. His hands dropped from my body and he stepped backward, and then walked over to my parents. "Mr. and Mrs. Monroe, I'm Vaughn McMichael. Your daughter is something else."

I flushed. My mom fought a smile. "Can we leave yet?" I asked.

"Stay here with your friend, Poly. We both need a break."

"But what if I don't want to stay here?"

My dad put his arm around my mother's waist and turned her away from us. "We haven't been in the store for a long time, either. Lots of memories have been shut in that apartment for years. Give us a chance to see what you saw when you first went inside."

It was a fair request. "I'll be there in two hours. Two hours. If I'm not there in *two hours*, come looking for me."

"You want to be independent one minute and you want us to look for you the next. It's tough growing up, isn't it?" Mom said, pushing my hair away from my forehead.

"If I'm not at the fabric store in *two hours*, call Sheriff Clark. His number is on top of the dresser in the bedroom."

"Poly, you're being dramatic." Mom tipped her head back and looked down her nose at me. "You really do need a haircut, though. Take an extra hour and see if one of the salons around here will take a walk-in."

They left me alone next to the donut shop with Vaughn.

I suspected he was watching me. I braced myself for the look on his face when I turned around but was surprised to discover that he'd left.

Whatever action it was I feared, it wasn't being left alone on the lawn of a donut shop. I leaned forward and walked around the side of the shop, expecting Vaughn to be standing there hiding from me. He wasn't.

"You okay? That was a nasty spill you just took," said Big Joe. He stood next to the spot where I had fallen down.

"I'm klutzy. I fall down a lot," I said.

"Maybe you do, but that fall wasn't your fault."

"Don't worry, I'm not going to sue."

"Wouldn't matter much to me if you did. I saw the whole thing out the window, and it was pretty obvious the McMichael kid tripped you on purpose."

"He tripped me?" I looked behind me to see if Vaughn had reappeared.

"Sure did. I didn't expect that of him. Seems you bring out a playful side that I've never seen."

"Did you see where he went?" I asked.

"There's only one way to go if you don't go back out to Bonita, and that's around the back, through the alley next to the sheriff's office. The Waverly House is across the street from there, and I bet that's where he went."

"So I have two choices? Leave out front or go that way and possibly end up following him?"

"There's a third choice. Come back inside and join the celebration, at least for a little bit."

I knew I owed Big Joe and Maria. Leaving their impromptu celebration was borderline offensive. "Do you mind if I use your phone first?"

"Follow me."

I went into the donut shop and followed Big Joe to the kitchen. He indicated a black wall-mounted phone with a rotary dial. "You need privacy?" I nodded. "Boys, let's go out front and see if your mother wants more donuts." He corralled his boys through the saloon-style doors that separated the customer area from the kitchen.

I picked up the receiver and dialed Sheriff Clark. When he answered, I identified myself. "Deputy Sheriff Clark, Ken Watts is trying to buy my store."

"I know. He told me."

"When did he tell you? It's supposed to be confidential."

I realized that even though this was a small town that rarely saw this assortment of crimes, the deputy sheriff was no dummy. He was putting two and two together faster than a room of kindergarteners who had just learned to add. "Mr. Watts told me his name might come up in my investigation based on his joint involvement with two other investors."

"How can he do that? It's a conflict of interest."

"You'll have to ask him."

"I plan to."

"Ms. Monroe, I found the guys responsible for the ketchup on your storefront."

"Who are they?"

"Couple of regulars at The Broadside. They said it was a joke. Kind of a 'welcome to the neighborhood' gag."

"That's it? They say it's a joke and you're going to let them go?" I waited for a second. "That's vandalism. Isn't that a felony?"

"It's a felony if the damages cost more than four hundred dollars. They used ketchup because they knew it wasn't permanent. I figure it took a handful of rags and a bucket of soapy water to clean it up. I checked it out myself. Have to admit, the gate looks better than it has in years."

"Did they confess to anything else, like vandalizing my car, abandoning kittens in my Dumpster, or locking me in Charlie's shower?"

"Ms. Monroe, their confession is a start. It's not the end. Like it or not, there's a difference between a practical joke and a felony. Give me something to work with and I'll use it."

"I don't have anything else."

"Give me a timeline of exactly what you've been doing since you arrived. Who you talked to, where you've been."

"Friday: arrived in San Ladrón. My car was vandalized that afternoon. Saturday morning I found Mr. Pickers behind the store. Saturday night I was trapped in Charlie's shower. Sunday I met Adelaide Brooks, visited Mr. McMichael, and had my storefront vandalized. Do you want me to go on?"

"I want you to take some time and think about this. Bring it to me. I'll be at the mobile unit until five."

I agreed to meet Deputy Sheriff Clark later that afternoon and hung up. I joined the Lopez family out front. It was evident that the hard work from the morning had morphed into a family affair, and I was little more than a stranger in the corner of the room for the next half hour. The attention that had been lavished on the boys when they'd presented the shoe box with the bracelet inside had worn off. While the women lounged against the tables, helping themselves to donuts from a tray on a table in the middle of the shop, Carlos and Antonio chased after each other.

"Penny for your thoughts," said Maria, sliding into the booth across from me.

I shook my head fast, trying to snap myself out of my thoughts. It only half worked, and I could tell from the look on her face that she expected some kind of explanation.

"I don't know what I'm looking for anymore," I said. "I thought I wanted answers about my aunt's murder, but I've heard the story and it's not enough. I need to know about Mr. Pickers, why he was killed when I first arrived. Nothing I've learned since I arrived explains that."

"When did you arrive in San Ladrón?" she asked.

"Friday morning."

"Were you planning to spend the weekend?"

"No. When I left Los Angeles, I thought I was going to take a peek inside the store, sign some paperwork, maybe grab lunch, and leave."

"Why didn't you?"

"My car was vandalized, so I had to stay."

"You probably have a friend who would have come to get you, or you could have rented a car and gone home. What about the paperwork. Did you sign?"

"No."

"Why not?"

"I didn't want to." All this time I'd seen the vandalism as the thing that kept me in San Ladrón. But maybe I had it backward. Maybe if I'd signed the paperwork to sell the store to Mr. McMichael, my car would have been left alone. Maybe the vandalism hadn't been intended to keep me in town but to punish me for not signing.

"Why did you stay? If you didn't know about the bracelet, then you couldn't have been looking for that. Why didn't you go home on Friday? Or Saturday?"

"Mr. Pickers's murder. I couldn't leave after that." I didn't tell her that part of the reason was that Deputy Sheriff Clark had advised me not to. "I'm in control of the legacy of the store. I can't let that legacy be about murder." It was the same thing I'd said to Adelaide.

"What do you want the store's legacy to be?"

"I don't know."

"I think I do." She leaned back in her chair and tucked her chin slightly so her stare was more direct. The action caused a double chin to appear above her neck. She blinked at me with thick lashes that could have been fake, then leaned forward and put her manicured hands on top of my own. "You came here looking for something, but you didn't know what. You found more than you bargained for. There are still questions, and you are still seeking answers."

"But why? I have a job, a boyfriend, and an apartment in Los Angeles."

"That might all be true, but it seems to me that you don't have a life."

"Hey!" I protested. Two of Maria's sisters—I'd lost track of who was who by this point—stopped their conversation and looked at me. The donut shop grew uncomfortably quiet, until I responded to Maria in a low voice. "I have a life. I have people who depend on me. Who rely on me to run their business, or to get paid, or to make sure there's a parking space at night. I have people who think I make the best macaroni and cheese in the world. I'm not a loser," I finished.

Maria sat back and held her hands up. "All I'm saying is that since you've been here your car has been broken into, you were locked into a shower, and your store was vandalized. People are whispering behind your back that maybe you had something to do with that man's murder. Your boyfriend and boss tried to convince you to go back to Los Angeles and you had a very lucrative offer to sell the store, but you're still here. I think I know why, too. It's as though you wanted something you could really care about to come into your life, and it did. Don't ignore that, Poly."

Twenty-four

I'd spent the last ten years hating the men who had robbed the store and killed my aunt. I thought they were lying when they said they didn't steal her bracelet. Now I had reason to believe they might have been telling the truth. If they didn't steal the bracelet, was there any truth to the rest of their story? Was the real killer still out there? Was he watching the store, hoping for a chance to get in and find the valuable piece of jewelry? Had Mr. Pickers been keeping a lookout hoping to right a wrong, to catch the bad guys trying to break in a second time?

Big Joe and Maria would go home tonight with their boys and chalk today up to a roller coaster of events and emotions in their town, but for me, it was different. I was the catalyst for these random acts of violence in San Ladrón. They started when I arrived. I had a feeling they wouldn't stop until after I left.

"Thank you both for what you've done for me today. I

don't know what I would have done—or how I would have done it—if it weren't for you two."

Maria held out her hand palm side facing me. "Stop right there. If you were the kind of person who was afraid of a problem, you would have left days ago. This is how we do things in San Ladrón. When one person's problem is big, we help out. If we need help, you can return the favor."

For a second I was rooted to the spot. The numb feeling in my chest was growing warm thanks to the friendliness of the Lopez family, and instead of saying anything else, I stepped forward and hugged each of them. I said good-bye and started my walk back to the fabric store.

It was after three. I crossed the street and passed a gas station before turning around and stopping inside for a bottle of Coke and a bag of popcorn. I added a jar of peanuts for my dad and a banana for my mom, wondered how fresh a banana from a gas station could possibly be, and retraced my steps to the store.

Deputy Sheriff Clark was right. The front of the store looked good. Not just because the ketchup graffiti had been cleaned away, but because years of grime had gone with it. I'd only been able to do so much on those first few days, occupied more with the task of getting the fence to open than the cleaning of the storefront. But now the surface was a whiter shade than it had been when I arrived. It was brighter than the stores on either side of it, finally the shining star on Bonita Avenue instead of the store thumb. I stuck my key into the lock and turned it, pulled the gate away, and unlocked the front door. The two kittens sat on the lower step of the stairs, staring at me. The gray one let out a peep.

"Hey, you two," I said, scooping each up with a hand under their bellies and pulling them to my chest. "Has your day has been nearly as exciting as mine?" I planted a kiss between the ears of each of them and started my ascent up the stairs. "Mom? Dad? You can stop worrying now. I'm back," I called.

My dad was sprawled across the sofa reading an old book. "Shhh. Your mother is taking a nap." He set the open book on his chest and folded his hands behind his head. I set both of the kittens on my dad's belly. He moved the book to the floor and ran a hand over the fur of each of their heads.

"Where did you find them?"

"I didn't. Vaughn McMichael did. He heard them in the Dumpster out back the afternoon after the murder. It would have been a funny story if it hadn't happened that day. I caught him digging around inside the Dumpster and accused him of going through my trash."

"Why would you have cared? Trash is trash. You threw it away, right?"

"I know, but I don't trust him."

"Has he given you reason not to? Sounds like maybe you don't *want* to trust him."

I stroked the gray kitten's head. "Now that I think about it, I still don't know if I believe he heard kittens in the Dumpster. They're not very loud, you know." I sank onto the carpet and moved my dad's book to the side, then bent my right leg over my left and tugged off my dirty boot. "He came here the first day I was in San Ladrón. Just showed up and walked in like he owned the place. And then I find out that his father had put in a bid on the store, that he actually did think he owned the place, because he assumed I'd take the offer and go back to Los Angeles." I stretched my right leg out and repeated the boot removal process on my left foot. "That all happened before Mr. Pickers was found dead out back."

"Why didn't you take the offer, Poly?"

"That's seems to be the question on everybody's mind." I was surprised by my father's question, considering he was one of the few people who should have understood. I put my boots together and tucked the toes under the sofa. "Doesn't it bother you that Uncle Marius kept this store for ten years to protect the memory of Aunt Millie? Or that the McMichael family wants to waltz in now that it's convenient and benefit from our family's tragedy?"

"No. What bothers me is that he kept it closed. If he wanted to honor her memory, he would have kept it open. Let people remember what it was she had built with him. I tried to ask him about it, but he was never willing to explain."

"But it was just him. He couldn't run it by himself."

"He knew your mother and I were willing to move here and help. This was the family business. It wouldn't have been the first time we'd pitched in and helped, and it wouldn't have been the last. The reality is that he didn't know how to function without her. Memories, if nurtured, have a life of their own. He made a choice to push the family away instead of letting us draw closer. And that's why we moved to Burbank."

"I didn't know you'd offered to help him run the store."

"For him, Land of a Thousand Fabrics ceased to be the day she died."

"So why do you think he left it to me? What do you think he wanted me to do with it?"

"Nobody can answer that question now that he's gone, but I think he realized her memory would die with him unless he gave someone a reason to keep it alive."

"Dad, I want to reopen the store."

"If that's what you want to do, then you'll do it. You've always been determined, and I don't doubt that you're smart enough to make it work. But consider this: the success of the store once was because Marius and Millie had made it their passion, their life's work. If you try to make it what they wanted, it will fail. The only way it can succeed is if you make it what *you* want."

The ping of a text message interrupted us. I looked at the broken screen of my phone. *Take a shower. Please*, it said.

I moved from the living room into the bathroom. A

trickle of water snaked down from the bottom of the faucet. I turned the handle on the sink and water spurted out in a rust-colored spray. The odd shade faded within seconds and soon a stream of clear water flowed into the basin.

I turned it off and called Ken. "It's about time," he said in lieu of hello.

"Thank you." I said. "I can't remember the last time I was so excited to take a shower. Or a bath," I added quickly, remembering the shower incident at Charlie's.

"I think the whole town's excited about you finally taking a shower."

Despite the favor he'd done for me and his joking tone, I couldn't help be angry about his secret business dealings with Carson. "Ken, why didn't you tell me you're trying to get a piece of the store for yourself?"

He was silent for a few beats. I pulled the phone away from my ear and checked the screen to see if we were still connected.

"That information was supposed to be confidential. Did your boyfriend tell you?"

"I found out on my own. I don't get it, Ken. You risked your real estate license to get in on his deal? Is the money that good?"

"I didn't risk anything. Your boyfriend convinced me he could get you to sell. I asked another agent in our office to draw up the paperwork so there wouldn't be a conflict if you took our offer."

"So win-win situation for you? I sell to Mr. McMichael and you earn the commission, I sell to Carson and you get part ownership and a potential big payoff when you resell the property?"

"Something like that." He took a deep breath and blew it out. "I wanted to tell you, honest. Your boyfriend said he'd have more leverage if you didn't know who the investors were."

"Sounds like Carson."

"How long are you planning to stick around?"

"I don't know. Are you that eager to get rid of me?"

"No, that's not what I meant. Felicity says I've been treating you too much like a client and not enough like a friend. She wants to invite you over for dinner." He paused. "She said if I mention you selling the store I'm sleeping on the sofa for the next week."

"I don't know how long I'm staying, but dinner sounds nice. Thank her for me."

"If you do come over for dinner, be sure to take advantage of that running water first."

"Good-bye, Ken."

I disconnected and propped the phone on the back of the sink, then turned the bathtub jets to full blast. Warm, clear water gushed from the spigot. I opened the door and padded down the Oriental carpet runner in my stocking feet.

As I made my way back to the front of the apartment, I paused to stare at the geometric shadows that were cast on the wall from the sunlight cascading through the cutouts of the decorative window at the top center of the building. I hadn't noticed the beauty of the window before, and now I couldn't look away. There was a certain perfection in it, in the small round loops framed with black iron, the peak at the center, and the repetitive cloverleaf pattern that filled the border. Houses like these could be renovated to minimize their original Victorian state, but a window like that would, most likely, survive a battery of home improvements through the sheer matter of it being hard to reach.

The window was recessed about twelve inches into the wall, leaving a narrow curved ledge around it. I would have liked to curl up on that ledge, to pull my knees up to my chest and stare out the pattern of glass at the view of Bonita Avenue, watching my neighbors go about the lives they had before I'd come to town, but I couldn't. A now-familiar construction truck pulled past the store. I watched it turn on the side street next to The Broadside and pull into the back. Soon a ladder was propped up against the side of the building. Looked like Duke was getting his roof fixed.

I turned back to the living room and found my dad asleep on the sofa, with the orange kitten spread-eagle on his chest. One of my boots had been knocked over, and a small gray tail stuck out of the shaft.

I left my dad in the living room and started a bath. I lowered myself into the hot water and lathered my head with a bar of Ivory soap. After scrubbing every limb, twice, I lay back against the porcelain, closed my eyes, and inhaled the scent of clean. When the water turned from hot to tepid, I climbed out, dried off, and dressed in clean underwear, a hooded sweatshirt, and black skinny jeans. I sat at the kitchen table and started my timeline for Sheriff Clark.

Friday: Arrived in San Ladrón. Saw Mr. Pickers by store. Car vandalized. Went to Charlie's Auto.
Saturday: Found Mr. Pickers behind store. Got caught in Charlie's shower. Had dinner with Vaughn in store.
Sunday: Left Tea Totalers, caught ride with Charlie to auto shop. Went to talk to Duke, Charlie interrupted me. Discovered Charlie's relationship to McM family.
Monday: Found bracelet.

I couldn't help noticing how frequently Charlie's name popped up. Why was she everywhere I was? Except for today. Charlie had been one of the few people I knew who was conspicuously absent from the donut shop.

But something was missing. Sure, Charlie had a connection to the McMichael family, but was there a connection between her and the fabric store or her and Mr. Pickers?

I tiptoed into the bedroom for the scrapbook Vaughn had

given me days ago. He said he had questions, too. Questions about what? His father's involvement? Were those questions related to Vic McMichael's guilt or innocence?

Careful not to wake up my mother, I hugged the book to my chest and sat on a spot on the floor that was painted with a ray of sun. My mom slept soundly, her breath almost, but not quite, a snore. The white shoe box from the donut store sat on top of the dresser next to the box of memorabilia I'd been digging through last night. I pulled the scrapbook onto my lap, and started to go through it a second time. These clippings were the closest thing I had to an account of what had happened in San Ladrón when my aunt had died. Now that I was past the shock of Vaughn's father's involvement, I might pick up something of importance from the clippings.

I scanned the titles again, flipping page by page past what I already knew. Vic McMichael had been suspected of involvement in the murder, but aside from gossip and innuendo, there had been nothing to link him to the crime. There was an article from the detective who had worked the crime that had a small red star next to it.

Based on the statement of the witness that placed Mr. McMichael's car in the area of the crime, the businessman has been investigated in connection to the murder. No evidence linking him to the crime has been found. It is our conclusion that the two robbers acted of their own volition in a robbery attempt that resulted in homicide. Further claims of Mr. McMichael's involvement led to an additional search of the crime scene to look for corroborating evidence to place him inside the store. Nothing could be found. The LA County sheriff's office has closed this case. We suggest that once the people of San Ladrón have mourned the loss of their friend and neighbor, they close the case against Vic McMichael, too.

A nagging thought pricked at the back of my mind and kept me from relaxing. I couldn't forget the way Vaughn's face had looked the day I accused his family of buying their way out of problems. He'd told me his father had bullied people into agreeing to his terms. If Uncle Marius had repeatedly said no to his offers to buy the store, had he escalated his tactics from bullying to something more threatening? Had he arranged to scare Aunt Millie with the robbery in an attempt to change her and my uncle's minds?

Twenty-five

My mom had turned to her side, her palms pressed against each other and sandwiched under her head. I covered her with the white eyelet afghan that had been folded at the base of the bed, and then crossed the room to the vanity and lifted the lid to the white shoe box and stared at the long-lost piece of jewelry Maria's boys had found. I scooped an assortment of charms with my left hand, forgetting for the moment that my mom was sleeping on the bed behind me.

All my life I'd believed that two men had broken into the store, robbed it, and committed murder. Even though they'd claimed that the store was empty when they got there and there was no money in the register, it all seemed too much like a lie. Of course they claimed they didn't do it. Of course they claimed they didn't steal anything. Of course they claimed they didn't kill my great-aunt. But no other evidence supported their claims, and they had gone to jail.

I'd found out more about that night in the past couple of

days that I'd been back in the store than I'd known my whole life, starting with the knowledge that Mr. Pickers had witnessed something the night the original crime was committed. And now Mr. Pickers was dead, too. No way did I see that as coincidence.

Had Mr. Pickers been keeping a watch on the store because he wanted to know what he'd seen that night? I closed my eyes and fingered the real charm. The gold had turned warm next to my skin. As I slid my thumb and forefinger over the rough surface I tried to imagine what might have happened that night.

My aunt had stayed late at the store, waiting for Mr. Pickers. Someone broke in. She would have been scared, but she would not have made it easy for the robbers. She would have put up a fight.

But how had Vic McMichael gotten a charm from her bracelet? Had one fallen off while she was fighting for her life? Had whoever committed the crime given it to him as proof that the deed had been done, or had he committed the crime and kept a charm as a trophy?

I opened my eyes and regrounded myself in the apartment.

"John, is that you?" my mother murmured.

"It's Poly. Sorry I woke you." I moved to her side and adjusted the afghan over her shoulders. She reached up and touched the charm that dangled around my neck.

"You took the bracelet apart?"

"No. Adelaide Brooks gave me this charm."

My mom sat up and blinked her eyes several times. She reached for her glasses, left upside down on the nightstand, and focused on the charm once she had them on. "I always wondered what became of that charm."

I pinched the medallion between my fingers. "What do you know about it?"

"Let's go downstairs."

I followed my mom down the carpeted hallway and down the stairs. She paused by a wall of taffeta and pulled the end of a bolt of seafoam green that changed color to amber in the sunlight. I'd always been mesmerized by how taffeta could appear to be two seemingly unrelated colors based on how the light hit it. I wondered if that's what I saw now: a situation that had two different sides that appeared to be unrelated.

My mom let the taffeta fall from her fingers. It floated down and covered the soft blue shade below it. "This place really is magical, isn't it?" she said softly. "I spent so much time in here, helping Millie run the store. Your father used to go on business trips before you were born and I'd come here and help out because it was better than sitting home alone. I still remember how Millie lit up when a new shipment would arrive."

"I thought they bought their fabrics on their trips?"

"The really spectacular fabrics, yes. But they also ordered from factories on the East Coast. This was before the Internet. She would talk to these men for hours, getting descriptions of their inventory. Occasionally something wouldn't be to her liking. But when something new, something special came in, she was like a little girl. It was so much fun to be around her! I think that's why people wanted to shop here. Some people came for the specialties, and others came for the company. More than a few times ladies would come in and have no idea what they were going to make. Millie would show them patterns, and she'd swirl around in her full skirts with her charm bracelet tinkling, and that would be it. She was so welcoming and gracious, women wanted to be like her. That was the secret of her success."

Mom ran her hand across the rose-pink washed silk that

hung on a roll next to the taffeta. Slubs of imperfections in the fabric made it rough and added to the beauty of the weave.

"Mom, you said something about this charm. What do you know about it?"

"Your father said he told you about the financial troubles at the store."

"He said Aunt Millie went to Mr. McMichael for help and didn't tell Uncle Marius."

"That was a hard thing for her to do, and ultimately it's what ended their friendship. Millie told me that rumors started about her and Vic. Marius was furious when he found out what she had done. She gave that charm to Vic as a way of thanking him and saying good-bye. She knew the friendship was over."

"She and Mr. McMichael didn't . . . ?"

Mom shook her head. "Millie was so in love with Marius, it was as if he'd hung the moon and the stars. Don't you think for a second that she would have violated that love. The only reason she went to Vic for help was because she didn't want them to lose the store. It represented their whole life together."

"That's why Uncle Marius could never let it go. Giving it up would mean letting go of their life together, but keeping it open would mean acknowledging that she wasn't there."

I turned around and took in the magnitude of the store. So much more than material made up Land of a Thousand Fabrics. Commitment, dedication, passion, and love were evident, too.

"Does the idea of staying in San Ladrón offer you something you've been missing?"

"Yes. From the first moment when I was here and Ken tried to rush me into signing away the store I knew I didn't want to do what he expected. And then I found Mr. Pickers's body by the Dumpster, and it didn't seem fair. Here's this old man who's lived here his whole life who got murdered behind the store. And I have to know why. It wasn't random, I know that much. If it were, my car wouldn't have been vandalized. I wouldn't have been trapped in a shower, or threatened at a bar, either. I'd probably be at home having— what day is it?"

My mom's eyes rolled up for a second. "Monday."

"I'd probably be at home having meatballs after a crappy day working for Giovanni. It would be just like any other Monday."

"Poly, listen to me. A man died, and that's a tragedy. And I'm sure it's difficult for you to process, especially since you found his body. But just because it happened on your property doesn't make it your job to find out who killed him."

"I told Dad I want to reopen the store. I mean it."

My mom tucked my hair behind my ear. "Millie and Marius would be proud."

It was ten minutes till five, and Deputy Sheriff Clark expected me to bring him a timetable of where I'd been for the past few days. I pulled my boots on and jogged down the winding metal staircase, ducking out the back of the store.

The sun had dropped considerably, dropping the temperature with it. I crossed my arms tightly to stay warm as I walked through the alley behind the store. The parking lot at the end of the street was vacant now. I passed the parking lot and walked behind the gas station, coming out on San Ladrón Avenue next to the Waverly House. I stood on the corner, staring at the Victorian mansion. The sign out front advertised it as the perfect place for wedding receptions and Sunday brunch. Another, smaller sign, closer to the sidewalk, announced an upcoming murder mystery weekend. I had always wanted to do that, but Carson had pooh-poohed the idea. Unsure as I was about the circumstances surrounding my time in San Ladrón, I felt like I'd been trapped in a play that had yet to be resolved.

I crossed the street and walked around to the side of the office, to the door where Deputy Sheriff Clark had let me in on my previous visit. I wrapped my knuckles against the glass a few times and waited. When there was no answer, I knocked harder.

"I'm over here," said a voice. I moved past the door to the parking lot under the carport. The deputy sheriff stood over the engine of one of the squad cars. The hood was propped up on a long metal arm. "You wouldn't happen to know anything about cars, would you?"

"Not really. Why?"

He pulled his sunglasses off and wiped the back of his arm across his forehead, then replaced his glasses and looked back at the engine. After shaking his head a couple of times, he pulled the arm out of the hood, laid it down in the track where I assumed it stayed, and closed the hood.

"My motor mounts are shot."

"I don't know what that means."

"See this metal thing? It holds the motor. There's a rubber cushion in the middle, gives the engine some give. Too many fast stops and starts, the rubber breaks, your engine just sits there. Whole car starts to shake."

"Can't you replace it?"

"Sure. I can replace this one, piece of cake. Only, you have to replace all of them at the same time. I'm not exactly sure how I'm going to get up underneath the car to get the one on the bottom."

"You have a mechanic across the street, you know."

"Who, Charlie? She's otherwise engaged at the moment."

I wanted to ask for details but didn't. I wasn't sure why we were standing by a police cruiser talking about motor mounts instead of going over my timetable, but I knew the reason I was there was to give information, not get it.

"Can we talk somewhere?" I asked.

"Sure. Follow me."

I dropped in line behind the deputy sheriff and sat across from his wooden desk. He stood by the coffee station, shaking powdered creamer into a small Styrofoam cup. I sat patiently, waiting for him to offer me my choice of beverages like the last time I had been here. He didn't.

After he finished stirring the clumps of powder around with a thin brown-and-white striped straw, he ran it through his lips and tossed the stirrer into the trash. The silence grew uncomfortable as I tried to figure out what I was supposed to say or do, until finally I couldn't take it anymore.

"I think there's a secret in the fabric store that someone doesn't want to come out," I said.

Deputy Sheriff Clark leaned back in his chair and folded his fingers behind his head. His eyes looked tired, but I could see the clarity in his stare.

"Interesting theory." The deputy sheriff took another pull on his coffee and set the cup down. I leaned forward and started to speak, but Officer Clark held up a hand to silence me.

"A couple of days ago you were sure this was about you. To be honest, it looked to me and a whole bunch of other people that you were working pretty hard at making yourself look like a victim."

"Why?"

"Because you kept crying wolf."

"No. Why would I want to make myself look like a victim? I inherited the store. Legitimately. When I said no to Mr. McMichael, that should have been the end of it. Maybe he'd be persistent and up his offer, that's what businessmen do. Meanwhile, someone tried to send me a message by vandalizing my car. And then Mr. Pickers was murdered behind the store. Now people are coming out of the woodwork trying to buy the place out from under me. The reason I'm at the middle of your investigation is because all of this stuff started happening since I showed up. I don't completely trust the McMichael family, but I'm starting to think this isn't their doing."

Clark raised his eyebrows and closed his eyes at the same time, nodding once, as though acknowledging that I'd made a point.

"You wanted a timetable of where I've been and what I've been doing? Here it is: I was trapped in Charlie's shower. I was threatened by construction workers when I went to talk to Duke. I went to see Mr. McMichael myself. If this is his way of hardballing me into selling the store, he's failing miserably."

"You didn't tell me you knew Duke."

"I met him yesterday. I stopped off at The Broadside Tavern. I thought maybe I'd learn something about Mr. Pickers."

"Before or after your gate was vandalized?"

"Before."

"Ms. Monroe, you aren't running an investigation here. I am. I should have you locked up for obstruction of justice." Clark picked up a yellow pencil from the side of his desk calendar and tapped the eraser end on the last Friday of the month. "Do you have anything else I need to know?"

I considered what I'd learned about Charlie and Vaughn's relationship. I knew it wasn't common knowledge, but I wasn't sure how uncommon it was.

"No," I finally said. I stood from the chair and shook Officer Clark's hand.

Outside, a crisp breeze blew my hair around. I wrapped my arms around myself and looked at the Waverly House. The majestic building beckoned me from across the street from the mobile sheriff unit, and a part of me wanted to walk right in, demand to see Adelaide Brooks, and lock her in an office until I got some answers. I took a deep breath for courage, exhaled, and crossed the street. A person stepped out from behind the carefully manicured shrubbery that lined the eastern property line of the historic building. Before I knew what was happening, a hand shot out and grabbed my forearm, pulling me into the foliage.

Twenty-six

"You're going to ruin everything for me," Charlie hissed.

"Let go of me," I said, shaking off her grip.

"Then stay still and shut up. They're about to leave and I don't want them to see me."

"Who's about to see you?"

"Vaughn and the old lady."

I followed Charlie's stare to the front steps of the Waverly House. Vaughn and Adelaide stood together. Her hand was on his upper arm. With one hand she reached up and pushed his hair off of his forehead, a maternal gesture that told me of their close relationship. I stole a glance at Charlie to see how she'd reacted. Her face looked stone-cold.

She was crouched down in the base of the shrubs, out of sight. Her heavy clumps of tangled, colorful hair were secured with a black rubber loop at the back of her head. When she'd pulled me back I'd landed on my butt. Moisture seeped through the seat of my jeans. I dug my heels into the ground and scooted backward until I was next to her.

"Why did you jump me?"

"Shhh," she hissed again, waving me quiet with a flapping hand. Her face was locked on the scene on the steps of the Waverly House. I wondered what was going through her mind. Vaughn and Adelaide hugged, and he turned away and walked the length of the sidewalk and turned to the left. Charlie didn't speak, didn't move. I could have called out to Vaughn if I thought I was in any danger, but I wasn't sure which one of them was more of a threat.

Charlie made a noise next to me. I turned to look at her. She blinked several times. I suspected she was fighting tears but already knew she'd deny it.

My mind buzzed with questions about Charlie. She clearly had anger issues with her birth parents, not only that, she could easily have vandalized my car and locked me in the shower.

"I haven't seen much of you today. Are you ever going to finish my car?" I asked, keeping my voice light.

"Tomorrow." She leaned forward, focused on the front door to the Waverly House. "Sometimes it's too much, hanging around this town where everybody's so proper, with their salon-styled hair and their afternoon tea. I don't belong here."

"Adelaide is your mom, isn't she?" I asked quietly.

She didn't answer.

"Charlie, I know. I got pulled over while driving your truck and I saw the name *McMichael* on the registration." I wasn't sure why I kept Vaughn's name out of it, but I wanted to hear what she had to say.

She turned on me. "Then you know what I know. My parents didn't want me. Do you have any idea what it's like, knowing you have two parents who wanted nothing to do with you? No, you don't, because you've lived a charmed life, Polyester."

"Whoa," I said, holding my hands up. "I don't know what's so charmed about losing a relative when I was in high school and being lied to about what happened." Even though I left out the references to being suspected of murder, it seemed Charlie had a pretty odd definition of *charmed*. "You're right, I don't know what you feel like. I don't know anything about your past. But sitting out here watching your family from under a shrub isn't doing anybody any good. I'd say you have two choices: get out of town and move on, or figure out a way to reconcile with your family."

"I found out Vic and Adelaide were my parents a long time ago. I've been living here for years and nobody ever had a clue."

"How'd you find out?" I asked.

"I spent my childhood in foster homes. I don't really remember anything before I was four. There were at least three sets of parents before I turned eighteen. That's when I went out on my own. Got a job with a mechanic in Encino. I kept showing up and just helping. I think he thought I was crazy. One day he asked if I wanted to learn about cars. I said yes and he taught me what he knew."

"So that's how you came to be a mechanic. How'd you come to be here in San Ladrón?"

"I remember telling him he was the father I never had. He asked about my real father and I told him I didn't know who he was. He asked if I wanted to know and I said I did. So he helped me figure out where the adoption agency was, we got into contact with the people who ran it, and I got my file."

"I'm surprised they let you have your file." Considering the distance Adelaide and Vic had put between themselves and Charlie, it seemed unusual that they would have left a paper trail that led back to them.

"It's not like I asked for it. I tracked them both to San

Ladrón and found out they'd been divorced for a while. Pretty much my whole life. Vaughn was around four when they split. They divorced while she was pregnant with me, and I guess that's why she gave me away. She didn't want any reminders of him."

She sat, staring at the Waverly House, silent. She pulled her knees up and started to rock back and forth. I didn't think she knew she was doing it. It was as if she was in a trance.

"Now everybody is going to know who I am and every-thing else is going to change."

I stood up, silent, wanting to hear what else she might say, afraid if I prompted her she'd snap out of it and re-member that I was there. I took another step back.

"Sooner or later, everybody's going to know what you did," she said, staring at the front door of the Victorian mansion.

"Who are you talking to?" I asked before I remembered I was trying to be silent.

Her head snapped up and she focused on me. Her eyes were dark. She let go of her legs and planted her right hand on the ground, and pushed herself up. "There's something I have to do," she said. "If you're smart, you'll forget you ever saw me here tonight."

I stood my ground, my adrenaline racing. I didn't want her to know I was afraid of her, even though a part of me was. She looked at the front doors of the Waverly House, turned and looked across the street at the mobile sheriff's unit, then trudged past me to the sidewalk and headed west—the opposite direction of her shop—on San Ladrón Avenue on foot.

I waited until she vanished from sight, somewhere about three blocks away. If she was planning to double back and be at the fabric store, then I was going to get there first and make sure the doors were locked. I spun around, my heel skidding on a patch of mud, headed the opposite direction to the corner, and turned right.

My parents were in the kitchen. My dad tossed the cross-word puzzle page from the newspaper on the small table that sat to my right. "Well, Helen, are you ready?"

"Ready for what?" I asked.

"To head back to Burbank."

"You're leaving me?"

"We both have to work tomorrow, and traffic from San Ladrón into Burbank tomorrow morning is going to be a bear," he said.

"Why don't you come with us?" my mom asked. "I'd feel better about you being with us than alone in this apartment. Your father can give you a ride back when your car is fixed."

He shot her a look.

"I'll be fine." I felt uncomfortable under her direct stare. "If things aren't any more settled by the end of the week, I'll sign Ken's paperwork and go back to Los Angeles."

"Do you think that's what we want you to do?" she asked.

"I don't know. Isn't it?"

"We want you to do what you want to do. Follow your heart. That's what Uncle Marius would have wanted."

I followed my parents down the hallway to the living room. My mom ducked under the long leather strap of her black handbag, wearing it cross-body style like me. She draped a scarf around her neck and scratched the tabby kitten's head.

The three of us headed down the stairs, through the store, and out the back door. The sun was dropping and the shadows were long. My dad's car was in the vacant lot at the end of the alley. I hugged them both when we reached it and promised I'd be careful. After my mom's parting words, which may have been about a haircut, I stepped away from the car and waved. I stood at the edge of the parking lot, staring at their receding taillights. They'd be back, I knew. I knew they'd be back because I knew I wasn't going to leave.

That meant I had two phone calls to make. I weighed the

words I would say to Carson when he answered. If he answered. As much as I didn't feel like getting into a thing with him, I knew there was something that had to be said.

"It's about time you called. Where are you? Do you want me to start dinner?"

"No, Carson—well, you can start dinner, but make it dinner for one. I'm still in San Ladrón." The other end of the phone was silent for a few seconds. "Carson? Are you there?"

"I'm here. You're there. Let's make this work for us. I called McVic after your meeting. Figured I'd do damage control. Here's what I found out: he wants the store. Badly. He's already lined up a couple of interested businesses, and I'm not talking mom-and-pop shops. Think big. Bull's-eye big. If you give me the go-ahead, I'll cut a deal with him. We can make a decent profit and you can leave your job if that's what you really want. Is that what you want?"

"No."

"I'm trying to meet you halfway here, Poly. I don't get your sudden interest in real estate, but let me help you with this. It's what I do best."

"That's not what I meant, Carson. I don't want to quit my job. I mean, I do want to quit my job, but only because I want to stay here and run the fabric store."

"I know the way I left wasn't good. I'm sorry about that— I shouldn't have gotten angry, so if this is about punishing me, putting me in my place and teaching me a lesson about your independence, then I get it. I love you, Poly. I didn't know you could be like this and it's a little bit exciting, I have to admit. But come home, honey, and we'll work this out. I'll be here waiting for you when you're ready for me."

I took a deep breath. "Carson, I don't think I'm ever going to be ready for you."

"I don't accept that, Poly. We're too good for each other, like yin and yang. I'm not going to let you go."

"Good-bye, Carson." I hung up the phone.

I thumbed through the contacts and called Giovanni's home number. If he was still at To The Nines, he'd be mad. Mad because I hadn't been there to put out fires and maintain productivity. Mad because he'd had to work for a change.

I pressed dial before I lost my nerve. He answered on the seventh ring.

"Poly? Jeez. You picked a heck of a time to have a family crisis. I'm going to need you at the workroom at seven tomorrow morning. The sewers need to see you working hard for me so they work harder for me. Got that?"

"I'm not going to make it to the workroom tomorrow, Giovanni."

"Where are you?"

"I'm still in San Ladrón."

"I don't remember approving an extended leave for you."

"You didn't."

I heard him grunt, and then cough twice, then clear his throat "This little fabric-store situation better be worth it. That's why you're still there, right? You're going through the inventory, figuring out what's salvageable? Your boyfriend should have told me you were going to be guarding the place instead of working here. Every day you're not here, I'm losing money. I'll give you today, but starting tomorrow I'm going to dock your pay for every hour you're gone. If you're not back by the weekend, you'll be paying me to have a job."

"I'll save us both the effort, Giovanni. I quit."

I pulled the phone away from my head and pressed the end call button. I turned around and chucked my already broken phone down the length of the parking lot. It landed a few feet past an ivory gift box that was propped against the back door to the fabric store. A creamy off-white ribbon was tied around the box. Both the box and the ribbon were familiar.

I grew wary. We hadn't locked the back door when we left and now, it seemed, I'd had a visitor. I looked up and down the alley for signs that I wasn't alone. Nothing. I crept past the store and picked up my phone. The glass broke apart into small, pebble-sized pieces. A couple of them fell out and landed in the gravel. The display of the phone was frozen on my home page.

Behind me, I heard a sound. I turned around and saw the toe of a sneaker by the back of the Dumpster. I fisted my keys. As I crept closer, I recognized the sneakers. Stan Smiths.

"You can stop hiding, Vaughn, I know it's you," I called out.

I stood in the middle of the lot, between the trash receptacle and the back door of the store. Vaughn stepped out from behind the Dumpster and stood to the side of it. There were dark circles under his eyes and his hair was messier than when I'd talked to him at the donut shop. If I trusted him more, I might have asked if he wanted to talk about what had been going on, but I didn't, so I didn't.

"Before you accuse me of spying on you or threaten to call the police and report me for trespassing, I just wanted to give you that." He pointed to the ivory box that was propped by the back door. "I've been driving around with it in my car since yesterday. It'll answer at least one of your questions about me."

I turned away from him and approached the back door. Before I reached it, Vaughn called, "Poly, watch out!"

I felt his arms around me, pulling me backward. I stumbled and stepped on his foot. A heavy bolt of thick decorator fabric fell from the roof and landed on the ivory box, crushing it.

Twenty-seven

The bolt of fabric, an almost-full roll of thick ivory damask wound tightly around a cardboard cylinder, probably weighed about twenty pounds. Had I been standing by the back door when it fell, I'd be looking at a bunch of little stars instead of a cloud of dust and a crushed gift box. I pulled away from Vaughn and looked up at the roof of the building, searching for an explanation where there was none. I crept closer to the fabric on the ground and looked at it from the side. A small, rubber-coated dumbbell had been jammed inside the cardboard core on the left side. I walked to the right side and found a matching dumbbell. Someone had weighted down the roll so it would do even more damage.

I needed to call the police. I knew the only way that bolt of fabric could be on the roof of the store, positioned to fall on me, was if someone went inside and carried it up there. Which meant someone might still be inside.

Or, that someone might be the person who had set the

ivory box by my back door, knowing I'd hesitate before walking inside.

I turned on Vaughn. His back was to me and he was on his phone. "Yes, the fabric store. Just now. I'll wait with her. No. No, I don't think so. No. Definitely not." He hung up and pushed his phone into his back pocket, then approached the bolt of damask.

"Who did you call?"

"The police."

"Then I don't think you should touch anything."

He pulled the crushed box out from under the bolt of fabric and walked it over to me. "You know that I put this here. I know that I put this here. And somebody else knows that I put this here. I will happily tell Deputy Sheriff Clark about it when he arrives, but for reasons I don't want to get into right now, I'd rather it not get carried away like evidence."

"What is it?"

"A mistake."

"Why, because you thought I'd pick it up and stand by the back door to open it and get knocked out by a bolt of fabric? Was that your plan?"

He ran his hand over his forehead, pushing his hair back. "You have no idea what you're talking about."

Before I had a chance to respond, the blue and red lights of a police car hijacked our attention. Deputy Sheriff Clark pulled into the parking lot and got out of the car. He nodded at me first, then Vaughn, and then walked past both of us to the bolt of fabric. He squatted by the end of it and stared at the five-pound dumbbells that had been shoved inside the cardboard tube. He looked up at the door, then back at the bolt, then at me.

"Tell me what happened."

Vaughn and I started talking at the same time and the deputy sheriff held his hand up to Vaughn. "I want to hear from Ms. Monroe."

"My parents just left. I walked them to their car, and when I came back I saw—" I looked at the box that Vaughn held, "I saw that box propped up against the back door."

"Why isn't it propped up there now?"

"I pulled it out from under the fabric," Vaughn said.

"What is it?"

"It's a gift for Poly." Vaughn turned red. "I didn't want it to get any more damaged than it might be."

Clark took the box from Vaughn. He slid the ribbon off and lifted the lid. I tried to look over his shoulder but only saw white tissue paper. Clark closed the box and handed it back to Vaughn. "What happened next, Ms. Monroe?"

"When I saw the box, I realized someone had been here in the short amount of time that I'd walked my parents to their car. I couldn't remember if any of us had locked the back door, so I looked around for signs that I wasn't alone. I saw Vaughn's sneaker sticking out behind the Dumpster."

"How did you know it was me?"

"I recognized your Stan Smiths."

"I'm not the only person in this town to wear Stan Smiths," he said under his breath.

"You probably are."

"When you two are done discussing footwear, can we get back to my questions?" Clark said, a hint of irritation in his voice.

"Sorry," Vaughn and I said at the same time.

"I told him I knew he was there and he came out. He said he wanted to give me the box. When I walked over to pick it up, the bolt of fabric fell from the roof."

"That's not exactly what happened," Vaughn interjected.

"You'll have your turn, Mr. McMichael," Deputy Sheriff Clark said.

I looked back and forth between their faces. As far as I could remember, this was the first time the deputy sheriff had called Vaughn by his surname. I knew that was protocol, but in a town as small as San Ladrón, things were more relaxed. This felt like it meant something, only I didn't know what.

"What else, Ms. Monroe?"

"That's pretty much it."

"What would you like to add?" he asked Vaughn.

"I didn't expect her to come back so quickly. I put the box by the back door. When I saw her turn around I ducked behind the Dumpster. I thought she'd pick up the box and carry it inside and I could leave."

"But you didn't."

"She said she saw me, so I came out. I noticed something out of the corner of my eye right before the fabric fell. I pulled her out of the way so she wouldn't get hurt."

Deputy Sheriff Clark made notes in a small notepad. He walked over to the fabric bolt again, this time on the other side. The dumbbell hadn't been packed as well and it had jarred loose from the tube. He stuck the end of his pen into the cardboard and tried to lift the fabric, but it was too heavy to budge with such a minor effort. He put his head close to the roll and aimed the beam of a small flashlight inside the tube. Before I could figure out what he was doing, Vaughn touched my arm and spoke.

"I know you don't want to hear this, but I think you're in over your head," Vaughn said.

I turned to face him. "You know what I think? I think your family is afraid of what I might find out. So what if the McMichaels have deep roots and deep pockets? Your family has been keeping secrets—from the world and from each other. Did you know your father tried to buy out the deed on the fabric store just like he tried to buy out Charlie? He thought his money made him better than Uncle Marius, but it didn't."

Vaughn handed me the now-crushed ivory box and walked toward the curb. I watched his back as he left.

Despite his stance that the box was a present for me, it felt more like a nuisance than a gift. Vaughn disappeared around the corner and I turned back to Deputy Sheriff Clark.

"Do you think he did this?" Clark asked, jutting his chin out toward Vaughn.

"He could have. He was here when I came back from saying good-bye to my parents. He was hiding. I don't know how he got into the store and got a bolt of fabric up to the roof, but he seemed to know it was going to happen. Maybe the goal was never to hurt me. Maybe the goal was to pull me out of the way all along, you know, so he looked like the good guy."

"Let me show you something."

Deputy Sheriff Clark gestured for me to approach the bolt of fabric. I walked to the left side of the tube where he squatted. With the click side of his pen, he lifted a small white tag that was attached to a piece of string that was tied around the roll. The tag said *Threads* in red ink, slightly lighter over the end of *decorators*, as if it had been done with a stamp and equal pressure hadn't been applied to the process. Under the imprint, in handwriting, it said *$12. 99/yd*.

"Does that look familiar to you?"

"No."

"Have you had a chance to look at the inventory in the store? Do you know how they're tagged?"

"I've looked at a couple. My aunt had a list of prices in a journal by the register. There are signs around the store, and the more mainstream bolts of fabric—the calicos, ging-hams, florals, and other basics—all come with the price printed on the end of the bolt. I've never seen a tag like this."

"Have you ever heard of Threads?"

"Sure. They're based out of Los Angeles. It's a giant warehouse filled with partially used fabrics, mostly the kind people would use to make curtains or bedspreads, or re-cover sofas."

"Is it possible Millie or Marius bought inventory from them to stock the store?"

"No way. Five years ago they were called Wholesale Decorators. They changed the name a few years after I started working for To The Nines. I only remember because they changed their focus and we weren't able to get cheap dress fabric from them anymore. Giovanni, my boss, wasn't happy. I don't think he ever paid the last three invoices that came under the Wholesale Decorators name because he figured the new owners wouldn't notice."

Deputy Sheriff Clark stood slowly. "I'd like to take a look at the fabrics inside."

"Sure." I yanked on the door, still not sure if it was locked or unlocked. The door didn't budge, and I realized my earlier fears about Vaughn possibly getting in were unfounded. I fumbled with the keys until I found the ones that unlocked the two locks, and then pulled the door open and let Clark enter before me. I hit the light switch on the wall and nothing happened. I clicked it up and down a few times. When the result remained the same, I checked the breakers. One had blown. I flipped it back to on and the store became bright.

"First time that happened," I said, and rejoined Clark by the wrap stand. I set the crushed ivory box on top of the counter.

"Can you show me the decorator fabrics?" he asked.

"Follow me." I led Deputy Sheriff Clark to the front right corner of the store, where large rolls of damask and tapestry lay on their sides, stacked by color. One table held shades of blue, green, and purple. Another held red, orange, yellow, A third held the neutrals: ivory, camel, brown, taupe. A full bolt of damask not unlike the one outside sat next to a collection of toile. Again, I thought of a French bakery, and how a couple of yards of fabric could help Genevieve re-envision her shop in the style she wanted.

"I don't know fabric like you know fabric, but that looks like what we saw outside, doesn't it?" He pointed to the damask.

"It looks like it, but it isn't the same. This one is silk and cotton. The one outside has a synthetic blend. It's a cheaper fabric."

"How can you tell?"

"From the way it feels."

He looked like he didn't believe me.

"I grew up in this world. I played with these fabrics. You can blindfold me and I can tell the difference between a silk/linen blend and a cotton/linen blend, the same way a sommelier can tell the difference between a cabernet/merlot blend and a cabernet/shiraz. Different people can do different things. That's what I do."

"I thought you designed prom dresses?"

I didn't defend my job or offer an excuse for why I did what I did. I knew why I'd taken that job. Security. And there was nothing wrong with security, only, since I'd arrived in San Ladrón I'd felt the polar opposite of security and discovered it made me feel alive.

"That bolt of fabric outside, where did it come from?"

"Up."

"The roof?"

"Maybe."

"Have you been to the roof since you've been here?"

"No. I wouldn't know how to get on the roof."

"Ms. Monroe, I'd like to take a look upstairs inside your apartment."

"Follow me." Halfway up the stairs I stopped and turned to him. "Watch out for the kittens."

I turned the knob on the front door and it swung open easily. I stood back and let the deputy sheriff enter. "I'm guessing you want to go to the kitchen."

"Why's that?"

"It's the room above the back door to the fabric store."

"Lead the way."

I wasn't sure what I expected to find when we reached the kitchen. An open window? Evidence that someone had pushed a bolt of fabric out of a narrow opening in the hopes of clobbering me? Or something worse? But when we arrived in the small room, I saw the empty juice glass I'd drunk from earlier and the kittens, who swatted at water that dripped from the faucet. The window was shut, and the collection of Spritzdekor pitchers that lined the shelf were untouched.

Deputy Sheriff Clark looked around the room. "Is this how you left it?"

"With the exception of the kittens, yes."

He nodded and looked around again, as if he was making a video recording of the interior with his memory. "Attic?"

"Pull-down stairs in the hallway."

He turned around and left. I stroked the tabby kitten and stared out the back window. I hadn't spent much time in the kitchen and didn't realize I could see the Waverly House from this vantage point. I turned to the left and watched a couple of cars drive down a side street. Men in hard hats and construction vests packed orange pylons into the back of a pickup truck, between a bucket filled with rope and a ladder. I recognized one of the men—the one in the red-and-black buffalo checked shirt and faded denim vest.

"Deputy Sheriff Clark—" I called out. I set the kitten down and ran to the hallway. The stairs were extended, and Clark's feet were visible on the second rung from the top. He climbed back down and looked at me. "I just saw a bunch of construction workers pack up a truck. They had a ladder. I recognized one from The Broadside. I saw him yesterday. Didn't you say those guys were responsible for the ketchup on the gate?"

He folded up the stairs and went back to the kitchen. "You sure it was the same guy?"

"Yes." I pointed to the road. "Wasn't there some construction around here?"

He nodded. "Duke's having his roof shingled."

"So whoever was doing the work on Duke's roof would have had the ability to get up on my roof. Right?"

"I'll check it out." He pulled his hat off and scratched his head, then replaced the hat unintentionally askew. "Ms. Monroe, are you planning to stay here tonight?"

I nodded.

"You wouldn't rather go to a hotel?"

"I'll be fine. I have the kittens to protect me."

"I want you to call me if anything happens."

I walked him to the back door and locked both locks after he was gone. If anyone came to find me, I didn't want to hear them. Now that Officer Clark had looked inside the ivory box from Vaughn, my feelings about the contents had morphed from nuisance to ambivalence to curiosity. I carried it upstairs and set it on the bed. I carried the kittens into the bedroom with me, pulled off my riding boots, wiggled my toes, and tipped my head back, rolling it from side to side to work out the kinks in my neck.

I moved the pile of ivory ribbon to the comforter. The gray kitten pounced on the frayed edge, flopped onto his side, and pulled it to his mouth. He chewed on it and shook his head when it hit him in the face. I pulled the ribbon from around the box and dangled it above him, then dangled the other end in front of the tabby. He swatted at me and tiny claws scraped my hand like the pins and needles in the box in the wrap stand where I'd found the hidden coin. I pulled my hand away, above them both, and slowly lowered it to pet each on the head. "Pins and Needles. I think I just found your names," I told them.

I turned back to the box and removed the lid. White tissue

paper fluttered up with the lid. I wondered if the McMichael family bought ivory boxes and white tissue paper in bulk. Inside the layers of tissue was something made of champagne silk. I flipped both layers of paper back and reached inside. It was a dress.

But it wasn't just any dress. It was the dress I'd sketched in the back of the turquoise journal from the wrap stand. I lifted it by the beaded shoulders. The beadwork was exquisite, exactly as I'd sketched it. Spirals of clear bugle beads covered each shoulder by the sweetheart neckline, right above cap sleeves. The champagne silk wrapped to one side and fell in a long cascade to the floor, pooling on the rose-colored Oriental rug.

I looked back inside the box and found a thick white envelope with my name on it. I set the dress on the bed, and then changed my mind and set it back in the box so the kittens couldn't mistake it for a play toy. I pulled the sheet of paper out of the envelope.

Dear Poly,

I found your sketch the night we had our Waverly House dinner in your store. My mother knows a seamstress who works out of a house a few blocks behind Bonita. I hope you don't mind that I had it made up as a surprise for you. If you ever decide you want to wear something other than black, you now have a dress.

Sincerely,
Vaughn

I set the card on top of the dress. I didn't want to feel the warm, cozy sensation that radiated from the center of my chest, through my arms, to my fingertips, leaving them tingling, but I did. I wanted to be angry at Vaughn. From the first moment I'd met him, in the back room of the fabric store, I'd wanted to find a reason to dislike him. If talking to Carson had been hard, then acknowledging the generosity of Vaughn's gesture, after accusing him of attempted assault, was going to be darn near impossible.

I picked up the card and read it again, then turned it over. There was a postscript on the back.

PS: While I would have liked to use fabric from your store, there was no way to do so without spoiling the surprise. This fabric came from a store in the Los Angeles garment district.

Twenty-eight

I dropped the card and it floated to the floor a second time. It caught on the side of the duvet cover and hung by one corner, like a leaf stuck to the hem of a dress. I stepped backward and thought about what it might mean. Vaughn had been to a fabric store in Los Angeles since he'd met me. He could have bought the damask.

I sank onto the bed. What did I really know here? Someone wanted me gone from San Ladrón. For a variety of reasons, it could be anybody. It could be Carson, who wanted me to come home, but I knew he wasn't responsible for the murder. It could be Mr. McMichael, who wanted me to sell the store. It could be Charlie, who had secret ties to the McMichael family, or Ken, who wanted his commission, or the bullies at Dukes. For all I knew, the Senior Patrol had rivals and Mr. Pickers was a casualty of *West Side Story: Senior Edition*. I couldn't afford to keep guessing at random. I had to figure out who had the most to lose by me keeping the store, and what Mr. Pickers knew that had made him a victim in the whole situation.

I could go through the apartment, but the murder didn't have anything to do with the apartment. It had to do with the store. And while I'd thoroughly cleaned the store, swept years of dust and neglect into countless piles of dust bunnies, there was one place I'd left relatively untouched. The closed-off room where Aunt Millie had been murdered.

The only time I'd gone back into the room after that first day when I'd met with Ken was when I was looking for the tabby kitten, who I now called Needles. I'd been creeped out by being there, and I'd been distracted by my fight with Carson, and after the kitten had run farther into the darkness of that area, I'd set out the can of cat food and thought I'd revisit him in the morning. The vandalism had changed my priorities.

Was it possible someone knew I was back there, that the vandalism had been a distraction so I wouldn't explore that room too much?

I grabbed the flashlight from the dresser and scampered downstairs in my stocking feet. The two thousand candle watts sliced through the darkness. After I hit the light switch I turned off the flashlight but carried it with me to the door that separated me from the back room.

I pushed the door open. To the left of me were the bookcases—white laminate, filled with plastic tubs of trim, buttons, snaps, tassels, and more. Each tub was labeled with Aunt Millie's handwriting on a white index card that had been taped to the plastic with clear packing tape. The edges of the index cards that extended past the tape had turned yellow, but under the tape the cards were still white. Straight ahead of me was a bin that held large bolts of decorator fabric like the ones out front. I trained the flashlight on the outline and, unlike the first time I was back there, I really looked at it. That was it. That was where she had died. In this back room.

My dad told me that Mr. Pickers had found my uncle next to her body. That meant at a time shortly after the murder, Mr. Pickers had been in this room.

Of course. Mr. Pickers had seen something. He knew something. But what?

My dad told me Mr. Pickers had been drinking pretty heavily that time. He'd said the only reason he went into the store was because he'd seen something the night before—a monster?—and he'd come back in the morning to check it out. People had dismissed his story as that of a drunk. But he'd been right. Something had happened at the store the night before. And he'd been the one to comfort my uncle the next morning. Maybe, just maybe there was a different reason he'd paid special attention to this part of the street. And maybe someone knew Mr. Pickers's story wasn't the hallucination of a man who'd had one too many glasses of bourbon.

I struggled to pick up a bolt of cotton from the floor. It was too heavy for me to put back on the table, so I dragged it to the wall and propped it between rolls of navy-blue and powder-blue silk that guarded the perimeter like sentries. The stiffness of the cotton was at odds with the delicate nature of the silk, but the shade of blue complemented the other two colors. Together, the three colors reminded me of the ocean.

I moved the flashlight over the rest of the fabrics, at least ten different shades of silk. I moved closer and looked at the labels. *Rare—from Germany*, said the sign that hung over the stock.

That's odd. Germany wasn't known for its rare silks. Silks came from exotic locals like India and Thailand. Not that it couldn't have come from Germany, or that my aunt and uncle couldn't have discovered it in an unusual fabric district on one of their trips, but still, it seemed off.

I noticed a small gold disc on the floor under the bolt of blue cotton. Another charm? I scooped it up and looked at

it. No, it was a button. I studied the elaborate *W* at the center
of it—the logo from Ken's blue blazer. It must have fallen
the day I'd first met him here. I put it in my back pocket to
give to him later.

But Ken hadn't been back here that first day. And if he
hadn't been back here that day, then when had he been back
here? And why?

To look for the bracelet.

I pushed the button in my pocket and searched my recent
memory for questions that fit this answer. All along I'd
thought of Ken as my friend. We'd known each other since
high school. His wife had invited me over for dinner.

But Ken had been responsible for the utilities being on.
He had a set of keys to the store. He had access to my car,
he'd been here when I found Mr. Pickers, he had warned me
about being friendly with Charlie, and he was one of Carson's investors.

And he'd been pressuring me to sell from the minute I'd
arrived.

I heard a sound from the store behind me. I spun around,
the flashlight beam bouncing off of walls and fixtures. Spools
of ribbon lined these shelves. Some were velvet, others were
beaded. An entire row was filled with fringe in every color,
from cotton ball white to peacock blue to coal black. But
spools of thread and fringe were of little consolation.

A figure in a black, zip-front sweatshirt with the hood
drawn into a tight fit around his head stood in front of me.
Backlit by light from the store, his torso was distorted like
a villain in a comic book. I stepped back, away from him.

"I know it's you, Ken. I just don't know why."

"You should have taken the offer, Poly. None of this
would have happened if you'd taken the offer," he said.

"You wanted me to sell the store so badly you killed Mr.
Pickers to scare me off? To give me a reason to sell?" I

asked. "What kind of commission did you think you'd get from the sale?"

"It's not commission I'm after. It's closure. Ten years of closure. Ten years of living with a secret. Tom Pickers saw me ten years ago. He's the only person who could place me here. Nobody listened to him. Crazy old man telling stories about a monster in black robes."

"You had ten years to get closure. Why now?"

"As long as your uncle kept this place boarded up, I was safe. Nobody knew what was in here. And nobody believed Pickers anyway. Then you came along. I thought you'd sign some paperwork and get out of my hair, but you didn't. You got ideas about reopening the store. If you started asking around, people would have talked to you. Pickers would have talked to you."

"And told me what? I've read his account of what happened. This whole town has."

"This town was willing to write him off as a drunk. But you—you wanted something to believe in. If he told you what he saw the night the store was robbed, you would have figured it out."

"You couldn't have been here the night the store was robbed. It was our graduation ceremony. There wasn't time. Once the ceremony was over we had half an hour to change and get to the dance. You were there. I remember. Everybody else was in a suit and tie, but you wore your football uniform under your gown," I said. The details of that night stood out like glow-in-the-dark craft paint on black velvet. I'd played them over and over in my head because that was the night my aunt had been murdered.

Ken advanced toward me. "That silly old man, keeping an eye on this store for all of these years. Telling everybody about his drunken hallucinations. I got away with it, too. Half this town still thinks Vic McMichael was behind the robbery. If I could have sold him the store when your uncle died, those rumors would be as good as cast into metal. He would have been paying me in more ways than he ever could have known."

A fire ignited my chest and a patchwork of memories came together the way pattern pieces formed a jacket. "Why, Ken? I have a right to know what happened."

"You have no rights. Nothing. If you'd have gone along with my plan, if you'd have sold the store and gone back to Los Angeles, things might be different. Tom Pickers would be alive today and you'd be alive tomorrow," Ken said. Black gloves covered his hands, a combination of Lycra and rubber, with a Velcro band around the wrist. "But this way works, too." He flexed his hands once, twice, and advanced toward me.

I looked at his hands closing and opening into fists. I stepped backward and stumbled when my foot hit the base of the wooden fabric bin. I stepped to the left. Ken came closer but stopped two steps away from me and laughed. I listened for sounds from outside the store—sirens or voices—but if they were there, the doors that blocked us from the outside world would keep them a secret. I was alone. With a killer.

"Some kids get cars when they graduate. Some get a watch. First day of senior year my dad offered me half of the real estate agency. I'd been working with him after school for a year. I knew I'd make peanuts on the kinds of starter houses around San Ladrón. I also knew the value of this building. I knew if I could cause a string of bad luck here, your aunt and uncle would either sell or the store would go bankrupt. Vic McMichael owned half of the street by then. I knew how valuable this property was before they gave me my diploma."

"But we were friends, Ken. You used to come to the store when I worked here on weekends. What happened?"

"You're right, I did. That's when I first heard your aunt and uncle talking about money being tight. I asked my dad about this stretch of property and he said he had a buyer interested in the whole strip. I went through his office and found the file. Vic McMichael had been buying up property on this strip for years. Once he owned the block, he'd stand to make a lot of money in the sale."

"He didn't own the whole strip then."

"No, he didn't." He chuckled. "A couple of other people wanted to hold on to their properties. Until the robbery. That changed a lot of minds." A smile took over Ken's face. "I didn't know which store I was going to hit first. I came here to figure out how to get your family to sell. When I heard them planning the big sale for our graduation weekend, I knew I had a perfect opportunity. All that cash in the register. Plus it would shake up the other stores on the street. They'd think it could have been any one of them."

I searched my mind for memories of that night. "We had a half day of school and then we went straight to the ceremony. The dance was that night. There wasn't time."

"Sports teams had photo ceremonies during the break."

"That's why you wore your football uniform under your graduation robe. You're the monster Mr. Pickers saw," I said. I felt cold and sick, my stomach twisted into a knot at the idea that the man in front of me had murdered my aunt and then shown up at a graduation dance and pretended to be my friend.

Ken wiped his nose with the back of his sleeve. "She wasn't supposed to be here. I hired those two thugs to rob the place. I told them it would be empty. But at our graduation ceremony when I asked you where your aunt was, you told me she stayed behind at the store. I had to get her out of the picture or everything would have fallen apart. I didn't have a choice. I cut out after the ceremonies and came here."

"The robbers said nobody was at the store."

"That's because I got to her first. I didn't plan to kill her. I wanted to scare her. But then I remembered that bracelet she always wore. When I demanded it, she said it was hidden someplace I'd never find it. That's when I hit her. If I hadn't had to get back to graduation, I could have searched the place and gotten her body out of the store but there wasn't time. I dragged her behind one of these fixtures and left."

He stepped toward me and I moved to the left. I reached a hand out for balance. My hands were on the edge of the wooden bin of fabric, guiding me along like a tentative ballerina might rely on a barre for balance. A splinter of wood from the fixture cut my thumb. I choked back a curse and kept moving.

"You killed Mr. Pickers because you were afraid he'd remember you?"

"The day you arrived, when I saw him on the street, I knew he was going to tell you what he remembered about that night. He's been watching this store for ten years hoping to understand what he saw. You might have figured it out then, I don't know. I couldn't give him the chance to talk to you. Mr. Pickers was an old man. When he died, what he saw would have died with him. His murder should have scared you off. You were supposed to want to sell, to get away from this store that's tainted with murder. You weren't supposed to stick around and start asking questions."

"If you wanted me to leave town, why did you damage my car so I couldn't leave?"

He shook his head. "I've got friends in very low places, Poly. I told them to make trouble for you and make sure it didn't come back to me. I couldn't believe they vandalized your car. You were supposed to be gone and they gave you a reason to stay."

"What about Charlie's shower?"

"A warning."

"And the bolt of fabric that almost fell on me outside the door?"

"Nice bit of poetry with that, don't you think? Good thing Duke's having his roof worked on. The truck with the ladder was already in your neighborhood. Cost me a couple hundred to get them to do the job."

"That could have killed me!"

"Would have saved me the effort."

"You're crazy, Ken. You aren't going to get away with any of this. The police are on their way."

I shuffled to the left, inches at a time. I had to get past him and out the door. The door was open and if I could get out of the back room, I could get to the back door, to the alley or the street. To a place where someone could hear me scream.

My eyes darted behind him, looking for something to fight him off. I was no match for him without a weapon. The wall of ribbon was too far. The bins of snaps and trim would do no damage. The scissors were in the wrap stand out front. It was me and Ken and a wall full of fabric.

He moved quickly. His gloved hands gripped the side of the bin and he peered into the corner. I spun around and grabbed the closest roll of fabric and swung it like a caveman clubbing a wildebeest. It struck Ken on the back. He bent forward over the bin. I watched his broad shoulders rise and fall.

I didn't give him a chance to gain his wits or breath. I swung the tube of fabric low at the back of his knees. His legs bent and he dropped, hitting his chin on the edge of the wooden fixture as he fell. He cursed. I ran past him to the door. His hand reached out and grabbed a fistful of my sweatshirt. My stockinged feet gained no traction against the exposed concrete floor and I propelled forward, my feet shooting out behind me. I landed on the ground. Ken yanked my sweatshirt backward. I fumbled for the zipper pull.

When I found it, I unzipped the sweatshirt and threw my shoulders back. The sweatshirt stayed behind in Ken's grip. I raced out the door and slammed it shut, threading the padlock through the hinge with shaking fingers. Seconds later I stumbled out the back. I made it to the end of the alley before my legs gave out from under me and I collapsed onto the gravel.

Twenty-nine

I opened my eyes and tensed. My head was in Vaughn's lap. His hand stroked my forehead. I tried to sit up.

"Don't move. It's okay. Deputy Sheriff Clark is on his way."

"But he doesn't know—"

"I called him when I found you."

"Where?"

"Right where you are."

"What are you doing here?"

"Charlie was waiting for me when I got home. She was pretty shaken up. I stayed with her until she calmed down. Truth is, I was mad at you for telling her you knew when I asked you not to."

"You came back to pick a fight with me?"

"Yes." A breeze ruffled Vaughn's hair. He shivered in his white crew-neck T-shirt. I tipped my chin and saw his navy-blue peacoat draped over me. I closed my eyes. It hadn't been a dream. It had been real. I'd gotten away. But that meant that Ken hadn't. I didn't know how much time he had in that sealed room, but I knew it wouldn't be forever. I looked back at Vaughn.

"We have to get into the fabric store."

"I don't think it's a good idea for you to move."

"I'm fine."

"No, you're not."

I turned away from him and stuck my hand out onto the ground for leverage. Blood spidered over my thumb and palm. My arm was bare. I picked up his coat and peeked underneath at my black bra. Without thinking, I glanced at Vaughn.

"At least you're consistent," he said with a smile.

Sirens blared from the street. Two police cars turned into the parking lot behind the store, followed by an ambulance. Deputy Sheriff Clark slammed the door to his car and approached me. This time when I tried to stand up, Vaughn helped. I fed my arms through the sleeves of his coat and buttoned enough of the navy-blue anchor buttons to keep the coat from opening.

"Ms. Monroe, what's this all about?" Clark asked.

"He's in the store."

"Who?"

"Ken. Ken Watts."

I felt the heat of Vaughn's stare against the side of my face, but I didn't have time to answer his questions now. "He's locked in the back room. The keys are on the corner of the wrap stand. You have to hurry."

Clark didn't wait for an explanation. He instructed one officer to wait outside with me while he and another officer entered the store. I heard the keys jangle against each other. I heard the pop of the lock opening. And then I heard nothing.

I pulled away from Vaughn and went inside. For the second time that day I threw the breaker, flooding the store in light. Beyond the wrap stand, two officers stood by the door to the partition. I approached them. "Is he alive?" I asked the officer closer to me.

He looked startled at the sound of my voice. "Who let you back here?"

"This is my store. I'm the one—" I looked around the door frame, into the room. Ken's body was on a stretcher. Blood stained the front of his shirt. His nose must have broken when he hit his face on the side of the wooden bin of fabric, right after I swung the bolt of fabric against the back of his knees. My sweatshirt was still clutched in his fist.

Deputy Sheriff Clark directed the men to take Ken to the ambulance. His eyes connected with mine as he passed. "I didn't expect you to put up a fight, either," he said.

Sheriff Clark stood next to the wooden fixture. His head was tipped back, his stare affixed on the window frame. "I'm going to need a statement about what happened here, Ms. Monroe."

"I know." I looked around at the room. The bolts of fabric that had lined the wall had fallen down like dominoes. I picked up the tube of cotton that I'd used to defend myself against Ken. The thin white ribbons tied around the ends had come loose and the fabric had unraveled. I stepped backward, away from the wooden fixture, carrying it underhanded. My ankle twisted and I fell backward. I landed on my tush. The cotton landed by my legs and unrolled across the floor. It hit one of Vaughn's white Stan Smiths.

I told Deputy Sheriff Clark what had happened: Ken trapping me in the back portion of the store and threatening to kill me. I told him about Ken's confession to the murder of Mr. Pickers. I told him how Ken had left our high school graduation, murdered my aunt, and returned with his football uniform under his graduation gown—the silhouette that had caused Mr. Pickers to think he saw a monster. I suspected more details would come to me in time but already

I felt my mind pushing them away, not wanting to face the truths I'd learned in the past hour.

"Ms. Monroe, do you have plans to leave San Ladrón before tomorrow?"

"No."

"I'd like to advise you to stay someplace else tonight."

"Stay at the Waverly House. I'll arrange it. It's the least I can do," Vaughn said.

"But—"

"I insist."

"Fine."

"I'll be in touch, Ms. Monroe," the deputy sheriff said to me, and left.

Vaughn waited behind the fabric store while I went upstairs to put on a shirt and pack an overnight bag. His peacoat was warm and smelled like pine needles, and if I'd been alone I might have kept it on all night. Instead I found a black velvet smoking jacket in a garment bag in the back of Uncle Marius's closet. I rolled up the sleeves until they fell just above my wrists and double-wrapped the belt to keep the jacket closed. I pushed my black nightgown into my messenger bag, along with a few cans of cat food and the bowls from the drugstore. I scooped Pins and Needles into the cardboard box, draped Vaughn's peacoat over the top, and lifted the box. Before I went downstairs, I spotted the champagne-colored satin dress hanging in the closet. I folded it down to the size of a dinner napkin, wrapped it in the tissue from the box, and slid it into my bag next to tomorrow's underwear.

Vaughn pulled his peacoat on and looked into the box. "How are they?"

"They're good. I think they finally know they're safe."

He reached a hand inside and scratched Pins's head. The

kitten swiped a dark gray paw at Vaughn's hand. Vaughn caught it and rubbed it gently between his thumb and index finger, until the kitten pulled his paw away and licked it clean.

Vaughn took the box from me. We walked to the Waverly House side by side. The silence between us was comfortable. I didn't fill it with words or explanations or apologies or blame and neither did he.

When we reached the Waverly House, he tapped on the front door and turned to me while we waited for someone to let us in. "Are you going to be okay?" he asked. "I can stay for a while if you want." he said softly.

I turned to him. "I'm going to be okay. I think maybe you should find Charlie and tell her what happened. She could use a family, too."

I looked past him, over the shrubbery separating us from the alley that ran to the back door to the fabric store, then back at Vaughn. There was more that I wanted to say, but I wasn't sure where to start. We said good night and I went inside.

It took an extra day for Charlie to finish up the repairs on my car, and I used that extra day to start getting used to the idea that my high school friend Ken had been charged with the murder of my aunt ten years ago and the recent murder of Mr. Pickers. It would take time to fully accept what it all meant, for both me and for the residents of San Ladrón.

Having closure on the subject of my great-aunt's murder meant something else to me. It meant I had a choice. Unresolved issues had been resolved. Questions had been answered. I could sell the fabric store to Mr. McMichael and move back to Los Angeles. He wasn't the villain I'd wanted him to be, and his offer on the property was both sound and generous. If he sold the property to a developer, new jobs would come to San Ladrón.

I could call Carson, apologize, and ask him to help me navigate the deal, and maybe even use the money to invest in a shop of my own like he'd suggested.

But behind door number two was the unknown: reopen the store that I'd inherited. It would take a lot of time and energy sorting through what remained of the inventory, and I probably wouldn't be ready to reopen it for months, but it would be mine. I'd have to write a business plan, apply for a line of credit, start developing contacts in the fabric world so I could stock new inventory, and get the word out that the fabric store was going to reopen. I'd also have to move to San Ladrón.

It was the easiest decision I'd ever made.

After getting my car back from Charlie, who demonstrated her soft side by comping the cost of repairs, I drove back to Los Angeles. In the weeks that followed, I broke up with Carson over Wednesday-morning waffles and moved all of my belongings from our apartment in Los Angeles to a storage locker on the outskirts of the city, with the exception of a two suitcases: one filled with my black everyday wardrobe, the other filled with the vintage thirties dresses I'd been keeping at the back of my closet. I collected payment for unused vacation time from Giovanni and moved into the apartment above the fabric store. I even made an appointment with Mr. McMichael to clear the air and ask him to look over my business plan. The cloud of suspicion that had hung over him for a decade was now lifted, and I could see that he'd only acted as a friend to my aunt Millie and uncle Marius. I hoped, with everything that had happened, he'd understand the way I felt about wanting to reopen the fabric store and not stand in my way.

Two weeks after moving to San Ladrón, I arranged to meet Vaughn at Tea Totalers. He was dressed in a suit and tie. He traded Genevieve a credit card for a red plaid thermos and a bag of carefully wrapped sandwiches.

"Stocking up for the week?" I asked.

"It's time for me to head home."

"You don't live here?"

"I rent a furnished apartment by the office. It works for me."

"Oh. I thought—I guess it doesn't matter what I thought."

"Lately I've been thinking about investing in something more permanent. I'm not sure what changed."

I tucked my chin to hide my smile and pulled a chair out from under a table. "Do you have a couple of minutes to talk?"

"Sure." He dropped into the chair opposite me.

"The night you brought dinner to the fabric store you said you wanted answers. Were your questions about your father?"

"Yes." He looked away, then down at his thermos, and then at my face. "I knew what people said about my father. I knew the only way the rumors would stop was if somebody found out once and for all what happened that night. I didn't think I'd ever know the truth. But then you showed up and you wanted to know what happened, too. I thought we could work together."

"I'm sorry about how I've treated you since I came to San Ladrón. I gave you a hard time."

"Yes, you did." He smiled. "What about you? You came here with questions, too. Did you find what you were looking for?"

I thought about why I'd come to San Ladrón: to inherit the family fabric store. I thought about the questions about my family that had kept me there and about the answers I'd found. In a matter of days I'd found a world I hadn't known existed and a collection of people I didn't want to leave behind.

I wanted to know what Genevieve would say when I showed her the fabric renovation I'd been working on for her tea shop.

I wanted to help Charlie discover the truth about her childhood.

I wanted to find a way to thank the Lopez family for their act of generosity.

And I wanted to reopen the store and make a life for myself in the town of San Ladrón.

"I didn't find all the answers I was looking for," I said, "but what I found is a pretty good start."

CRAFT PROJECT: HOW TO MAKE AUNT MILLIE'S GLAMOROUS THROW PILLOWS

Beginner/Intermediate Sewing Level
Will Take About an Hour

½ yard white velvet
½ yard white watered silk or taffeta
1 white marabou or ostrich feather boa (at least
    50 inches long)
1 12x12 pillow form
1 vintage or vintage-looking brooch
Sewing machine
White thread
Needle (for hand stitching + basting)
White 12-inch zipper

Cut a 14x14-inch square out of the white velvet.

Cut a 14x14-inch square of the silk.

Place right sides together, and pin along one side.

Baste pinned side.

Pin closed zipper face down over basting stitches on wrong side.

Sew zipper in place.

Remove basting stitches.

Open zipper.

Measure 50 inches of the boa and cut.

Pin the boa around the edge of the RIGHT SIDE of the velvet, leaving a ¾-inch allowance at fabric edge. (HINT: Pin from the underside of the fabric. Space pins 1½ to 2 inches apart.)

Baste the boa into place. (HINT: Baste from the underside. Use your pins as a guide.)

Remove pins.

Pin the right sides of the fabric together, leaving a ½-inch seam allowance. (Tuck the boa feathers inside the fabric squares with your fingers as you go.)

Sew three sides of the square using the sewing machine.

Flip inside out along the side with the open zipper.

Stuff the pillow form into the pillow.

Zip shut.

Attach the pin/brooch to the center of the white velvet.

Nestle pillow on your bed by your sleeping pillows and enjoy a touch of glamour!

Turn the page for a preview of Diane Vallere's

next Material Witness Mystery . . .

CRUSHED VELVET

Coming soon from Berkley Prime Crime!

The crash was louder than I expected.

Two men stood poised on the top rung of their respective stepladders on either side of the *Land of a Thousand Fabrics* sign—or where the sign had been ten minutes ago. The man on the right had lost his grip on the *L* in *Land*, and it fell to the sidewalk in front of the store, cracking the concrete. The effects of weather and time—a decade since the store had closed for business but almost half a century since the store had first opened—had rusted the cursive iron letters in the logo. Bird poop and leaves were almost indistinguishable from the decorative font, and one of the metal posts that anchored the massive sign to the storefront had broken sometime in the past week while I was in Los Angeles. Since then, *Thousand* hung in a diagonal slope downward. The men on the ladders were hired to remove the rest of the anchors so the sign could be replaced with my new sign, *Material Girl*, before I opened for business in six days.

They'd rescheduled the job twice, and now I had less than a week before the registers were scheduled to ring.

It was eleven thirty on a Monday morning. The first time I had scheduled this job had been on a Monday, too, because I knew most people would be at work, and the handful of hair salons on the street would be closed. I'd alerted the business owners on either side of me: Tiki Tom, who sold Hawaiian ephemera to my left, and the Garden sisters, Lilly and Violet, who ran an antique shop called Flowers in the Attic to my right. They'd both agreed to close for the day. The construction crew canceled at the last minute, leaving my neighboring stores out of a day's business. I made it up to them with ten yards of a fabric of each of their choice. You work with what you have.

Two weeks later, an unexpected February downpour kept the crew from showing up for the job, which meant it was today or nothing. I didn't love that a sidewalk of tourists and nosy neighbors had a front-row seat to my sign troubles, but the small town of San Ladrón had codes and zoning regulations, and a job like this had to happen Monday through Friday between the hours of ten and four. If it wasn't today, I wouldn't have a proper sign when I opened at the end of the week.

"Polyester Monroe?" said a voice to my left. I turned to see a man in a red plaid shirt, faded jeans, and a yellow construction hat. He held a clipboard under one arm. His phone was velcroed onto his belt below a generous belly. "Zat you?"

"Yes, I'm Polyester Monroe," I said. "But call me Poly."

"Is your legal name Polyester?"

I nodded.

"Then that's what I need you to sign. Here, here, and here." He pushed the clipboard in front of me and tapped the paper with the end of the pen.

I scanned page one of the documents. "I already signed

the contract for the sign removal and a few notices from the city. Is this for something else?"

"This is the release form for the contractors. If anyone is hurt in the course of the job, you're responsible. If any property is damaged in the course of the job, you're responsible. If any—"

"But the city council recommended you for the job because you have experience with this sort of thing and they said you could work on my deadline. The store opens on Sunday and I need a sign."

"Lady, this is San Ladrón, not Times Square. You turn on your lights, you open the front door, and you hang out a shingle. If people want what you're selling, they'll come in and buy it. But if you want me, you still gotta sign the release."

I signed my full legal name by the Xs and wrote the date after my signature. The rest of the construction workers were scattered around the sidewalk, moving large chunks of concrete that had broken loose when the large iron *Land* had hit the sidewalk. My attempt to make the fabric store look new again, to make it more of a shining star than a sore thumb on Bonita Avenue, wasn't exactly going according to plan. Tiki Tom and Lilly Garden stood out front, surveilling the scene. Neither looked particularly happy about the work being done. I suspected the good will I'd accrued with the gifted ten yards of fabric had worn off. Good thing I'd arranged for my friend Genevieve to bring a couple of gourmet baskets for them from her tea shop.

"You look like you could use a pick-me-up," Genevieve said to me after handing over two of the three baskets she held.

Genevieve Girard was the owner of the small, French-themed tea shop called Tea Totalers about two blocks from my fabric store. I'd befriended her a few months ago when I first inherited the store. She and her husband had met at the World Tea Expo, and after a typical courtship that involved flowers, candy, and twenty pounds on her curvy frame, they married and set up shop in San Ladrón, her husband Phil's hometown. They plunked their savings into the tea store, but a poor economy kept them from making it the joint project they'd hoped. He went back to driving a taxi and occasionally picking up delivery jobs and she ran the store. A nice, patchwork resume, the new reality for the small-business owner.

"Genevieve, you have no idea how happy I am to see you."

She set the picnic basket on a public bench and flipped the wooden handles open. When she lifted the lid, the scent of buttermilk biscuits and mulled cider filled the air. Mugs, saucers, flatware, and napkins were attached to the inside lid of the picnic basket by elastic loops that had been sewn to the red-and-white checkered interior. She removed a mug and saucer, filled it with cider, and handed it to me. I took a sip, savoring the rich apple and clove flavor.

"This is heavenly," I said.

"Try the biscuit. It's a new recipe: I added pureed loquats to the batter."

I took a bite. The flavors of loquats and cranberries complemented each other perfectly. "You're a genius," I said.

"Can you take out an ad in the *San Ladrón Times* and tell people that? I could use the endorsement."

"Business is still slow?" I was mildly surprised. "I thought it picked up after you started promoting your proprietary blends of tea."

"The only person who's responded to those ads is a food distributor who wants me to sell out to the big grocery stores, and that's not what I want for Tea Totalers. I need to get people to the store. Right now I have about five regulars—not that I'm complaining, so don't you even think about not showing up tomorrow!—and a handful of walk-ins a week. It's barely enough to pay the bills, let alone buy the supplies I need."

Out of the corner of my eye I saw two men standing on scaffolding that had been suspended from the roof of the fabric store. They looped thick ropes around the iron letters of the parts of the sign that hadn't crashed to the sidewalk and slowly lowered the word *Thousand* to the ground. When I turned to watch what happened next, I saw another group of men move the iron word to the back of their truck, where they'd put *Land*. It was after twelve now, and there was one word left. I'd specifically asked that they take *Fabric* down last in case there were any snafus. Better branding than *of* or *a*. Now they could remove the iron bolts that jutted out from the façade and mount the sign I'd designed during the nights when I was too excited about the prospects of opening the store to sleep.

I did a quick calculation. At the rate the construction crew was working, we'd be at it for hours. Removal of the sign was one thing, but removal of the scaffolding was another.

"Wait here," I said to Genevieve. I walked over to the foreman.

He held up his hand palm-side out. "Hard hat," he said, and pointed to a yellow helmet resting on the back of the truck.

I tucked the front of my auburn hair, cut in a style made famous by Victoria Beckham a few years ago, behind my ear and set the half-lemon-shaped hat on top of my head. The hat was bigger than my head and almost covered my eyes. I tipped it back so I could see. The foreman waved me forward.

"How long do you think you're going to be?" I asked.

"This is an all-day job."

"How can that be? The words are down and that had to be the hardest part."

"We gotta finish removing the iron. Then we gotta get your new sign in place and run the electrical. Then we gotta test everything. Then—"

"So, what does that mean? Three? Four?"

"At least. We go into overtime at five."

"Zoning laws say you have to be done by four."

"Then we're going to need to pick back up tomorrow."

I put my hands on my hips. "Not. Acceptable. This is a one-day job. You said so when you gave me the quote. You canceled on me twice."

"Once. Couldn't do much about the rain, lady."

"You started at nine. You will finish at four. And by finish, I mean finish. Gone. Cleaned up. Out of here."

"Those wall mounts are pretty rusted through," he said. He pulled his hat off and rubbed the back of his arm across his forehead.

"Good. That means instead of trying to save them, you can save time by just cutting them off."

He looked at the picnic basket behind me. "We could work a lot faster if we had food."

"Don't worry about food. I'll take care of that. But this job? Done by four."

He scratched his head and pulled his hard hat back on. "Deal." He turned around and yelled to the workers. "Hey! Pick up the pace! We're on a time table."

Genevieve was halfway through her third biscuit when I returned to the bench. "Can you do lunch for—" I twisted around and counted the various colors of flannel, "nine men on short notice? I'll pay menu prices."

"Poly, I can't let you be my savior. You're putting all of your money into the store."

"Let me worry about my money. You worry about lunch for nine."

"Fine. Lunch for nine. Can you drive to the store in half an hour? You know Phil took the truck to LA to pick up your fabrics."

"See, you guys are my savior, too."

When the lease had come due on their Saab, Genevieve had convinced her husband, Phil, to turn it in and invest in a van they could use for deliveries. She'd had the logo for her tea shop painted on the side and hoped it would help raise her shop's profile. As it turned out, most delivery orders could be handled by bike and the truck spent more time sitting behind the shop than cruising the streets of San Ladrón. Ever pragmatic, Phil still took the occasional moving and delivery jobs in the greater Los Angeles area to justify the price of the vehicle.

When I'd first decided to reopen the fabric store, my parents had helped me sort through the bolts of fabric that had been in the store for decades. My Uncle Marius had closed the store ten years ago, but left the interior intact. A surprising amount of fabrics were still in sellable condition. I hoped to one day be able to take the kind of trips that Uncle Marius and Aunt Millie had taken—Thailand for silk, France for lace, Scotland for cashmere—but until I established a cash flow, I had to do what I could on a shoestring budget. I sorted through the old inventory and then contacted many of the dealers in New York and New Jersey, spending hours selecting whimsical cotton prints, Pendleton wools, and a glorious spectrum of silk de chine. I offered to buy any bolts they had with less than five yards if they'd make a deal on the price and a few of them did. A few of them remembered my aunt and uncle and deepened my discount when I told them I was reopening the store. It was a start.

Still, I needed a hook, something to make people come to me. After two weeks of stopping by Tea Totalers every morning for a cup of Genevieve's proprietary blend of tea, I got my idea. A proprietary blend of fabric.

It was no coincidence that I owned a fabric store and my name was Polyester. The store had been in my family for generations and I'd been born inside on a bed of polyester. Growing up, I'd been teased on a regular basis and often wished I'd been born on a less controversial fabric. Was there a person alive who didn't think of the seventies when they heard the word *polyester*? Still, it was what it was. Instead of fighting my name, I decided to use it for a PR opportunity. I reached out to all of my contacts and finally found a mill willing to weave a custom blend of velvet using ninety percent silk and ten percent polyester.

I had experience working with cheap fabrics in my former job at To The Nines, a somewhat sleazy dress shop in downtown Los Angeles, and I knew that ten percent of a synthetic woven into a fabric could change the drape and wearability of the cloth without dramatically altering the appearance. Fabrics that were woven with a synthetic blend resisted wrinkles and held color better than their pure counterparts. My former boss liked to use mostly synthetic fabrics that came cheap (and sometimes defective). Having grown up around the best fabrics in the world when Land of a Thousand Fabrics was in its prime, I'd always wanted to work with top-quality weaves. This was my opportunity.

My custom velvet had arrived in Los Angeles on Friday afternoon. The warehouse was closed for the weekend. Genevieve had mentioned that her husband was going to Los Angeles for supplies for Tea Totalers today and I'd arranged for him to pick up the fabric. It was a win-win.

Even though the store was locked up tighter than a drum, I had a few misgivings over leaving the crew to pick up the lunch. The foreman saw me watching them and gave me a thumbs-up. I smiled a thin smile and walked around the back of the store to my yellow VW Bug. Five minutes later I was parked in front of Tea Totalers.

The tea shop was actually a small house that sat away from the street. A narrow sidewalk led to the front door. Small white iron tables and chairs with mismatched, faded cushions were scattered around the front interior. Inside, Genevieve had hung checkered curtains by the windows and tacked a few French posters featuring roosters and chickens on the walls.

Genevieve was a self-professed Francophile, and her shop was a testament to her love of the country. I'd secretly been working on a fabric makeover for her store, including curtains, cushions, aprons, placemats, napkins, and tablecloths from toile, gingham, check, and linen. I even found a bolt of place-printed cotton canvas, too heavy to use for apparel, with images of roosters on it. I planned to stretch the images over wooden frames and suggest she hang them like art. I couldn't wait to share the concept with her, but I wanted to get it all together before it was done, and I wanted to find a way to use the new velvet in the design.

Genevieve was stacking sandwiches wrapped in parchment paper, sealed with stickers that featured the Eiffel Tower on them, into a wooden crate.

"I hope you don't mind that I didn't go fancy. I'm low on a couple of supplies. Jambon sandwiches with Brie and Dijon mustard on crusty French bread, with a side of pommes frites. Is that okay?"

"That's not fancy?" I asked with a smile to my voice. "I think it'll do. What time is Phil expected back?"

"Hopefully this afternoon. He left yesterday so he could avoid traffic and be at the suppliers first thing this morning."

We loaded jugs of iced tea into a separate crate and packed them into the back seat of my Bug. I returned to the store and parked out front so we could unload. Two men lowered the scaffolding and sign removal ceased while a line formed by Genevieve. I stood behind, assessing the work that was left. In the background, a generic white van turned the corner. It pulled up to the curb behind the flatbed. The logo on the side of the truck, a white rectangle that covered the area to the left of the passenger-side door, said *Special Delivery*. Underneath it said *Have We Got a Package for You! Call Us 24 Hours a Day*.

The driver of the truck cut the engine and got out. "Is there a Polyester Monroe around here?" he asked.

"I'm Polyester," I said.

"Rick Penwald. Have I got a package for you. Bunch of fabrics?"

Genevieve approached the truck. "My husband was supposed to pick up her fabrics. Where's Phil?" She looked at the logo on the side of the vehicle. "Where's his truck?"

"He called me this morning, made arrangements for me to make the delivery for him. He said he had some business in Los Angeles and wasn't coming back right away."

"But that doesn't make any sense," Genevieve said. "He left yesterday because of this job. Why would he call you to finish it for him?"

"Not sure." Rick pulled his black mesh hat off his head and wiped his forehead with his palm. "He probably wanted to surprise you with something."

He held out a clipboard with sheets of paper attached and handed me a pen. "Sign by the Xs."

I glanced at the form and then back at Rick. "I already paid for the fabric and I paid Phil for the delivery up front."

"If I make a delivery, I gotta have proof I made the delivery. Has nothing to do with payment. That's proof of the delivery. The form's in triplicate. You sign the top one and take the pink copy in the middle. Press hard."

The top copy was white, the middle pink, and the bottom yellow. Along the upper-left side, the logo, website, and phone number for Special Delivery had been rubber-stamped in red. Across the center of the page, written in ballpoint pen in surprisingly neat printing that tipped slightly backward, it said, "12 bolts velvet. Prepaid. Signature for delivery confirmation only." I zeroed out the totals field and signed my name at the bottom. I tore the pink page from between the white and yellow and set the clipboard inside the open window on the passenger-side seat.

I folded the paper up small enough to fit into my back pocket and followed Rick around to the back of the van. He flipped through a ring of keys and tried three in the padlock before he found one that worked. He took the lock off and hooked it on one of the belt loops of his jeans, and then flung the back doors open.

Sunlight hit twelve large bolts of multicolored velvet, propped along the left-hand side of the truck. On the right were crates of vegetables, spices, and dry goods.

"Where you want it?" he asked.

"Inside the store," I said. I unlocked the hinged metal gate in the front of the fabric store and propped the entrance open with a small black vintage sewing machine I used as a doorstop. Behind us, the colorful flannel army of construction workers sat alongside of the building watching. Nobody volunteered to help. Rick grabbed a bolt of velvet by the end and yanked on it, then positioned it over his shoulder and carried it inside the store. Behind him, Genevieve screamed. I ran to the back of the truck and looked inside.

Jutting out from under the bolts of fabric was an arm.

I scrambled inside the truck and rolled the bolts of fabric out of their stacked-lumber formation to the side of the truck with the dry goods. The arm belonged to a body that had been hidden under the fabric.

And the body belonged to Genevieve's husband, Phil.

From *New York Times* bestselling author
Ellery Adams

MURDER *in the* MYSTERY SUITE

A Book Retreat Mystery

❧

Tucked away in the rolling hills of rural western Virginia is Storyton Hall, a resort catering to book lovers who want to get away from it all. To increase her number of bookings, resort manager Jane Steward has decided to host a Murder and Mayhem Week, where mystery lovers can indulge in some role-playing and fantasy crime-solving. But when the winner of the scavenger hunt, Felix Hampden, is found dead in the Mystery Suite, Jane realizes one of her guests is an actual murderer...

PRAISE FOR THE NOVELS OF ELLERY ADAMS

"Enchanting."
—Jenn McKinlay, *New York Times* bestselling author

"In one word—AMAZING!"
—*The Best Reviews*

elleryadamsmysteries.com
facebook.com/TheCrimeSceneBooks
penguin.com

M1509T0614

From *New York Times* Bestselling Author
Jenn McKinlay

DEATH OF A MAD HATTER

A HAT SHOP MYSTERY

Scarlett Parker and Vivian Tremont, co-owners of a London hat shop, are creating the hats for an *Alice in Wonderland* themed afternoon tea. The tea is a fund-raiser hosted by the Grisby family, who wants a new hospital wing named after their patriarch.

When the Grisby heir is poisoned, evidence points to Scarlett and Viv, and the police become curiouser and curiouser about their involvement. Now the ladies need to find the tea party crasher who's mad enough to kill at the drop of a hat...

"A delightful new heroine."
—Deborah Crombie, *New York Times* bestselling author

jennmckinlay.com
facebook.com/TheCrimeSceneBooks
penguin.com

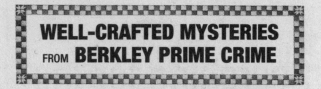

WELL-CRAFTED MYSTERIES
FROM **BERKLEY PRIME CRIME**

- **Earlene Fowler** Don't miss these Agatha Award–winning quilting mysteries featuring Benni Harper.

- **Monica Ferris** These *USA Today* bestselling Needlecraft Mysteries include free knitting patterns.

- **Laura Childs** Her Scrapbooking Mysteries offer tips to satisfy the most die-hard crafters.

- **Maggie Sefton** These popular Knitting Mysteries come with knitting patterns and recipes.

- **Lucy Lawrence** These brilliant Decoupage Mysteries involve cutouts, glue, and varnish.

- **Elizabeth Lynn Casey** The Southern Sewing Circle Mysteries are filled with friends, southern charm—and murder.